FLAME
IN THE WIND

JAMES NOBLE GIFFORD

℘

FLAME IN THE WIND is the story of a neurotic Park Avenue debutante inextricably ensnared in a web of too much money and too little responsibility, who seeks fulfillment and happiness through many illicit loves and unnatural emotional experiments.

FLAME
IN THE WIND

James Noble Gifford

AUTHOR OF

"Caviar for Breakfast"

AND

"Made for Love"

1932

WILLIAM GODWIN, INC.

NEW YORK

TO BENNIE HALL

In appreciation of her invaluable help and unfailing
kindness.

FLAME IN THE WIND

"For the flame of love tossed by the wind of passion casts
grotesque shadows on the screen of life."

FLAME IN THE WIND

CHAPTER ONE

It had been a warm, sunny day with a soft spring-like quality in the air which was quite unbelievable in the first week of November. Now at six o'clock the buses along Fifth Avenue were crowded with workers going home by this most comfortable route, and proving for a moment that all New Yorkers are not necessarily in a hurry. And to-night it is interesting to ride up Fifth Avenue because, for one night at least, all the mansions are blazing with light, and there is an animation seldom seen at other times. To-night is the opening of the opera season, and wealth will have its proudest moment. The golden horse-shoe never glitters so grandly as it does when a so-called hard winter is in prospect.

A bus ran along slowly, preparing to stop at a corner. On the upper deck a gay group of young people were laughing and joking, and pointing out houses they knew. A Jewish girl with thin features and dark tousled hair pointed quickly to a house.

"That's where the Bronsons live. I bet none of you knew that one."

Her companion squeezed her arm. "Gee, I bet you sit up nights readin' 'Who's Who.'"

"Why not?" a girl in front flashed back. "It does you good to know who wastes the money we slave for."

"Hurrah! Hurrah! Speech!"

"Down with the rich, up with the garment union!" cried a deep voice mockingly.

The first girl stood up in her excitement. "Did you see

to-night's paper? Mr. Bronson says the depression is being made worse by helping lazy loafers. Every one must work."

There was a derisive whistle and a babel of voices.

"Try and find work."

"Three cheers for Thor Bronson, God of Thunder!"

"And a tiger for Lil! She makes it all so plain."

"Yeah!"

But the girl had found a new interest. She leaned far out of the bus which was still held up by the traffic signal. "Hey! look at the woman getting off now. She was sitting in front of us and got up when we began to talk about the Bronsons. Look! She's ringing the bell! I bet she lives there."

"Maybe it's Mrs. Bronson, been out gettin' a marcel."

"Aw, she's got a maid; maybe two or three of 'em."

"Well, maybe she got a marcel just the same."

"Don't be a sill, she has a maid for that."

"Yeah? Well, maybe the maid don't know how to do it."

The girl laughed. "Of course she does. I know a woman that has a maid...."

Loud groans interrupted her. "My Gawd! Rose is doing her society stuff again."

"You mean you know a maid that has a job."

"All right, be silly if you want to."

The bus pulled slowly out of sight in the press of cars, and the voices were lost in the sharply defined traffic sounds. As the woman the girl had pointed out stood waiting for the door to open, she felt she had almost rather it didn't, so she might cross the avenue and sit on a bench she remembered. It was probably still there, and to-night might be the last night of the season on which one could sit out quietly and think about things. Those raucous young people on the bus had disturbed her more than she cared to realize. She had almost forgotten how unpleasant so many American voices were. There was no rest, no quietude in them.

The door swung open, and the old butler was framed in the space with the light flowing out around his portly figure.

"Good evening, Greenleaf. Mrs. Bronson is expecting me."

He stepped aside a little. "I'm not sure, madame, if Mrs. Bronson . . . why, why, it's Miss Downer!" He closed the door quickly behind her and accepted her proffered hand. "This is indeed a surprise, May-May; we all thought you had quite settled in England. Are you coming to us again?"

She smiled quietly, and her thin beautifully modeled face was suffused with light. "I really don't know until I've seen Mrs. Bronson. I've only just arrived on the *Berengaria*. It was so warm I came up on the bus."

He immediately was all dignity again, but there was a ghost of a smile on his lips, as if he was truly glad to see the woman again. "I'll tell the madame you're here."

"And is Cynthia—in?" She hesitated slightly before the word, as if there were so many things she wanted to know about Cynthia, and then finally compromised on a mere question of whereabouts.

"No, May-May, but she will be coming at any moment to dress. The opening of the opera to-night, you know."

The woman smiled a little after the butler's retreating figure. He hadn't changed a bit in the three or four years since she had seen him, nor indeed in all the years she had known him. He was ageless and changeless, like fine furniture, good china, real silver, or any of the good, true, permanent things of life. After the ride on the bus with the raucous group flinging disturbing ideas about with no respect for those of whom they spoke, or who might be listening, it was good to see Greenleaf, a very balance wheel in the tottering social scheme of things. Even in England his type was rare enough.

The butler knocked and entered Mrs. Bronson's dressing room. The lady was sitting in a low chair, with one maid working on her hands and another arranging her reddish-brown hair in some gleaming waves to deny its clipped shortness. Could Rose on the bus have been able to see through the heavy green silk draperies, her ideas as to rich women and their maids would have been completely vindicated; or at least some of her ideas. Mrs. Bronson looked up quickly from a study of her elegant slippers which were scarcely more than jeweled straps to hold a paper-thin sole and high heel in place. Her large eyes were as beautiful and as unvital as mist on a summer hill-top.

"Miss Downer has come, Madame."

"Will you tell her to come right up, please." There was a slight pause. "And Greenleaf, Miss Downer will be staying with us for a while, in her old room if possible. I know I can trust you to see she is quite comfortable." There was a vague upward twist to her words.

"Thank you, Madame."

A minute or two later Miss Downer entered the room quietly. The lady held out her free hand cordially.

"May-May, I'm so glad to see you. Do find a nice comfortable chair, so we can have a real chat while I'm getting my social armor on to face the battle of a new opera season. Now tell me how you are."

"I've been enjoying very fine health, Mrs. Bronson. I hope you feel as well as you look." Miss Downer sat with demurely folded hands.

The lady shook her beautiful head slowly. At forty Aurelia Bronson still had a head of the type sculptors

dream about, set firmly on a beautiful white throat and
with features of chiseled perfection. Her hair was a deep,
dusky, reddish-brown and waved tightly about her skull,
as short as a Greek boy's. And her eyes had a faint glint
of sun behind the mist on the hill-top.

"Now that will never do, May-May. You're much too
formal by far. Try to remember you've come all the way
here to do me a favor. And you two girls," she cried, ad-
dressing the maids, "haven't even spoken to May-May.
Have you forgotten her, or am I the hard-hearted social
ogress who would snap your heads off if you said 'Hello'?"

Thus encouraged, Marie and Olga greeted May-May
and soon a more friendly air was in the room, even as
their mistress desired. A few minutes later they finished
her hair and nails, and she told them to run away for ten
minutes. When the door had closed behind them, she held
out her hand again.

"Come, May-May, sit here beside me. I want to talk
to you very seriously. Now please remember you are not
Cynthia's governess any more; you are here as her friend,
and as my friend. I'm asking a favor of you now."

"Thank you."

The lady sank deeper in her chair and cupped her chin
in one long elegant hand. "I don't know just where to
begin. I suppose my letter and cables didn't make things
very clear, did they?"

She looked eagerly at the older woman and then went
on. "No, of course they didn't. I was hoping you'd guess,
but then English people don't guess, do they?"

"I came by the very first boat, Mrs. Bronson." She said
this quietly, as if it somehow answered both questions.

"Then you do understand?"

Again the faint smile. "I only understood I might be

of some service to you or to Cynthia. That was all I
needed to know."

"Good faithful May-May!" She patted her hand. "I
knew I could depend upon you. It's about Cynthia, and
by the way, she doesn't know you're here. I've thought it
best that we surprise her." For a full minute they both sat
in silence, the lady thinking deeply and the older woman
watching her intently. Finally Mrs. Bronson spoke.

"Would it be too much to ask you to pretend you came
back to America of your own accord to see Cynthia?
She'll believe it quickly enough, and it would help."

"Yes—if you wish it."

"And will you really stay with us for a while?"

"I should be happy to, thank you."

Then Mrs. Bronson burst out, "May-May, I've needed
you so badly! Something has come over Cynthia, and you
must find out for me. She barely speaks to me any more.
She sits hours and hours by herself and won't see any
one. The other day she was almost killed riding a vicious
horse, and she didn't seem to care. When the policeman
saved her, he asked, 'Are you all right now?' and she
said, 'No! But I would have been in another minute if
you'd stayed away.' ... The policeman told me he thought
she had made the horse run away. And she's so pale and
silent now, May-May, I don't know what to do."

"Is she ill, perhaps?"

"No, she's not sick. It's as if something were preying
upon her mind, and I can't think what. I'm worried, terribly worried. She isn't the same girl at all that she was
when you were here with us, not at all the same."

"She's three, almost four years older," reminded the
older woman practically. "She couldn't remain a child."

"It isn't that. I know it isn't that. Now I want you to

win her confidence, make her love you as she did before, make her act to me as she did before."

Her voice rang out sharply in her eagerness and the large, cold gray eyes flashed as few people had ever seen them do. Her associates would scarcely have recognized the statuesque Mrs. Bronson in this eager, bewildered, pleading woman. Miss Downer replied slowly.

"Do you want me to pry into her mind and then tell you?"

"No! No! Not that at all. How could you even think of it, May-May? I simply want her to be a happy laughing girl again as she was before. I want her to be gay and play like the other girls of her class. The way she is now she worries me. I'm afraid."

"Afraid of what?"

The two women looked at each other steadily for a few moments without a word. Mrs. Bronson opened her lips to speak, then closed them again. The old governess bowed her head ever so slightly and murmured, "I understand." It was like the hard, dry rustle of dead leaves in an autumn wood.

And just at that moment there was a quick knock and the door flung open. Mrs. Bronson jumped to her feet with a glad cry.

"Jane, I'm so glad you came early. And how well you look in that gold dress, almost like some Chinese mandarin." She ran on quickly, words tumbling eagerly over each other as if to blot out her thoughts of a moment before.

The woman smiled vaguely. She was very tall and angular with harsh, rugged features and coal-black hair which she wore sleeked down on her head. A gown of dull-gold metal cloth seemed like a suit of armor on her bony figure. A monocle glittered in her left eye as she greeted her hostess.

"I see May-May is back." She stressed the name ever so slightly.

"Yes, Miss Talbot," the older woman spoke very quietly. "I came for a few weeks to visit Cynthia."

"I thought you only liked to live in England," sneered the angular woman, standing with feet spread wide apart.

Miss Downer bowed serenely. "Quite true, but I like to *visit* in America and I trust Cynthia will be glad to see me." She stressed the girl's name ever so slightly.

"Of course Cynthia will be overjoyed," put in Mrs. Bronson nervously. "She has always talked about you and hoped you would come to see us. We have both hoped so."

The woman in the gold dress smiled down on her quizzically. "How very touching, Aurelia. Such a beautiful thought, but very much out of the last century."

Miss Downer rose slowly. "And don't you think there were so many better things and better ways thirty years ago?" She eyed Miss Talbot quietly for a second then turned to Mrs. Bronson. "Perhaps Cynthia is home now. I had better see."

"Of course, May-May. You will have your old room next to Cynthia and you know I want you to be right at home with us. Tell Greenleaf anything you want."

"Thank you, Mrs. Bronson," and with a quiet nod to Miss Talbot she passed out of the room.

For a moment there was a tense silence, then Miss Talbot's sharp laugh barked out roughly. It seemed as out of place in that dainty room as the scuff of muddy boots.

"Well, I never. Aurelia, I simply can't understand you at all. After you once safely got rid of that meddlesome old fool, why have you brought her back here again?"

"Why, Jane, I didn't bring her here. How can you

say such a thing? She told you she just came to visit Cynthia. I think it's a most natural thing to do. You know how devoted she always was to Cynthia."

"Really!" There was a wealth of scornful meaning in the highly inflected word. For a moment the two women were silent while Mrs. Bronson tried to stare her friend down. Their glances crossed, rapier-like, and then she lowered her eyes, and with a faint sniff picked up a lace handkerchief from the little table by her side and furtively dabbed her eyes with its perfumed filminess.

"You have no right to talk to me like that. I think you're just too cruel."

Miss Talbot rose slowly and began to stalk about the room in an abrupt manner, while one somehow felt instinctively that she wanted to thrust her hands deep into some missing pockets. For even Jane Talbot had not yet gone to the extent of having pockets put in her evening clothes, though they were prominent enough in all her street costumes. Finally she turned, with feet wide apart, and again one felt her costume betrayed her; felt certain that brogues were the logical footwear of this determined woman. Her monocle glistened like some infuriated Cyclopean eye.

"Aurelia, sometimes you make me very tired. Now I suppose your sense of propriety will force you to burst into tears and ruin your face after your maids have been working on it for three hours."

"I think you're horrid. You know my maids have not been working three hours. Three hours ago I was with you and ..."

"All right then, not three hours, only two hours or an hour and a half, or an hour; what the devil does it matter? The point is for once talk sense and don't start weeping. Tears disgust a woman like me—you know that."

"But you insinuated I was lying about May-May coming here."

"Did I only insinuate?" she mocked, sprawling into a low chair. "Then I'm afraid I wasn't definite enough. Aurelia Bronson, do you take me for a fool? Well, I'm not enough of one to swallow that story about May-May just happening to come to America to visit Cynthia. I know how these retired English governesses feel about the money they've saved up, and especially this one. I always thought she was the nosiest, most domineering creature I'd ever seen, and I hardly should think I'd need to remind you how she acted the last year she was with you. Why, you hardly dared breathe in your own house for fear of what May-May would think or say. And now you try to make me believe she's used her savings to come here to America, and just to visit poor dear Cynthia." Mrs. Bronson's eyes flickered a little under the withering sarcasm of the last sentence, and she moved ever so slightly in her chair, but Jane ran on coldly, with every word dropping bitingly off her beautiful teeth.

"And now may I know who paid her to come here? You —or Bronson?" She leaned forward in her eagerness.

"I did."

The words dropped simply, calmly into the glittering pool of irony. Their very simplicity made Jane Talbot hesitate an instant before she plunged on again.

"Well, at least we're getting a little truth now, and I suppose it's a little better that she's here on your invitation rather than on Bronson's. Now, why in the devil have you brought her here? That's what I'd like to know."

Mrs. Bronson rose slowly from her seat, and, walking quietly over to one of the big windows, held back the heavy green silk draperies and looked out. The lights in the park looked dim and golden and, somehow, faintly

alluring, glowing softly against the dark shadows of de-
nuded trees. The window was open a little, and the warm
unseasonable air floated in turgidly, mingling its damp
gasoline-tinged breath with the fragrant femininity of the
room.

Jane Talbot sat back in her low chair, her gaze
fixed steadily upon her friend standing at the window
with one arm raised shoulder high, a round smooth arm,
beautiful as alabaster. It was like a stage-setting, like one
of the theatrical tricks of Ethel Barrymore in her heyday.
That was one of Aurelia's faults: she couldn't resist theatrical effects, and they were only the more irritating as they
were beautifully done. Her foot in its elaborately gold-
strapped sandal tapped impatiently, then she spoke sharply.

"Aurelia, I asked you a question!"

Mrs. Bronson slowly turned away, as if reluctant to face
her own life again, and leave the dimly imagined things
out there in the mocking warm darkness of the park dotted
with golden lights. The heavy curtain fell into place again
as she walked toward her chair with a faint sigh. Out
there in the darkness there were no questions.

"What was the question?"

"Aurelia, for Heaven's sake, come down to earth.
You're not acting in a Barrie play now. I said, 'Why have
you brought May-May here?'"

"I can't tell you."

"Can't tell me?" The voice rose incredulously. "Can't
tell me? Do you mean that you can't, or that you won't?"

"Maybe won't is more accurate. I won't tell you. It is
purely my own affair."

Jane Talbot rose slowly, amazement vividly painted on
her bony features. "Aurelia Bronson, are you mad, talking
to me like that?"

"Hardly. You merely asked something which is none

of your business, and I'm telling you so." She sat down again, and, picking up a buffer, began to rub her nails idly. For a full minute the silence held, then Miss Talbot planted herself squarely and demanded truculently, "Are you going to answer my question?"

She looked up sweetly and then moved her left hand to get a better light on the nails. "I have answered you, Jane. Now will you please ring for Marie, or I'll never be dressed in time. Dale Eustis is coming with us and Prince Ladislov. I think I told you about the Prince, and I think you may know Dale Eustis. Tuxedo and athletic. Strange but true."

Miss Talbot determinedly screwed her monocle in her eye. "I'll be damned if I ring for any one. Do it yourself. And I'm going." She strode across the room and snatched up her wrap. "I'll see you again when you've come to your senses and realize you're not Jane Cowl in a Maugham play. I hate evasions, and I hate chit-chat."

She flung open the door and then started back as she saw Thor Bronson standing there with a quiet smile on his usually grim face. He entered and then bowed ironically toward the still open door."

"So glad to see you're going, Miss Talbot. Don't let me detain you—it's so seldom I have a chance to see my wife alone, I've almost taken to sending in my card."

Mrs. Bronson had risen to her feet and stood clutching her tiny handkerchief in one hand. All her quiet assurance was gone now; all the quiet self-possession which she had gathered while looking out over the park, and buoyed up by which she had faced Jane Talbot so calmly. There was a nervous tension in her voice.

"What do you want, Thor?"

"I want to talk to you the minute the ever-charming

Miss Talbot has favored us by taking her departure. I'm sure some one must be impatiently awaiting her."

Miss Talbot eyed him from head to foot, her monocle gleaming and her wide mouth twisted into a strange smile in which complete insolence and mocking tolerance were scornfully mixed. Mrs. Bronson broke the silence sharply.

"Thor, don't be a fool. Jane is here to dinner and is going to the opera with us. What's the matter with you to-night?"

He bowed ironically. "To be sure. Naturally the opera wouldn't dare begin unless Miss Talbot were in our box." He pulled out his watch ostentatiously. "But are Miss Talbot's clocks all wrong, or is she in need of a book of etiquette to tell her, among other things, how early to arrive at dinner parties? I understand she has a very comfortable apartment."

Miss Talbot waited until he had finished, then threw her wrap over a chair and sat down. "I've changed my mind, Aurelia, I'm staying."

"Please do, Jane. Thor, you're too disgusting, and I'm glad Jane doesn't take you seriously." She glanced nervously from one to the other.

He sighed lugubriously and planted his feet more firmly in the rug. "I wish she would take me more seriously for the benefit of both of us, but one can't expect too much. But is the drawing room so crowded she can't wait for you there? It looked rather empty as I passed."

Mrs. Bronson crossed swiftly and rang the bell. Then she faced her husband. "Sorry, Thor, but Jane waits up here, and I must get on with my dressing. I'm late as it is. Dale Eustis and Prince Ladislov are coming to dinner. You haven't much time to change."

"And suppose I should happen to want the unusual

pleasure of watching my wife dress?" His heavy lips curled.

"Don't be a fool, Thor."

Before he could answer the two maids appeared in the door and walked swiftly into the room. With their coming the atmosphere changed at once, and it was as if a clean, cold breeze of efficiency had swept through the heated sogginess of a greenhouse. For a minute or two the man stood as if bewildered by the sudden change and then wandered out irresolutely, slamming the door behind him. The maids went on with their work quite as if oblivious to everything around them; as if neither Thor, nor Jane Talbot, were anywhere about.

Fifteen minutes later Mrs. Bronson was ready to receive her guests, and with a wave dismissed her two maids. She had not spoken a single word to Jane Talbot since her husband had slammed the door of the room. Now as the girls closed the door softly behind them she turned with half a smile.

"Well, Jane, how do I look?" In her voice was the supreme confidence of a woman who knows just how well she does look.

Outside the door one of the two maids watched down the corridor and the other knelt with her eye glued to the keyhole. There was a moment's silence, then they walked slowly toward the servants' stairs. Their feet sank silently into the heavy carpet.

"Well!"

Marie sniffed eloquently. "That Talbot woman was kissin' her, of course. Disgusting, I calls it. If I was him I wouldn't put up with it; indeed I wouldn't."

"Well, you ain't him," mocked Olga primly, and I guess you know which side yer bread's buttered on. Anyway, his goin's on is as bad or worse. Ye know I saw

that Smith woman in the theyater the other night. Some
class to her. It's diamonds like hers what makes ya wonder
sometimes."

Marie paused, hands on hips. "Well, now, and what do
you wonder? I'm sure it would be most interestin'!"

Olga sniffed. "Wouldn't ya like to know? Don't you
fret, I've had my chances." She nodded her head por-
tentiously.

Marie laughed. "Be yerself and stick to Pat. If ya get
too gay I may get him away from ya. He may be broke,
but he can manage to warm a poor girl's heart."

They both laughed as they ran down the stairs.

CHAPTER TWO

WHEN Miss Downer passed out of the room leaving Mrs. Bronson and Miss Talbot together she stood for a moment irresolutely outside the door and then began to walk very slowly toward the stairs. There was no doubt her composure was ruffled, however little it might have shown during her brief altercation with Jane Talbot, and it took very strong feelings to have the slightest effect upon the gathered quietude of forty years of training and guiding the lives of others. And the trouble went even deeper than that because her pride was touched in its proudest point. May Downer was a woman of few vanities, but she was definitely, if quietly, vain of her sure composure, and when she realized her emotions were stirred sufficiently to break through the steady quietude of her manner, and so, perhaps, make her a matter of comment to others, she was resentful of the cause of her untoward feelings. To put it bluntly, she resented Jane Talbot.

Indeed she had always objected to Jane Talbot on what she considered good and sufficient grounds, and she knew the feeling was reciprocal. When she had agreed to come back to America and leave the simple cottage in Sussex where she had intended to flow gently into the calm, peaceful old age to which she had always looked forward, she had not forgotten about the woman who had so deeply disturbed her last year or two in America. Very few things in her life had ever touched her so intimately, not even the World War. That ghastly struggle had been on such a huge scale as to remain almost impersonal to any one

who had had no intimate part in it, and she had done her
share quietly, steadily, in the way of a million other
women. But Jane Talbot had struck deeper than her mere
concept of personal safety. A war-time enemy might
threaten your life, but they only made the flame of your
principles burn more brightly. It was only little personal
things that could really hurt you, or people like this woman
who struck at the very basis of all your spiritual life, who
defied the basic principle of all life, laughed at God's law,
and gloried in their mockery.

No, she had not forgotten Jane Talbot when she agreed
to return to America for a while in answer to Mrs. Bronson's appeal, accompanied as it was by the most generous
monetary offer, which, if all went well, would enable her
to have a number of little comforts she had thought to
have to do without. Perhaps the thought of those little
comforts had dictated her line of reasoning, but in any
event she had figured that Miss Talbot would long ago
have lost her influence over Mrs. Bronson, and things
would go on as they had before her advent. Mrs. Bronson's deep concern for her daughter had led her to think
this, as much as her quiet faith that time would mend most
troubles, even including Jane Talbot. Mrs. Bronson had
always neglected, indeed ignored Cynthia, especially under
the Talbot influence, therefore her extreme interest in the
girl could only indicate the removal of the influence. It
had seemed so plain.

Such had been her specious reasoning, and she now realized how faulty it had been. All her plans and expectations
were at once changed and would have to be discarded. As
she descended the stairs, she wondered if it might not be
better to return to her little English cottage and forget the
whole stupidity of the madly complicated life which she
had escaped three years before with such a sigh of relief,

and which now threatened to close round her once more. It would be much the simplest thing to do, and yet somehow it was the coward's way. A stupid rhyme jingled in her head:

> "He who fights and runs away
> Lives to fight another day."

She thrust it aside with an impatient gesture of her white, bloodless hand. She must see Cynthia and talk with her. Everything really depended on how she had changed in three years. Perhaps that was really why she had come.

And even as she brushed away her clinging, confused thoughts with a sweep of her hand, she revealed completely the true depths of her perturbation. In her code one did not gesticulate no matter what the cause, and above all, ladies did not. It pronounced you as either foreign or theatrical, equally horrible imprecations.

Greenleaf was standing in the hall as she reached the bottom step.

"It is nice you're going to be with us, May-May. It will seem like old times to have you next to Miss Cynthia."

"Thank you, Greenleaf. Has Cynthia returned yet?"

He shook his head slowly. "Not yet. And the maid is already fussing for fear she won't have time to dress. But it's a short dinner; opera night, you know."

"Yes." The word fell from her lips absently, almost mechanically. She glanced at the butler standing easily and half smilingly before her. Good old congenial Greenleaf; time had not changed him in the least, nor, she smiled a little at the quotation as it popped into her head, was custom likely to stale his infinite variety. He was such a splendid butler, and at the same time so genial, so warm, so human; not at all the stage variety of ramrod-backed automaton. He served meals as if he were the host, somehow taking the place of Thor Bronson sitting glumly at the head of the table, devouring greedily or scorning what was placed before him.

There were so many things she wanted to ask Greenleaf, so many points on which she needed enlightenment if she was to be comfortable in this house after an absence of three years. But there was no need to ask him now, and it was surely neither the time nor the place. Cynthia would be coming in, and Mr. Bronson. She turned toward the stairs.

"I think I'll wait for Cynthia in her room. Has my luggage come?"

The butler smiled. "Just a minute or so after you did. Hortense is unpacking for you. She's a new maid, but I've told her about you, and she'll see you're comfortable. Do you want to go up in the lift?"

It was her turn to smile now. "I see you still will have your little joke. No, I haven't changed a bit, on that point at least. I still despise lifts in private houses and refuse to use them." She went up the stairs slowly.

The butler walked across the hall and stood in the dining-room door looking over the elegantly laid dinner table with a critical eye. It was perfect, as usual, but quite in the modern, rather bare taste. There were moments when Greenleaf regretted the magnificent repasts of the days before the war when to be a real butler implied so much knowledge of ceremony. Then a dinner table had been indeed the scene of veritable feasts, and the beautiful carefully-aged wines had followed one another in sumptuous procession until the ladies swept from the room radiant as charmed peacocks, leaving the gentlemen to their port and gay stories. It all seemed so far away now. Dinner now might begin with a salad; there was no limit to

the eccentricities. To-night dinner was to be merely a cup
of soup, duck, plain salad and dessert. No more lingering
over port. Coffee would be gulped at the table or not
touched at all in the scramble to get to the opera three
quarters of an hour late. Why couldn't people move the
dinner hour forward on opera nights and dine calmly, with
due consideration for the proprieties, and for the exigencies of digestion? Why not arrive on time at the opera and
show originality in some truly original way? Greenleaf
smiled just a little at the patent absurdity of his own
thought.

Just at this point he turned and walked to the door, but
not quickly enough to reach it before it was flung open to
admit a tall slim girl. She was dressed in a severely
tailored suit of dark material with a dark hat pulled down
on her head accentuating the strange ungirlish pallor of
her face. Her features were cameo-like in their cut, and
of faultless perfection, if one sees it not as a fault that
they seemed too sculptural, with the strange haunting quality of alabaster. And her rigidly tailored clothes seemed
only to accentuate her pallor and almost unearthly quality.

"Hello, Greenleaf, were you dawdling about for me?"

As she spoke she pulled off her soft hat, and a pro-
fusion of soft brown hair seemed to spring into life about
her face. It was a regular habit of the girl whenever entering any place where she felt in the least at home, be that
place her own room or a railroad station, and to all who
saw her, it came in the nature of a complete revelation.
And she always said something as she did it, which only
made the effect the more startling, as her voice was soft
and low, with a vague vibrant undercurrent of warmth
which seemed to match the glowing softness of her lovely
hair and join in passionate protest against the classic life-
lessness of her facial beauty. No one ever saw the thrill-

ing transformation without surprise, even for the thousandth time.

A French count expressed it perfectly. "When she enters a room she is a beautiful statue; just so beautiful and so lifeless. When she speaks, you realize the statue is alive, thrillingly alive, and you are stirred."

Perhaps something of these thoughts flashed through Greenleaf's mind as he bowed in answer to her question. "Yes, Miss Cynthia, I was afraid you would be late for dinner. Opera night, you know."

She sighed even as she smiled faintly. "I am not likely to forget. But I can dress in time."

He stood watching her as she walked slowly up the stairs, and then turned away with a shake of his head. It was for the best that May-May had come back at least for a little while. Something was bothering the girl.

When Cynthia entered her room she stood still for an instant, staring with open eyes, then flung her hat away and ran to embrace Miss Downer with open arms, a glad cry on her lips.

"May-May, darling, where have you come from? Oh, I've wanted you so much, so much, and so often."

The woman kissed her gently, then held her off at arm's length. "How beautiful you are, Cynthia! I can't believe it! I'm sure I expected to find my long-legged gawky girl still about. Instead—well, it's too marvelous."

Cynthia shook her head until her brown hair danced. Laughter and tears were mingled in her large brown eyes. "Then are you disappointed, May-May?"

"How could I be, child? Only now I shall have to share you with a thousand cavaliers waiting on your doorstep. There won't be much left over for an ex-governess, even one all the way from England."

The girl suddenly looked serious, and the laughter died

in her eyes. "Have no fear of the thousand 'cavaliers.' There isn't even one. But even the thousand couldn't tear me away from you." Her face lighted up again. "Now tell me why you've left your little dreamy cottage in Sussex to come back here. It looks so adorable in the pictures you sent."

They sat down on a big deep sofa as the woman replied, "Why, to see you, child."

The girl put her long beautiful hand in that of the older woman. "You always were a darling. But why did you come now, just at this time?"

There was a moment of deep silence, then Miss Downer turned slowly and took both the girl's hands in hers. Their eyes met quietly.

"Because I knew you needed me. I think I had to come. Was I wrong? Something seemed to tell me."

This time the silence was so prolonged that she began to wonder if the girl was going to answer or no. She kept her gaze full and steady on the large brown eyes until suddenly they dropped, and she felt a slight tightening of the girl's clasp.

"I do need you, May-May. I'm so glad you came. For a thousand reasons I want you."

"Do you, really?"

"How much I can't tell you."

The woman rose. "Then don't try, child. At least not now, when you're already late for dinner." She glanced at a tiny clock. "You must hurry, Cynthia. Now let me help you, as I used to."

"Will you really?" she cried, jumping up vivaciously. "Won't it be just like old times? Do you remember when I wore my first evening gown, and we laughed so because I looked like a plucked chicken?"

"How could I ever forget? You know I have your pic-

ture in that dress on the shelf over the fireplace in my
little cottage. I'm sure you'd just love my cottage."

"Oh, I know I should. It must be so quaint and sweet
and quiet—just like you."

"My, what a pretty compliment. You have grown up
indeed. And one of these days you must come to visit me."

The girl laughed lightly, then continued seriously, "But
how could you leave it and come back to all this—this use-
lessness?" She waved her arm in a vague, sweeping gesture
which seemed to take in her whole life.

"I wanted to be with you for a while. I've seen your
mother, and I'm to have my old room next to yours.
Won't that be lovely? It will be just like old times."

The girl opened her mouth to speak, then checked herself. "Then mother knew you were coming?" She said
the words slowly, as if they hurt in passing her lips.

For a swift instant Miss Downer hesitated and thought
quickly. But then she spoke so quietly one would never
have known of her perturbation and swift decision.

"Of course, child. I wanted to surprise you, but it would
hardly have done to have surprised mother, would it?"
She watched the girl carefully.

"I suppose not."

"Of course not, Cynthia. And I had to have an invitation, didn't I?" The smile was a little surer now.

The girl swung round passionately. "You could have
asked me. You could have been my guest, instead of
mother's. Now everything is all wrong and tangled up,
like things always were. Don't you see you can't be
mother's guest, and mine too? It can't be. Not any more,
not any more."

The woman moved carefully. It would be so easy to
do the wrong thing now, and spoil everything. "But, child,
I couldn't have stayed here without mother's invitation."

"There are hotels. Hundreds of hotels. I would have gone to see you anywhere, or maybe you doubted that."

"How could I, Cynthia?" Then she saw her opening and walked into it. "I suppose I'll have to confess. You always were so precise you won't leave a poor old woman a shred of pride. Your mother had to pay my passage here. I couldn't afford it, much less living in a hotel. These days in England we just manage to get along, and there's nothing left over for travel, least of all to America. Now you know."

The girl flung herself on her knees before her and looked up at her with brimming eyes. In a moment she was completely transformed.

"Please forgive me, May-May. You know I always was mean and selfish, and I haven't changed a bit, you see. I wanted you all to myself, and I'm such a little fool I didn't even think of the practical side of it. I'm so sorry, so terribly sorry."

The woman brushed the girl's beautiful hair gently with her strangely white hand.

"Poor Cynthia, still the most generous and self-accusing girl in the world. I really don't mind telling you I'm poor. In England we say every one is, so it's just taken for granted. And now let's get on to something important. You have just seven minutes to dress. Haven't you a maid?"

The girl rose quickly. "No, no maid. I can't bear them fiddling around me. After all, you taught me to be self-reliant you know. You're to blame."

And in a minute more they were laughing as they rushed happily about. Cynthia was ready just in time, and as the footman tapped at the door she flung it open gayly, crying, "Ready and waiting—for once!"

Then she turned. "May-May, I wish you were having dinner with us. I hate social formalities."

The woman smiled. "Then why try to drag me into what you hate? I'm going to a little restaurant I remember, and then on to a play. I'm really quite excited about my first night in New York in three years. Who knows how gay I may be?"

"Darling May-May. You'll probably be as wicked as Sir Galahad." She held out her arms and as she stood so for an instant the woman was fascinated by her ethereal beauty. The simple white silk gown billowed luxuriously about the slim, girlish figure, and the pearls about her throat seemed to draw life from the delicate flesh on which they nestled so glowingly. The girl half-turned slowly, and then glanced smilingly over the delicate curve of her shoulder.

"Are you pleased with your pupil? Do you think any one will ever want me?"

"What a beautiful creature you are, Cynthia. Whose heart are you going to break to-night?"

"Well, I have a choice between a football star and a Russian Prince. I might try both. What do you suggest? I've never even seen the 'gridiron hero' as the papers call him, but he looks very cave-mannish in his pictures, you know, tousled hair, no shave, and a sort of 'grrr' light in his eyes."

May-May laughed. "He does sound fascinating. I'm sure he'll be irresistible."

"I hope so," the girl cried as she ran down the corridor.

CHAPTER THREE

A SPORTS-WRITER had once written of Dale Eustis, "It is hard to imagine a more perfect specimen of the true football player. It is as if God had decided that the perfect sport needed a perfect type by which others might be judged and measured. A great, powerful body, and yet with legs to run like a track-man; a clear, quick brain and gifted with true imagination; limitless endurance coupled with infinite patience and capped off by the best disposition on or off the football field."

To be sure that sports-writer was an enthusiast, but there was much truth in what he said. Dale Eustis was indeed the perfect football player, and his name was on every one's tongue, even as his image was enshrined in every youngster's heart. And with it all he was the quiet fine fellow he had always been, sure of himself, able to take care of himself, and the gentler for that very reason. Because of all this he was dining in New York and going to the opera, which is certainly contrary to the usual training standards of football players. When he had asked his trainer, Mike Mulligan, for permission, the tough little Irishman had grinned until he showed most of his broken ugly teeth, as well as giving some indication of the depths of his good nature. He had laid his hand on Dale's arm. "And does dinner and the opera really mean just dinner and the opera?" The man was clever enough to ask in just that way.

Dale had smiled then. "I think I can safely promise you that." The two men laughed a little.

"Then run along, my boy, and when you come back you can sing us a few tunes."

Dale had thanked him in his earnest quiet way, and so seven-thirty found him in Mrs. Bronson's drawing-room, talking to Jane Talbot. His elegantly cut evening clothes merely accentuated the grace of the powerful body they clothed.

"It's fine meeting you again, Miss Talbot. I remember how you used to beat me at tennis that summer in Tuxedo." He ran a hand through his rough fair hair.

She smiled. "We did have good games, didn't we, and you really played awfully well? But you shouldn't remind me of those days; you make me feel ancient."

"I couldn't be so unjust. You haven't really changed a bit. It seems yesterday that we said good-by at the club."

She laughed her strange, harsh laugh, and turned the gleam of her monocle full on him. "How nice of you to say that. We must play again soon. I still manage to stagger about the courts a little."

He grinned at her, and it suddenly flashed through her mind what a big, grand boy he really was, seemingly as untouched as when she had played tennis with him, during her last year as a guest in Tuxedo Park. His words came lightly to her, and the years seemed to fall away.

"I'll bet your tennis is still tournament-form. You were one of the real top-notchers."

She crossed her legs carefully before answering. "That was not so clever, Dale. Don't you know never to remind a woman of what she was? It hurts."

"I'm sorry."

"Don't be. I was asking for trouble when I suggested playing with you again, but I couldn't resist trying to turn back a few of life's pages. Isn't that the way the sentimental novelists used to express it? How old are you, Dale?"

"Twenty-two." He proclaimed it almost defiantly.

"Isn't it sad. You're only a child still. Do you still take orders from your mother?"

He grinned again, half sheepishly, half mockingly. "No, it's my trainer now. His name's Mike Mulligan, as you probably know, and I ask him, 'Please may I go to New York to have dinner with Mrs. Bronson and go to the opera?' I use my meekest voice of course."

"And what did he say?" she laughed.

"Oh, something about being a good boy and going to bed early."

"Did he add 'alone'?" she mocked.

"It was understood."

The slight stiffness of his tone amused her, but she made no reply. She got up and he rose with her. "I say, Miss Talbot, why don't you ever come to Tuxedo any more?" Once more the tone was lightly conversational; quite proper."

"I'm not invited. Quite simple, isn't it?" She shrugged her shoulders.

"And suppose I invite you?" He was earnest enough now.

She stared at him a moment, then laughed again. He wished she wouldn't laugh so harshly. It had a strange quality, like the jangle of iron bells.

"I forgot—you're over twenty-one now. But you won't invite me, so it doesn't matter. Speak to your mother. As I remember, she's quite an authority on why one isn't invited places. I really think she ought to get a book out on the subject. It would make a fascinating stir, especially if illustrated properly, with Tuxedo scenes."

She noted that he looked uncomfortable as she spoke,

but such a thing had never deterred Jane Talbot, and least of all when she was speaking of some one whom she disliked as heartily as she did Clorinda Eustis. But she had liked Dale as a youngster, and he seemed to have developed beautifully, so she laid a hand lightly on his arm and turned towards the stairs where Cynthia was just descending, a vision of white loveliness.

"There's your reason for being here. Feast your eyes."

The young man stared a moment as if fascinated, then breathed softly, "God, what a beauty!"

Miss Talbot glanced at him searchingly. "I thought you'd think so." Then she walked swiftly into the hall to meet the girl.

"Cynthia, you are a real vision of loveliness."

They stood a moment. "That's sweet of you to say that, Jane. I want to look as happy as I feel to-night."

"Then you've succeeded."

"Oh, Jane, do you know May-May is back?"

The woman nodded grimly. "Unfortunately, I do. We'll all go Victorian again now, with just a piquant dash of Queen Mary for good measure. But I won't disturb your rapture in her return." She lowered her voice a little. "Can you have lunch with me to-morrow, just we two?"

"Why, Jane, I'd love to." Her eyes brightened.

"Good, but don't advertise it. One o'clock." Then she turned toward the drawing-room and raised her voice. Dale Eustis stood looking out at them as if he couldn't take his eyes off the girlish figure in white.

"Come, Dale, and be presented to your queen of beauty, for whom you must do deeds of great valor. Cynthia, here is the reincarnated Sir Galahad."

He bowed deeply as the girl held out her hand with a warm gesture. "I'm just thrilled to meet the famous Dale

Eustis. I saw you play two weeks ago. It was just wonderful. I couldn't sleep a wink all night."

Miss Talbot clapped her hands lightly. "I'm sure you've rehearsed it, Cynthia, it's just too pat. And now, Sir Galahad, what have you to say, even as you hold the lady's hand?"

A deep flush mounted above his crisp dress collar. "I'm so glad to meet you, Miss Bronson."

Cynthia laughed, and her voice was ravishing music to his ears. "But I'm really Miss Thorpe. Mr. Bronson is my step-father. I thought every one knew that."

The flush mounted higher as he half stammered, "I'm so sorry, Miss . . . Miss Thorpe."

Miss Talbot shuddered mockingly. "Dale, what a disappointment you are. Like Sir Galahad, you are all virtue and no poetry."

Cynthia smiled. "Not to me, Jane." She slipped her hand through his arm coquettishly. "Now you must take me in to mother, Mr. Eustis. I see mother so seldom we almost need to be introduced."

As they passed into the drawing-room, Greenleaf appeared to announce dinner. Cynthia nodded gayly to her father and mother and extended her hand to their other guest, Prince Ladislov, who bowed over it elegantly.

"Miss Thorpe, you are as beautiful as a spring dream."

She curtsied laughingly. "When Prince Ladislov honors us, I dare not be less." She just couldn't help liking the dignified, sad-eyed Russian.

Every one laughed except poor Dale who was still in a fascinated daze, and Mr. Bronson who rattled his keys in his trousers' pocket and muttered, "Can't we save the comic opera until later?"

Mrs. Bronson laughed tinklingly to cover the remark as she took the Prince's arm. "Thor's right, we must hurry

if we want to hear the big solo in the first act. Prince
Ladislov, do you remember how well Sembrich used to
do it?"

Bronson turned to Miss Talbot as the others entered
the dining-room.

"I don't suppose you need an arm to lean on?"

"Not unless you insist," she mocked.

"I'm not likely to insist," he barked, and strode into the
dining-room ahead of her and straight to his place at the
foot of the table.

The butler and two footmen began serving dexterously
with that silent almost motionless swiftness of perfectly
trained servants.

And as dinner progressed there could be no doubt that
Cynthia had captured the thoughts and fired the imagination of the unanimous choice for All-American right
half-back. He had eyes for nothing else and quite in the
tradition of romance neglected the dinner shamelessly. The
butler was quite put out by his careless refusal of the wine,
because, as high-priest of the fast decaying art of dining,
Greenleaf felt that wine was one of the few really sacred
things in life, and the more so because careful legislation
had made it accessible only to those rich enough openly
to defy constitutional amendments. He could well understand how one might refuse a rare vintage sadly, with a
lingering look at the luxury one was denying oneself, but
to nod it away carelessly in the middle of a sentence was
too much. After dinner was over he confided to the cook
that he was "afraid Miss Cynthia was too much taken up
with Mr. Eustis. He might be a good athlete, but ..."

"Afraid" was the word he used with carefully lugubrious stress on the second syllable, but Molly Dennison was
of the generation of cooks who must peep into the dining-
room, and so she either ignored or was completely insensi-

tive to his meaning. She merely remarked with feeling that
Eustis was "the grandest man she had ever seen," and
something in her tone intimated that even if she was a
cook, one need not presuppose that she had not seen plenty
in her time. But Greenleaf refused to take up her conversational lead, even as she had scorned his, and so nothing
came of either remark, to the vague disappointment of
them both. He returned to his pantry with a feeling of
futility.

Meanwhile, at the opera enough people stared at her
little party to satisfy Mrs. Bronson's deepest cravings.
They were photographed as they entered from Fortieth
Street, and inside the lobby an energetic reporter in a
sufficiently badly fitting dinner jacket stopped Dale to
question him as to why he was at the opera in the very
height of the football season. His manner intimated an
article on athletes who break training rules, etc. Mrs.
Bronson was a little annoyed at this interruption of her
sweeping progress through the lobby where there was a
good-sized crowd of those who considered it more important to watch the million-dollar late-comers than to
listen to the music within; but she stopped with a smile
and spoke to the Prince.

"Dale Eustis is so popular it must bore him dreadfully
at times. And yet I suppose it's a wonderful thing."

Prince Ladislov had been watching him with sad weary
eyes. He smiled down upon his hostess.

"It must be wonderful to be so vitally alive. He seems
quite taken with Cynthia. They both look so happy."

She laughed lightly. "And why not, my Prince?"

"Why not indeed? For myself, I love too, but oh so
hopelessly. In these days to be a Prince is less than
nothing."

"And must you always jest about my poor daughter?

But she does look so happy to-night. I'm afraid I hope it's Dale."

It was rather unfortunate that she did not hear that young man rise to the occasion when asked why he was breaking training. He smiled on Cynthia before facing his interrogator. "Do I need a more perfect reason?"

The reporter agreed and plunged into a telephone booth to give his city editor the results of his interview with Dale Eustis, "the idol of a million fans."

But if Mrs. Bronson did not hear the remark and Cynthia's happy laugh which followed, Jane Talbot did and turned to her unwilling escort.

"I hope you have plans for Cynthia and Dale."

He sniffed. "Well, what of it? Have you any objections?"

"None in the least, but I happen to like Dale, and whether she likes me or not, I think I understand his mother."

"Which means you don't like Cynthia. Is that it?"

"On the contrary, I do like Cynthia."

He stopped and faced her for just a moment as he spoke. "I'm very sorry to hear it. I would be much happier if I were sure you hated her."

She said nothing, and a moment later they entered the box. As they did so waves of applause swept across the crowded house. The first act of the opera was over, and as Miss Talbot expressed it with acid irony, they were just in time. As the applause died down, the lights went up into their full glowing warmth, and every one turned this way and that and frankly stared. Mrs. Bronson sat with lightly folded hands and beamed upon the world, the happy world in which she found herself so happily placed. She was rich and she looked her best. Her husband was rich and powerful. She had a beautiful daughter with her, and a very rich young man who was also a popular idol; a Russian Prince who looked the part; and Jane. That was all important. They had quarreled, but she had carried her point. For the first time she had faced Jane determinedly and carried her point, carried it so completely that Jane had given way, and been the one to offer to make up. It gave her an uncanny sense of triumph.

And it was good to have May-May back. How happy Cynthia had looked as she came down the stairs, and how beautifully her meeting with Dale had gone off. She glanced at her daughter with her head slightly tilted back and a delicate smile on her lips as she listened to Dale's comment on something or other. They certainly were much taken with one another, and it looked like a case of love at first sight. She sighed ever so little. How perfect if it were really so, and her dark troubled thoughts had been unfounded. Maybe there was no need for May-May after all, and yet it was for the best if she stayed—at least for a while.

CHAPTER FOUR

JANE TALBOT looked very much at home in the brown tweed trousers and open-necked white shirt she affected in the privacy of her cozy apartment on Central Park West. She wore Basque sandals with rope soles which are always so popular on the Riviera, and moved lightly and noiselessly about in her big living room. Seeing her there it was as if you saw her for the first time as she really was and not as if made up for some highly sophisticated and pretentious masquerade. There was a surety and ease about her movements now which no one who was to judge her by her behavior of the night before could quite understand. She was at home.

The sun flooded in at the big windows which faced east and south and so gave a maximum of sunlight, which was one of the things Jane Talbot wanted most out of life and which she intended to have if it was humanly possible. She was always annoyed, for example, at Aurelia Bronson. "How can you bear to have a bedroom which doesn't get the morning sun?"

The first time she asked this vehemently Mrs. Bronson had been surprised. "But you can't have it on Fifth Avenue. All the houses face West."

Miss Talbot had tapped her foot impatiently. "But you can have a bedroom at the back of the house and so have the sun. And it would be quieter too."

Aurelia had been really surprised. "Don't be silly, Jane. Every one would laugh at me if I had my room at the back of the house. That's where the servants' rooms are. Besides, I want to look out on the Park."

She smiled. "Aurelia, I'm sure you don't look out of your windows twice a week. No one on Fifth Avenue ever does for fear some passer-by will see her. Well, why not live in some place like Central Park West? I get sun and view and still can have a front bedroom."

"But Jane, one can't live on Central Park West. You know that." She was very serious.

And Jane had laughed her loudest and harshest at this. It was so delightfully like Aurelia Bronson to feel she'd die if she couldn't live on Fifth Avenue. What use was there in trying to remind her that she had been born in Brooklyn. She had not only striven to forget when she was born but where as well, and had been completely successful in both.

Now this day as Jane Talbot sat in her sunny living room she thought of it again, and laughed a little grimly. The sun felt good to-day as the weather had turned much cooler during the night, and now it was cold enough to make one appreciate the flooding sunshine and a sparkling log fire as well. She leaned back in her chair comfortably with legs outstretched and ankles crossed.

A few minutes later the telephone rang and she thought she knew who was calling as she walked over to the table where the instrument stood. There was a faint smile on her lips as she heard the voice of her caller. Her imagination had not been at fault. When she put down the instrument five minutes later her smile had widened into one of complete triumph. She took a few quick strides up and down the room.

So Aurelia Bronson had come to her senses after her display of bravado the night before and had telephoned suggesting she come for lunch. For an instant she had wondered if Cynthia had told her mother of her luncheon engagement but had instantly decided it was highly improbable as there was no bridge of affection between the two across which careless confidences were likely to pass. No. It was far 'more likely that Aurelia was merely contrite and suggested she come to lunch with her as a friendly gesture. Aurelia was hardly capable of anything much more subtle than that. Every play she made was so obvious.

Unless one considered the return of May Downer a little more carefully. Was it really just a silly show of affection on the part of the old Englishwoman whereby she got her former employer to finance a trip to America in order to break the monotony of life in a little cottage; or was it something much more important than that, some scheme of Aurelia's? Was it possible the woman had been brought back to bridge the gap between mother and daughter; was it possible Aurelia had sent for her in a belated fit of maternal interest? The idea was almost too fantastic to any one who knew Aurelia.

And yet it would account for so much. She rose to her feet suddenly and crushed out her cigarette with an air of determination. If Aurelia was reaching out for her daughter she had delayed just a little too long, as her little luncheon to-day would prove. A little frankness last night might have made all the difference in the world, but Aurelia had chosen to be secretive and clever.

She was glad she had been so short with Aurelia. "Sorry, but I can't ask you to lunch as I have guests coming. . . . No, I'm sure you wouldn't fit in. . . . All right, we can go out to dinner if you really wish it, but I'm afraid I'll be tired." Yes, that was the only way to talk to Aurelia— with utter indifference. Jane Talbot swung through the room and into the little kitchen to talk to her colored maid about preparations for lunch. Rosalind might be a ridiculous name for a colored servant but if she could be utterly faithful and discreet and cook divinely, what did it matter

what she chose as a name? Jane Talbot would not have resented Ganymede.

The trim ship's clock over the fireplace was just about
to ping its two staccato notes indicating one o'clock when
Rosalind, now resplendent in passionately starched cap and
apron, ushered Cynthia into the room with sweeping
African ceremony.

"You look lovely, Cynthia. Have you walked here across
the park?" Jane shook hands warmly.

"And ever so much further too," the girl cried as she
flung off her coat and sank into a deep chair. There was a
faint touch of color in her cheeks which lent a human
touch to her usual strange pallor. And it seemed to correspond with the rose in the button-hole of her crisply
tailored, tweed walking costume which lent a delicate fem-
inine touch otherwise strangely absent. There was a little
silence broken only by the crackle of the bright fire. Then
the girl rose impulsively and walking to the cheery blaze
stood for a moment with her back to it, English fashion,
hands clasped behind her and slowly rocking on her heels.
She looked very determined.

"I'm awfully glad I was coming here to lunch to-day.
Mother sailed in on me dressed in one of those regular
Ethel Barrymore negligees and tried to play the doting
mother. I can't bare her to kiss me and I wish she wouldn't
do it. I told her so to-day and she went off in a huff. It
was all too ridiculous and with May-May there, too. Why
must mother be absurd at times?"

Jane Talbot leaned back in her chair with her sleek head
against its down back-cushions and her eyes closed. "Cynthia, aren't you a little hard on your mother?"

"No. Why is it hard on her that I merely want to be let
alone? It isn't very much to ask."

A strange smile twisted the woman's lips. "That is,

strange to you, isn't it? But mothers are like that, at least
I suppose so." Her lips hardly moved as she spoke.

"But mine isn't, and you know it. Mother hasn't a spark
of love in her body for me and not only we know it, but I
guess all the world does too. At least all our little stupid
world and we're so tied down we never get a chance to
know any other."

"Then maybe your mother realizes that—now."

"Now it's too late," the girl cried passionately. "Nine-
teen years ago was the time for that, or fifteen, or ten, or
five, but not now. It's too late now, so terribly too late.
The first thing I can remember in life was crying for my
mother, and she never came. I yearned for her and when
I got older I prayed for her to come to me, because I
needed her so much; because there were a thousand things
every day I wanted to tell her. And she never came. I used
to hide behind curtains to watch her walk through the hall
as beautiful and as aloof as some glittering star. I'd run
away from May-May and hide in mother's room so she'd
find me and maybe give me a hug and a kiss like one hears
about mothers doing, but it was all of no use. I was merely
sent back to the nursery and May-May was scolded for
letting me get away from her. Then I'd cry myself to
sleep.

"When I began reading I always wanted stories of
mothers who were devoted to their daughters, foolishly devoted if you please, but to a lonely little girl no devotion
can possibly be foolish. And I always wanted May-May to
tell me of her mother and how good she had been to her,
especially about the time when she wandered off with the
gypsies who didn't realize she was with them until they
built a fire under the stars to cook their supper. Then they
took her back to the village where she lived and found
every one looking for her. Her mother was so happy she

covered her face with kisses. I can't ever forget those words. I always used to pretend I didn't hear and ask 'What did your mother do when you got home?' I knew those words so well. They sang like little birds in my heart, but I wanted to hear them again.

"Then I wanted to run away, too, so I could be brought home to my mother. What gypsies are there to run away with in New York? It's so funny now when I look back. I didn't know where to run because I didn't want to go away at all; I just wanted to be brought back and as soon as possible. So I slipped out of the house and sat on a park bench just across the street with my eyes glued on mother's windows. It was a warm spring day and the curtains were blowing back a little at the open windows. Once I caught a glimpse of mother and I couldn't help waving. I thought maybe she'd see me and come rushing out and cover my face with kisses. Yes, and 'clasp me to her bosom.' That was another phrase of May May's which used to pluck my heart strings. I used to lie awake nights haunted by visions of impossible tenderness."

She raised her hand quickly to her eyes to touch away a tear. "Am I boring you Jane?"

The woman still lay with closed eyes. "No indeed. Please go on. You were just sitting on the park bench looking across Fifth Avenue up at your mother's windows."

"Well," she sighed, "that was all there was to that. The butler came out and took me back to the nursery. I remember he carried me in his arms just as if he was entering into the game a little, too. We met mother on the stairs. I held out my arms to her but she merely spoke to him and swept on down. She said, 'Greenleaf, I do wish you wouldn't carry Cynthia. She's spoiled enough as it is.' That was all. He said, 'Yes, madame,' but he didn't put me down until he reached the nursery. I'll never forget that."

Again there was a silence. Then the girl's voice sobbed out, "That's why it's too late now. Now I'm a woman and mother's only just another woman, a complete stranger. I can't bear her to touch me, her kisses sicken me now, Jane. Jane, I don't understand it. I can't understand it."

The woman rose quickly and faced her calmly, trousered legs wide apart. "Why try to, Cynthia? Why try to understand anything in this muddled life? When the sky is blue and the sun glowing why want to *know* anything, in the vain italicized sense of the word. It is enough to know your need for love and to refuse to be denied the natural opening of your heart. Maybe I'm lonely too."

The girl looked up quickly. "Oh, but you have a mother."

Jane stood very still a moment, then asked quietly, "And do you hate me, too? Don't be afraid to say it, not to-day when we are speaking right out of our hearts."

"No." The girl spoke very slowly now. "How could I hate you? I feel as if you were more than a friend; more like a—brother." There was a strange hesitation before the word.

The woman's gruff laugh rasped out. "Very well put, Cynthia, and I'll try to live up to it. You were very happy last night, weren't you? Let's think about that."

"Oh, yes."

"And it wasn't entirely for La Traviata, was it?"

"No, indeed, Jane. Don't be silly."

"Or for your May-May whom you like so much and I so little?"

"No," the word fell hesitatingly from the girl's lips as she watched Jane closely. She started a little when the clock pinged sharply three times. She could just hear Rosalind speaking to some one in the little outer hall of the apartment."

"Then let's be happy," Jane laughed, and turned toward

the door. "Come in, Dale Eustis, luncheon is waiting for you. Luncheon and a very wonderful surprise."

Cynthia's eyes opened wide as the young man walked smilingly into the room. As he saw the girl he stopped and his expression instantly changed.

"Cynthia!" he cried.

"Dale!"

Jane Talbot watched them staring at each other with strange startled eyes for a moment, then her short laugh barked out raucously.

"I thought so. Well, children, stop staring at each other and let's have some lunch. I, for one, am famished."

As she spoke the young man pulled himself together and advanced to meet her with outstretched hand. "I'm so sorry Miss Talbot, but I was really startled to see Cyn— I mean Miss Thorpe."

The woman shook hands in her firm, hearty manner. "Quite all right, my boy. You wouldn't be the first man whom Cynthia has startled even though you are the first here."

"Jane." the girl's voice snapped across the room.

The woman turned slowly, setting her monocle firmly in her eyes as she did so. "Don't worry, child, I'm not in the least flustered even if I am very well pleased, and in any case Dale and I are old friends and he's a senior at the university now. Am I right, Dale? I thought so." She spread her hands palms upward, fingers wide apart, with a strange exotic gesture which yet was characteristic of her vibrant personality. "And there you are."

The girl smiled faintly and crossed to Dale whose eyes had never left her. "Well, Mr. Eustis, it is a surprise to see you so soon again, and a happy one."

Before the young man could speak Jane burst out, "Dale,

I'm surprised at you. That's the speech you're supposed to make."

He faced her with a little flush and a faint laugh. "I certainly am very remiss to-day." He turned toward Cynthia and bowed. "How do you do, Miss Thorpe, I didn't realize how much the gods were to favor me to-day."

They all laughed and just then Rosalind entered to announce luncheon. Jane slipped an arm through one of each of her guests and led them toward the dining room. "But I must say I will allow no more of this Miss Thorpe and Mr. Eustis. It's all very well for the average wishy-washy colorless people, but not for two dear friends of mine, both with endless charm and personality. It's now Cynthia, Dale, and Jane. See how well they go together, almost like Tom, Dick, and Harry. Now, Cynthia, you sit there, and Dale, you there. Now we're all set and let's hope Rosalind doesn't fail us."

All during the meal which was most delicious, Cynthia wondered about it all; that is, wondered as much as her happiness would allow her to do. It was all so very strange, and still harder to account for Dale being here for lunch. But he was and her happiness did not allow her to question too deeply. From the first moment she had met him last night she had been stirred as never before in her life and when he bade her good night after the opera the mere touch of his hand had become magic to stir her blood and let the warm depths of her stifled emotion move within her. It was all so unexpected coming as it did immediately on top of May-May's happy return and just when, only a few hours before, life had seemed utterly dull and purposeless.

She smiled at Jane in response to one of her gay sallies. She had never known Jane to be so jolly and amusing as to-day, and yet until Dale's arrival she had been so serious and had listened so patiently to her passionate outburst against her mother and against the long dreary years of neglect which had been her childhood.

It seemed she had always wanted to confide in some one as she had in Jane to-day, and there had never been any one, not even for a day, to whom she might have talked. There had always been May-May, of course, but you couldn't confide your heart-aches to some one who was a witness to most if not all of them; to some one who seemed to be trying every minute to make up for the very thing which you wanted to talk about; to some one who was in the employ of, and received a salary from, the very one of whom you needed to complain. No, for all the long years of her love-starved girlhood there had been no one to whom to turn.

And now she had blurted out her secret to Jane, and Jane had understood so much more than she had said; had seemed to understand those hidden inmost thoughts which she never dared to put into words in her own mind, since even as vague ghostly pictures they were bad enough and needed no gilded frame of speech to make them clearer. For a moment she had been a bit terrified at the seeming extent of Jane's understanding and the vistas of thought opened by it. Jane's questioning had seemed either so purposeless or else so terribly purposeful and all the while she was simply leading up to a striking entrance for Dale, an entrance which seemed to say, "You have asked for love, and it is here."

Dale. What strange thoughts and emotions suddenly twined themselves about the tiny word which made up his name. How sweetly her own name had fallen from his lips, how spontaneously, as if it had hung like a drop of water trembling on the edge of his mind. And his name had leaped to her lips involuntarily to blend with hers like

flame to flame, and they had stared at each other forgetful
of all else. It was like a flash of lightning, too terrifyingly
sudden to be real, and yet with trembling nerves to testify
to its reality.

What a gay happy person he was. How his wide mouth
laughed and his eyes laughed as he listened to Jane talking
vivaciously, snared with her droll sense of humor which
always lent charm and interest to the most ordinary chron-
icle of daily events.

She was deep in her thoughts when she noticed Jane had
stopped talking and they both were watching her with an
amused expression. Jane laughed.

"Wake up, dreamer; or are your dreams so much pleas-
anter than the reality of our company?"

She half started from her chair. "Why, Jane, you really
frightened me. I must have been daydreaming."

"I should think so," Dale cried, "Jane has been telling
us a very funny story and you never even smiled. Come,
'fess up, as they say, and tell us who was the lucky one."

She looked steadily at him. How blue his eyes were and
how clear and bright, like a sun-flooded sky. "I was thinking about you," she said quietly.

A startled look came into his eyes and he opened his
mouth as if to speak but no word came. Jane fixed her
steady gaze on the young girl.

"Well, Cynthia, I must say you are refreshingly candid
to say the least. You certainly speak right out."

"Why not?"

Jane's short laugh barked out, "Indeed, why not? I
agree with you, but look what you've done to Dale. He's
quite speechless."

"Not quite, Jane," he said slowly, but even as he spoke
his eyes never left Cynthia's face. "I'm not sure I don't

like it. Anyhow, I know I've never met a girl like Cynthia, never."

He repeated the last word with a vague, soft emphasis which touched some chord in Jane's heart. She reached out her left hand and touched Cynthia's lying on the table. The girl's eyes raised slowly to hers.

"Now see what you've done, Cynthia, child. I know you've simply ruined a great football player. He'll do nothing but dream about you now. I know how it is. The minute a man decides a girl is different, there is no hope for him and now I'm sure Dale will pick up the football and run in the wrong direction, or whatever it is one does to correspond to trumping your partner's ace!"

They all joined in the laugh with the relief every one feels when an apt remark has broken the tension and one can sit back and relax. It's good to laugh easily.

"I'm sure Dale never runs in the wrong direction," cried Cynthia. "They only do that in silly moving pictures."

Dale grinned. "Don't be too sure. It does happen once in a while and then it's much funnier than any picture could be. A chap did it in one of our practice games early this fall."

"There you are," Jane cried. "But, Dale, please let us know ahead of time when you're going to do it, so we can be sure to be there."

"And I'll give you a scarf to tie around your arm like the knights in the old days," mocked Cynthia.

In the general laugh they rose from the table and passed into the drawing room where Rosalind was busy arranging the coffee table.

"Do you dare drink coffee, Dale?" asked Jane.

He bowed. "To-day I dare do anything, even as I have stayed over to-day when I should have gone by the first train this morning. But I certainly don't need any more stimulation and I've got to run along now. It's all right to miss classes, but football practice . . ." he shook his head, "not this time of year. Saturday's one of our big games."

He remained standing with a smile on his lips. Cynthia swung toward him. "And won't you stay over if I ask you? Won't you stay for dinner with me?"

He bowed. "I'm sorry I can't."

"But you stayed over for lunch with Jane," she pouted.

"That was a glorious stroke of luck and I don't dare tempt the fickle goddess again. Now I can go back to my duty with a singing heart."

Jane caught up the word lightly. "A singing heart," she cried. "Dale, you're really becoming a poet."

He clicked his heels together. "Man is tempted to be worthy of his inspiration." Jane applauded.

The young girl turned toward the big windows a little wearily. "I'm tired of the game of fine phrases. I'm asking you to stay over and take me to dinner. I've never asked any one before."

In a stride he reached her and caught her hand. "Cynthia, don't talk like that. I can't tell you how much I want to stay but I must go back." He pulled out his watch. "I've just time to catch my train." He dropped her hand as if suddenly realizing what he was doing.

She turned and to his surprise he saw she was now smiling. She held out both her hands heartily. "Run along then, and good luck. Call me up whenever you're in town."

A moment more and he was gone. Jane sank into her chair and began pouring coffee. "It's one lump of sugar, isn't it, Cynthia?"

The girl stood staring out of the window down into the street. The blazing sunshine flooded her slim elegant figure and brought out the golden lights in her soft wavy hair.

She answered without turning, "Three lumps please—to-day."

Jane glanced at her strangely. "And a Benedictine, perhaps?"

"Please. It would be fine, if you have any."

The woman rose and walked swiftly across the room to a beautifully inlaid cabinet and drew out a bottle. Her face was lit with a strange look of triumph as she poured out the fragrant liqueur. The girl still stood at the window bathed in the glory of the sunshine.

CHAPTER FIVE

CYNTHIA burst into Miss Downer's room and flung her arms gayly about that woman's neck.

"Oh, May-May, I'm so happy I don't know what to do. I just want to shout and sing and dance forever."

And suiting the action to the word she began to dance wildly about the room, her eyes sparkling. Miss Downer stood very still in front of the chair from which she had risen, with one hand still holding the sewing on which she had been working before the girl's tempestuous entrance. When Cynthia finally quieted down a little breathlessly, she put the sewing carefully into a basket.

"I'm certainly glad to see you so gay. Now you are more like the little girl I was always so fond of."

Cynthia caught both her hands. "And I'm not going to be glum or morose any more, May-May, never, never, never. I've decided life was just meant so we should live it and be gay every minute of the time." She paused a moment in thought then went on slowly, "When the sky is blue and the sun glowing, why want to *know* anything in the italicized sense of the word."

The woman smiled. "That sounds like a quotation."

"It is, May-May, and I knew you'd guess it. But there is another line of it, I think I can remember: 'It is enough to know your need for love and to refuse to be denied the natural opening of your heart.'"

Miss Downer sat down again. "I don't like that part of it, but then you probably knew I shouldn't. It sounds like something out of a novel, one of those modern novels."

Cynthia flung herself at the woman's feet with a gay laugh. "Dear, kind, old May-May. You haven't changed a bit. But this time you're wrong, because it doesn't come out of a book. Some one said it to me and with great fervor, too. You should have heard."

"I'm rather glad I didn't. It hardly seems to me like appropriate luncheon conversation. You were out to luncheon I understand."

"Yes, May-May, I was out to luncheon, and it was the most thrilling meal I've ever had in my life. I just hoped it would go on and on forever, but it didn't, and seeing everything must come to an end I brought it to an end happily—with Benedictine."

The girl sat still for a moment, then ran on again: "But the quotation isn't from luncheon conversation. It was before lunch that we had a serious talk."

"Is it permitted to inquire whom you were lunching with?"

Cynthia shook her head. "It seems funny, but it is a secret. I don't particularly see why, but it is."

"Was it some one of whom your mother approves? I'm not asking you, of course, but just reminding you."

The girl laughed joyfully. "It's strange, but I'm not sure I can answer that question. At any rate mother knows the people and they are guests here. Does that satisfy the requirements?"

"Certainly. There should be no doubt of that."

"Then all is well," cried Cynthia, jumping to her feet. "What does it matter, anyhow, as long as we're as happy as we are now? Won't you be gay with me, May-May?"

"Why of course, child."

"That's the gay sport. Now let's see what we can do. Let's have dinner in some nice, grubby place where no one will know us and then we'll go on to a play. We'll have

dinner early and walk around and see all the lights and
stare in all the windows as if we came from the country
or Staten Island or some place like that. How does that
sound?"

Miss Downer rose quickly. "It sounds wonderful to an
old woman from a little English village. Are you sure you
want me instead of some nice girl friend?"

"But that's just it. I want only you and no one else. Do
you remember how you used to take me to the circus when
I was a little girl and we'd feed peanuts to the elephants?
That's the mood I want to go in to-night. Now you've
come all the way from England to see me and I just want
us to be gay together and not think of any one else."

A happy smile wreathed the woman's face. "What time
do we start out from here?"

"Five-thirty," laughed the girl. "And we won't have any
tea so we can get hungry very early. And remember, no
dressing up. Put on your worst hard-times costume."

She waved her hand lightly and flashed from the room.
Miss Downer sat down again placidly with her sewing.
There was an hour she could use before beginning to dress.
But though she worked steadily enough any one watching
might have seen her lips curve into a quiet smile a dozen
times or more.

It was only half past seven when they came out of the
Italian restaurant on 49th Street and joined the throngs of
people on the crowded streets. Cynthia had been as happy
as a lark all through the table d'hote dinner and many of
the people in the restaurant had turned to stare at her,
lured by the sound of her light silvery laughter. And for
once Miss Downer forgot her English reticence and didn't
really mind as she sat smiling easily, happy in the girl's
happiness as well as in her own thoughts. There could be
no doubt now that Cynthia trusted her and would turn to

her when the opportunity came to confide in some one. Everything was going smoothly. Already she thought she understood the girl's real difficulty and felt in her heart that she would be able to cope with the situation when it arose.

So both were extremely happy as they threaded their way through the Broadway crowds, being jostled every minute and minding it not at all. Cynthia sailed ahead with sparkling eyes and laughing lips as several young men with pale faces and much-too-large overcoats bumped into her and commented in a loud voice.

"Say, Jerry, there's a swell looker."

"Yeah! What about it?"

"Huh! Where's your nerve now?"

One of them whistled softly, then they laughed uproariously as the girl passed out of earshot in the rush to cross the street before the traffic signal changed. Miss Downer caught up with Cynthia a little breathlessly and took her arm.

"Child, you walk so fast. I'm all out of breath and feel pushed until I'm sure I'm coming apart."

"Isn't it grand?" the girl cried with slightly disconcerting irrelevance. "Don't you just love it? I think this is the real way to go to the theater and not like we do in the big car and stare out of plate glass windows at people who don't jump out of the way quickly enough." She looked into May-May's eyes and her face was radiant with the glorious discovery of the joy of living. "May-May, I'm sick of plate glass windows and cushions and chauffeurs and limousines. I want to get down in the street and rub shoulders with life, with people, men and women. It's all so exciting. I want to feel bodies rubbing against me and—"

May-May stopped still, aghast and hardly able to believe her ears. Cynthia faced her with dancing eyes.

"Cynthia! How can you talk so, and in the street?"

"But it's really so private in a crowd like this, May-May. Nobody knows who you are, or cares for that matter."

Miss Downer opened her mouth to speak, but was suddenly pushed in the back and found herself literally propelled along the thoroughfare. She tried to swing around to find Cynthia but only succeeded in getting her hat pushed awry and almost tripping. A crude voice cried, "Hold everything, lady."

But a moment later she felt the girl's arm slipped through hers and they clung together until they were below Forty-second Street and the crowd suddenly thinned out. They leaned against a shop window a little breathlessly.

"There, now, wasn't that grand?"

"I hardly think so." The woman smiled faintly.

"Poor May-May, I'm afraid we'll never make a real pushing shoving happy-go-lucky New Yorker out of you. You'll always be English."

"But London has crowds too," retorted Miss Downer with a faint touch of asperity in her tone.

"Surely, but not like here." She looked serious, "Do you know, I just can't imagine you pushing and shoving in a crowd for the sheer love of it."

"Certainly not," cried the woman.

"Well, there you are. I feel I want to push into the mob where it's thickest and have some one slap me on the back and some one else step on my toes at the same time. I want to live, make up for all the long lost years."

"It all sounds rather silly to me, child. Whatever has come over you to-day?"

"Don't you know?"

"Indeed I don't. Something seems to have turned your head at luncheon to-day."

"Now you see you do know. To-day I was reborn, am reborn, whatever you want to call it. But I can't tell you about it, May-May. I just want you to be happy with me."

As if by common consent they moved on slowly and soon turned up Broadway again toward the theater which housed the play of Cynthia's choice.

After the play she suggested walking home up Seventh Avenue and then cutting through Central Park over to Fifth Avenue. Miss Downer agreed a little reluctantly for various reasons, but tiredness was not one, and she was sorry therefore. She knew she would only have to mention being tired and Cynthia would at once be all contrition and they would go straight home in a taxi. But much as she felt she didn't want to walk and talk any more with Cynthia that night in the girl's present mood, she was much too honest with herself to invent an excuse for getting home at once, especially such an unworthy excuse as fatigue.

The play had been one to make matters much worse, a thoroughly frank discussion of a woman thrusting aside all moral obligation in her pursuit of happiness, her desire "to live naturally and triumphantly as a flower." So Cynthia had put it in her enthusiasm during the intermission just before the last act. And she had entered freely into conversation with a young man who sat next to her. During their conversation Miss Downer had kept silence ostentatiously, but her marked disapproval certainly had no effect upon Cynthia who not only gave her own opinions freely to the young man, but quoted at length those of Miss Downer, and her reasons for them. The rising of the curtain had come as a blessed relief to the perturbed woman who did not know that Cynthia made no attempt to withdraw her hand from the young man's fervid clasp during the entire act, at the end of which the man classified her as tepid but interesting.

Now as they turned into the Park, Cynthia took her companion's arm and held it tightly.

"I wanted to walk home to-night so I could just pour out my heart to you. Do you mind terribly, May-May?"

"Of course not, child, I'm proud to have you want to 'pour your heart out' as you say. But you do sound so dramatic."

She patted the girl's hand softly and there was a world of encouragement in her voice which belied the troubled feeling in her heart. But Cynthia needed no further encouragement. While they walked slowly along the twisting concrete paths she talked rapidly in a low quiet voice which carried the more intense conviction for its very low monotonous tone. When they emerged from the entrance at Seventy-second Street she shook her head just a little as a swimmer shakes the water out of his eyes when he rises to the surface after a deep dive. Then quite suddenly she stopped still.

"And there you are. Now you know as much about the real me as I do myself, and certainly more than any one else in the world. Now, what do you say?"

The woman stood staring numbly down the street, watching the shining beautifully-cared for cars swing out of the Park entrance and into the main stream of Fifth Avenue traffic, or else cross it at the proper signal and head straight down Seventy-second Street. Her wandering thoughts followed the crosstown traffic. Maybe some of the cars would go as far as the river because the expensive apartment houses ran all the way down and seemed quite to have forgotten the habit of former years when Lexington Avenue was the extreme limit of respectability. Times were changing and respectability was expanding, enlarging, or maybe it was just growing careless in an era of success and heedless of where carelessness was leading. She was recalled by Cynthia's sharp voice.

"May-May, haven't you heard what I've been saying?"

"Yes, child, every word. Though I wish I hadn't," she added slowly, regretfully. The girl tapped her foot impatiently. "Don't be like that. I want you to help me; I need you to help me. What am I to do?"

"I don't know. How can I say? You talk so strangely, so wildly, I'm sure I do wrong even to listen to you. I'm sure your mother wouldn't want me to," she added lamely.

"Mother! Mother!" cried the girl scornfully. "What has she to do with it anyway? She has her problem and I have mine." Then she began to talk very softly. "May-May, don't you see that I have no one but you to turn to and you are failing me. I was so sure you'd understand me, and you don't, you don't at all. Don't you see you're failing me?"

Miss Downer was touched. "I'm sorry, Cynthia, but I don't know what to do. I've never heard any one talk as you have to-night, not even on the stage. I simply can't believe it." She paused a moment while a Fifth Avenue bus lumbered noisily by. "Come, let's go in and forget about it all. I really think you've just been teasing your poor May-May. I remember how you used to do it even when you were a little girl." She smiled faintly in retrospect and at the same time hoped deeply, terribly, that such was a true explanation of the girl's words. It was too incredible to even consider such things as anything but a joke.

Cynthia looked at her steadily a moment. "Oh, if it were only as easy as that, May-May, but it isn't. And we always trust the wrong person, don't we? Take the young man I talked to in the theater. He would understand what I mean.

I'm sure of it. Why can't I just go home with him and lie in his arms with his warm body against mine and tell him what I want out of life; tell him . . ."

"Cynthia!" the woman cried in an agony of spirit. "I won't listen to another word like that. When I went away you were so refined, so quiet, so self-controlled, and now—well, I don't understand you at all. This isn't a joke any more."

The girl laughed loudly and hooking arms ran her quickly across the avenue. "May-May, when you knew me I was dead, starved in the most horrible way. Now I've just waked up and it's so sudden I'm drunk with the joy of it. I suddenly see what I want, what I've always wanted, what it's too late for you or mother or father or any one like that to give me any more. I've been cheated of childhood, but no one shall rob me of my womanhood."

"Stop!" the woman was aghast. "How can you talk so and in the streets, too? You must be mad."

"Sane! Sane now!" the girl cried wildly. "And plain damned happy. I'm going to be happy from now on."

Miss Downer rang the bell for the butler twice. She felt she couldn't trust herself with speech. It was all too utterly preposterous that their evening should have ended so disastrously. When Greenleaf opened the door Cynthia ran lightly past and up the wide staircase without a word. Greenleaf had a message for Miss Downer.

"May-May, Mrs. Bronson would like to see you. She said to tell you as soon as you came in provided it was not too late." He smiled a little wearily as if he needed rest and quiet after the long day.

"Thank you, Greenleaf. I'll go to her directly."

She started slowly up the stairs, a little sorry to-night that her irrefragable principles would not allow her to use the lift even when she was very tired. For she was tired

now, with a feeling that went far beyond mere bodily
fatigue. She wanted to lie down and close her eyes while
she tried to collect her scattered thoughts and reassemble
her tumbling principles and integrities. She certainly did
not want to talk to Mrs. Bronson before she had time to
think, but there seemed to be no help for it, so she knocked
softly on her door. The maid, Olga, opened it and smiled,
frigidly, and for an instant she was buoyed up by a mad
hope that Mrs. Bronson would be in bed and Olga would
send her away. It might be all easier in the morning. Olga's
rough voice shattered her hope.

"Come right in. Madame is waiting for you."

Mrs. Bronson was lying on a chaise-longue propped up
with pillows holding a novel in the careless way of one
who reads merely while waiting for something more important to happen. As soon as she saw Miss Downer she
dropped the book casually on the floor and held out one
beautiful round arm as a gesture of welcome. The wide
sleeve slipped back and nestled in filmy folds about her
shoulder.

"Come in, May-May, and let's have a nice talk. We
really haven't since you've been here, you know."

Olga quietly left the room while the lady gracefully
arranged the trailing draperies of her dressing gown, a
filmy creation of shell pink and silver, which glowed softly
under the subdued lighting of the room. May-May sat
down stiffly on a little straight chair while the soft alluring
quiet of the room flowed gently around her, isolating her
grim British practicality, marking and stressing every
crude angle of her serviceable walking costume.

But the warm fragrant atmosphere brought her no comfort, no desire to absorb it and sink languidly into an easy
chair and easy conversation. She was alien to the elegant
languor of the room and through a distinct effort of the

will became even more so. It was no comfort to know Mrs. Bronson was lying there at ease waiting for her to speak. She closed her eyes.

"Well, May-May, do say something." The words came slowly, filtered through a silken screen of smiling lips.

"What about?"

Mrs. Bronson stirred restlessly on her cushions. "Come, May-May, don't be so English. I know you went out with Cynthia to-night. Tell me what you did, where you went."

Miss Downer's folded hands rested quietly in her lap. "We had dinner at Giolito's, then walked about on Broadway, then went to the theater, then walked home through the Park." She spoke as if ticking off the items on a laundry list, so many collars, so many shirts, etc.

"It doesn't sound very gay or exciting," laughed Mrs. Bronson lightly. "Did you enjoy your escapade with Cynthia, because I'm sure you both viewed it in that light?"

"Yes, everything was very nice."

"Well, May-May, I must say you don't look as if you'd had a good time. You look as if you'd seen a ghost."

"I suppose it's just because I'm very tired. I'm not used to walking so far," she explained, rising to her feet.

"Don't go yet. Surely you're not too tired to talk a little while, or I've never known you to be so before."

Miss Downer sat down rigidly and once more folded her carefully gloved hands. Mrs. Bronson watched her a moment with a smile, then shook her head slowly.

"It's very clear, May-May, that you're hiding something and the more you try to hide it the more I feel it's something important, something I should know."

Miss Downer swung round slightly in her chair. "Mrs. Bronson, I think it would be better if I went back to England. I'm afraid my coming here was all a mistake."

Mrs. Bronson stared at her a moment in astonishment,

then swung her feet to the floor and sat up with the lithe grace of a panther. Her voice was very tense and low.

"Just what do you mean? I don't understand you at all. Why should you talk about returning to England when you've only just come?"

"I just think it's for the best."

"And I think there must be some reason. You are not a creature of whims and impulses; you never have been and no one can convince me that you are now. Something has happened and it must have been while you were out with Cynthia to-night. Don't you see you must tell me now no matter what it is? Has Cynthia been rude to you or hateful in any way?"

"No indeed. She could not have been kinder."

"That's just it." The lady rose and commenced to pace the room slowly, thoughtfully, her trailing draperies catching and jumping as they caught in passing over the thick piled rug. "Cynthia is very fond of you and I knew I couldn't be mistaken. It is something you are trying to hide, I am sure of it. Why don't you speak out?"

"I can't."

"Can't!" Mrs. Bronson swung around dramatically. "I don't see why you use such a foolish word. Why should there be anything you can't tell me, at least in this connection? After all, Cynthia is my daughter," she added, and her voice rose a little as she spoke the words.

May-May rose quietly, calmly. "And at the same time, Mrs. Bronson, I am not your paid governess now, and so I speak or do not speak as I choose. In this case I do not care to discuss my conversation with your daughter to-night beyond saying she was perfectly kind to me." There was a little pause. "You see I told you it was best if I returned to England at once."

Mrs. Bronson crossed to her swiftly and laid a soft hand

lightly on her arm. "Come, come, May-May, let's not be foolish. You are here as my friend and my guest so how can you suggest going away like this for no reason at all? Let's not be like silly women and quarrel over nothing at all. We're both too old and too sensible for that, let's hope. Now let's sit down and look at this thing sensibly." She sank back on her chaise-longue and drew Miss Downer down beside her. "Now tell me you're not angry with me."

"Of course I'm not angry, Mrs. Bronson," replied the woman, a faint glow in her pale cheeks.

"That's better, much better. Except I really don't think you should call me Mrs. Bronson so formally. Do call me Aurelia as all my friends do. It's much nicer."

"Oh, it wouldn't be proper at all."

"Why not? Don't be foolish. And now that's settled, you do realize that as Cynthia's mother I naturally should be interested in my child, shouldn't I?" There was a world of coaxing in her tone of which no one would have dreamed her capable. But May-May's answer was the single word, "Yes."

"Of course you do," the lady's smile was positively glowing. She put her hand gently on the woman's knee. "And don't you see I realize Cynthia has reached a point in her life when great decisions are made, overwhelming decisions? I know that; no one could know better. I am sure she has talked about herself to-night, told you her dreams, her emotions, her feelings. Isn't that true?"

"Yes."

"Of course. Now don't you think you should tell me what she said?" Mrs. Bronson leaned forward to look into her companion's eyes as the words melted from her lips.

"No!" the word almost rang in the stillness of the room.

After a moment's hesitation the lady threw her arms wide in a gesture of resignation. "Very well, then, May-

May, I can only assume that you have very good reasons for your decisions."

"I have indeed."

They both rose slowly. "Then let's not worry any more about it. But since we are being very frank I think I can still ask one question. Did Cynthia bring me into it in any way, or," she hesitated an instant, "or Jane Talbot?"

"No, she only talked about herself—and men."

"Men!" Mrs. Bronson spoke the word slowly as if fully to comprehend some long train of thought behind its expression. Then a slow smile lingered a moment in the graceful contours of her beautiful mouth.

"Good night, May-May, and thank you so much."

"Good night, Mrs. Bronson."

CHAPTER SIX

MRS. VENTNOR was quite conscious that she looked regal in sables so she was very glad it was a rather cold day and hence they would be quite correct, especially at a football game. She didn't particularly like football and consequently didn't take very much trouble to understand it, but she saw most of the important games within motoring distance of New York. She didn't really like anything in which she could not take active part but there were certain things she felt obligated to do from a sheer sense of duty and so used her opera box every Monday night, attended Theater Guild First Nights and sat through Toscannini Symphony Concerts at correct intervals. In exactly the same way she went to football games and since she had an exact idea of her own importance she was always the smiling, gracious hostess. Noblesse oblige.

As she descended her marble stairs she was sure she was quite correct in everything. She could hear her daughter and some girl friends laughing in the library, her Hispano Suiza and Mercedes with the two chauffeurs and footmen in attendance glittered before the door in the keen morning sunshine. All was very well indeed. With a smile she entered the library crying in her best gay-young-matron voice, "Are we all ready to go?"

There were confused cries of greeting and waves of the hand from some, but her daughter, Agnes, summed up in her cool, direct way, "We're waiting for Cynthia, mother."

A tall girl rose and picked up her sumptuous chinchilla coat. "It seems that all we do is wait for Cynthia lately.

I say let's wait out in the cars. That may get under her skin."

Mrs. Ventnor looked properly restraining. "Now, Gloria, isn't that unkind? I always remember Cynthia as the one girl of all of you who is very prompt and proper, and so beautifully quiet and restrained, too."

There was a general laugh. "Proper and quiet," snorted Gloria. Wait 'til you see her since the last few weeks. What a change! Now she's sort of Dancing on Life."

The lady looked confused. "Why what happened?"

"God knows." Gloria Glendale was correctly dramatic. "And he won't tell."

The voice caused them all to turn quickly toward the door where Cynthia stood legs apart, her hat caught in her hand, her hair soft and fluffy about her flushed cheeks. For a second every one seemed held by embarrassment and the vision of this flaunting, half-wild beauty. Mrs. Ventnor got herself under control first and held out her hand with her most gracious smile.

"Come in, Cynthia. We are all waiting for you."

The girl advanced into the room quietly. "So I heard. In future I'll be careful to be on time."

Agnes Ventnor caught her hands deftly. "Don't be a goose, Cynthia."

"Is there something I should apologize for?" inquired Gloria in a high voice.

Cynthia laughed shortly. "Yes. No one at your age should be allowed to own such a sumptuous chinchilla coat."

Mrs. Ventnor led the laugh happily. "Come, come, children, we mustn't delay any more. Now I'll take three of you in the Hispano and Agnes three in the Mercedes. Who's coming with me?"

"I shall be glad to," cried Gloria.

"And I *must* stick to Gloria," laughed Cynthia, "or else she'll tell you something about me and why I'm not proper any more."

Gloria took her arm mockingly. "All right, come if you dare because I'm going to talk about you anyway."

"Then we all want to go, too," cried the others, and began dancing about crazily. "We all want to hear about Cynthia and her crush on the football team. What's his name, Gloria?"

"Don't you dare," cried Cynthia suddenly flushing.

"Why not? Every one knows you've been raving around about Dale Eustis for several weeks. Maybe that's why you've been so gay."

"How lovely," said Mrs. Ventnor. "I wish he were playing to-day. I've heard so much about him but I haven't seen him in years and I dare say he's quite forgotten me."

"Mother, please," remonstrated Agnes. "We're going to the game to-day *especially* because Dale is playing. Mother, you go to all the games but you never seem to understand them." The girl's voice rose almost in a wail but her mother only smiled understandingly and put an arm around her shoulder in vague, comradely fashion. In her happy moments like these she knew how absurdly important games were to young people.

"I stand penitent and repentant. Now what must I do for my sins? Maybe I'd better fall in love with Dale Eustis, too."

In the general happy laugh they all ran out of the door and piled into the two waiting motors which glided away a minute later and began the swift drive to the game. The skillful chauffeurs were used to keeping together, even on congested roads, and they arrived at the university town in time for the early luncheon which the game necessitated. It was a meal as gay as only one can be where young

people are happy and hungry and fairly bouncing with
energy and the desire to get into things. Mrs. Ventnor felt
the years literally falling away from her until she, too, was
just a young girl radiant at prospect of a delightful game.
After luncheon the streets were packed, for this was the
last and most important game of the season.

The great bowl was filled to overflowing when the first
kick-off came and the stands fairly rocking with anticipation, that maddest of all stimulants. And even the most
ardent admirers of the game could not but be satisfied by
such a spectacle as they witnessed that day. The two teams
were at the peak of form and flung themselves into the
scrimmages with all the impetuous abandon of gladiators
of old proud to be dying before the eye of Cæsar. And
indeed they were battling, but before a new Cæsar with
ninety thousand heads and twice as many eyes. When
stretcher bearers rushed on to the field to carry off a limp
figure sadistic cries of triumph and ecstasy flamed into
the keen, biting air and pocket flasks were passed manfully.
Then when Dale Eustis' toe kicked the goal and added the
winning point to what he had already earned by a thrilling
broken field run the crowd went wild and there was an
overwhelming, swelling scream of triumph. 7—6 the score
remained.

As the final whistle blew, Cynthia found herself in the
very heart of the shrieking, pandemoniac mob. She glanced
quickly at her girl friends about her, their faces alight with
the hectic excitement, their voices hoarse and strident from
joining in the yells and cheers. What a strange, mad world
it was. She knew her own eyes were dancing, and her
cheeks flushed, and her hair tousled but she had reasons,
reasons which they did not know and which they could not
understand, perhaps. To her it was a personal game, a

personal victory. It was Dale's hour of triumph and therefore it was her hour of triumph.

Mrs. Ventnor reached over and patted her hand as they rose and joined the throng pouring out of the stadium gates. There seemed to be miles and miles of parked cars. The girls were all shouting excitedly to each other now as they threaded their way through the throng until Mrs. Ventnor, with the unerring instinct of years of practice, guided them safely to the waiting motors. Cynthia spoke quietly.

"Let's have tea at a place I know near here. I'm almost frozen."

"Splendid." Every one agreed and Mrs. Ventnor added that if they didn't linger over tea they would reach town in time for dinner and she would take them somewhere to dance. She threw off the suggestion as if it had just occurred to her.

"But what about partners?" Agnes was again mildly reproving.

"I think that will be all right." There was a little light of triumph in her eye as she thought of the select group of young men she had invited to dinner at her favorite club. It all required rather close timing and made a long, strenuous day of it but she was sure the girls wouldn't mind having to jump into evening frocks. It was the way they really liked to do things even as their present enthusiasm showed. Only Cynthia seemed a little too quiet suddenly.

"Doesn't it appeal to you, Cynthia?" she asked.

"Why of course, Mrs. Ventnor. I think it's just a perfect idea to finish off such a gay day."

But somewhere out of sight, in her heart perhaps, the girl smiled quietly and wondered a little at her own duplicity. It was a little strange even to herself how calmly and assuredly she was shaping events to please herself.

Only in a small way, perhaps, but it was the particular small way which was all important, the rest of the things and the ways of the world didn't matter, not now at any rate.

How swift the few weeks had been since she had met Dale at her house and then, far more important, at Jane's. That day was never to be forgotten in her life. She had blurted out her heart to Jane and to May-May, and how strange it was that Jane to whom she had said the least had understood the most. Jane had given her a password on which to mold her life and May-May had shrunk from it in horror without understanding at all.

May-May had failed her as was only to be expected if she had thought the thing out carefully enough. May-May was her nurse and had brought her up from babyhood. May-May had watched her grow, and develop, and expand, and all so carefully, so minutely day by day that she couldn't quite believe that the smiling, gurgling baby in the cradle had turned into the vibrant young girl who viewed life suddenly in a new passionate way inspired of her new and poignant passion. How May-May had shied away from that single, clear word; how coldly unwilling she was to listen to the demands of the body expressed in clear terms; how unwilling to allow herself to see things in their true proportion. Cynthia smiled to herself and looked out of the car window into the falling twilight through which the masses of cars moved slowly. How foolish she had been to turn to an elderly virgin, an English one at that, and expect to find understanding of her needs, her desires, her necessities.

Then quite suddenly the two cars stopped outside the tea room and they all piled out gayly. The tea room was crowded, but space was made for them somehow in the laughing groups and in a few minutes they were eating little sandwiches and cake. Cynthia rose quietly and went to the cashier's desk near the door.

"Have you a note for me? I am Cynthia Thorpe."

The busy woman looked carefully at the lovely questioner as she adjusted her spectacles. "Yes. But I almost wonder if I should give it to you. You look so pretty and I know the writer. He brought it here himself."

The girl laughed. "You sound as if the man were an ogre instead of my friend. Is his reputation in town really so very bad as all that?"

"No. But this is football night and released heroes are very human." She smiled a little grimly as if to say she knew what she knew.

"Then I am the Delilah of the piece. That makes it almost funny, doesn't it? You see his hair is so short now."

Gloria strolled up inquisitively. "What are you gabbing about, Cynthia?" The old woman stood watching them.

For a moment the two girls faced each other squarely, then Cynthia said quietly, "I'm just getting a note Dale was to leave here for me and I'm explaining my honorable intentions."

"Oh!" There was a wealth of meaning in the simple word. "So that's why you brought us all here. What would the proper Mrs. Ventnor say?"

Cynthia shrugged her shoulders and as she did so the woman opened a drawer of her desk and handed her a letter. Gloria watched carefully. She murmured,

"Want to go to the ladies' room to read it?"

"Certainly not. I'll read it here." She ripped the envelope roughly and opened the single sheet it contained. She read the few lines at a glance then walked back to the table. Agnes cried, "Look, Cynthia has a letter."

"Yes. And I'm sorry to disappoint you all but Dale Eustis won't be able to join us here for tea."

"Here?" they cried in unison while Mrs. Ventnor added, "Cynthia, did you ask him here for tea? Is that why you wanted to come here?" Interest struggled with propriety.

"Certainly. He told me about this place which he likes. He's quite a pet of the woman who runs it."

"How grand," cried Agnes, while her mother tried to look a little shocked to cover her desire to grin at the girl's cleverness. The others were all talking now of how they had almost had the great hero of the hour for tea and what a sensation it would have caused. In the confusion Cynthia slipped away to the ladies' room and when she returned she looked as one of the girls said as if she had seen a ghost.

Mrs. Ventnor was quite concerned as Cynthia explained in a whisper that she was suddenly taken sick and would have to go home at once and by train. It was all whispered and rather garbled especially in the noisy room, so before the confused lady could quite realize what it was all about the girl had walked swiftly out of the door and was lost in the traffic. Hurrying to the door Mrs. Ventnor was just in time to see her climb into a taxi which swung quickly away in the direction of the railroad station.

"What's the matter, mother?" cried Agnes.

The lady hesitated an instant, then said quietly, "Cynthia doesn't feel well and has gone back by train. She slipped out so as not to break up the party."

"But, mother, if she's ill some one ought to have gone with her at least." Agnes had definite ideas on such things.

"I don't think so." Gloria spoke with complete assurance. "I think I understand her better than any of you. When she doesn't feel well she simply wants to be alone and not have to talk or anything. I know I'm like that."

Her tone carried conviction and for once Mrs. Ventnor was only too glad to accept any explanation of her too lax chaperonage. She really should have gone with her herself, of course, if the girl didn't feel equal to the ride home by car, but, she remembered weakly, it was very hard to do anything with a determined girl like Cynthia and in any event her mother was not likely to want an explanation.

A few minutes later they left the tea room and soon were rolling swiftly back toward the city and the gay dinner dance which awaited them at Mrs. Ventnor's favorite club. In the gayety of planning for the evening Cynthia was almost forgotten. Her little note from Dale lay carelessly tossed on the table and there the woman who ran the tea room found it after the crowd had thinned out and she had time to leave her cash register and think calmly. She read it carefully then deposited it in the waste paper basket behind the cash desk. It only said he was sorry he couldn't get to the tea room as he would be tied up after the game, but he would call her up in New York very soon. The very was underlined but that was all.

And in the Hispano Suiza with Mrs. Ventnor Gloria Glendale was quieter than the others and sat for miles looking out of the window into the chill darkness of the country. They seemed to whirl through various little towns, a flash of ridiculously bright main street and they were gone, the darkness closing round them again. Gloria smiled as she thought how she had stepped into the breach and explained things when Cynthia had dashed out so wildly. She didn't particularly like Cynthia, so why had she done it? She thought of the others and their gaping, questioning faces. Some one had been needed who could understand; that was all. She had been the one; it was as simple as that.

. . . .

Several hours later the annual football banquet was in triumphal progress at the usual hotel and about the doors leading to the banquet hall a crowd loitered, dully hoping to catch some vague scraps of the hidden gayety. The successful players were indeed the idols of the hour, for had they not come victorious through a whole season of play? And had not the schedule been so difficult that it seemed to spell disaster on its announcement? Never had the university been more perfectly represented on the gridiron and now in their hour of complete triumph the team as a unit and individually must be fêted by grateful alumnæ, preceptors, and associates.

At the focal point of the speakers' table sat the coach and his star product, Dale Eustis the superman, two quiet men from such different walks of life come together to make history in sport. The other players were seated to left and right of them, for every man who had fought so gallantly for his Alma Mater would be expected to say something. It was an experience most of them dreaded worse than the hardest game, but there was no escaping the immemorial responsibility.

At the end of a particularly eulogistic speech there were wild roars of applause and shouts for "Eustis" but Dale only shook his head quietly to indicate to the old alumnus who was directing proceedings that he would not speak until his turn came in the regular order of events. During the singing of a rousing song the coach whispered in his ear, "What's the matter, boy, you look worried?"

He smiled faintly. "No, I'm all right."

But the harassed expression of the coach did not lift. "Is that shoulder bothering you?"

"No. I'm fit as can be. There's nothing the matter."

"No?" The word rose on a quizzical inflection. "Now I know there is something the matter. Why not trust me with it? It's that dame, isn't it?" He watched him closely.

"I don't know what—"

"Keep your shirt on, boy. I know how it is. You're all

wrought up, and you're tired, and you want somethin' out
of life, you don't know just what. Most of these guys'll
just go out and get drunk and that'll satisfy 'em, but I
know you're different and that's why you're a great football player, one of the very best."

Dale grinned a little. "Save it for the speech."

"All right. Only I thought you might want to go to New
York to-morrow. Maybe I'm wrong."

There was a strange light in Dale's eyes as he gripped
the man's rough hand. "Say you are the real stuff, aren't
you?"

"Sure. But to-night you belong here, don't you?"

There was a nervous lift to the end of the question, but
the coach didn't get any answer. A waiter serving coffee
slipped a note to Dale but not cleverly enough to escape
the shrewd eyes that were watching. The coach laid a hand
on Dale's arm very gently, almost protectingly.

"I wouldn't read that if I were you."

The waiter had glided away as quietly as he had come
and some one on the other side of the big banquet room
was leading a band of alumnæ in a song. The whole room
came under Dale's eyes as he swung his head slowly
around to face the coach squarely. Then he said quietly:

"Why not?" A strange undercurrent of excitement ran
through the simple words.

The man shrugged resignedly. "It's your note, boy, do
as you please. But here's my suggestion," and he whipped
out a cigarette lighter and snapped it on. The tiny flame
leaped and danced as he held it out and for an instant the
young man watched it with fascinated eyes. Its leaping,
licking tongue of color seemed to be drawing his hand
toward itself, the hand in which the little note was held so
tightly. Then all at once the temptation was gone and he
felt very calm. He lifted his hand from beneath the table

and read the single line of writing. The coach snapped out
the lighter and returned it to his pocket simply. Dale rose
quietly. "Hail our Alma Mater," the words of the song
rang out.

"I'll just sneak out for a minute."

The coach merely smiled and turned to the man on his
other side. It would be a relief to talk to Kirby who was
all football and nothing else. Anyway the season was over
and it didn't matter so much now.

"Where's Dale goin'?" Kirby asked.

"Just out for a minute," the coach said, and joined his
applause to that of the others at the conclusion of the
alumnæ song. Kirby grinned sheepishly and turned away.

Dale found his way out as quietly as possible through
the service entrance and inquired his way to the card room.
That usually crowded place was deserted to-night, except
for a stolid foursome playing bridge in complete oblivion
to the gayety of the rest of the city. In the corner of the
room he found Cynthia. She seemed like some rare exotic
flower in the stupid room.

"I came as quickly as I could," he said when he reached
her and held out his hand cordially.

For answer she glanced quickly at the absorbed card
players and then fell into his arms. He caught her as she
murmured, "Dale, darling." The scent of her swept over
him.

He sat down quickly with her on a narrow couch, his
arms still holding her. "What's the matter, Cynthia, you're
all trembling?" His voice shook a little as he spoke, though
he didn't know it.

She held her face up to him as she whispered, "I've been
waiting so long, so long. I'm cold." He felt her body
tremble.

For a moment their eyes held each other and then suddenly he caught her head with his cupped hands and kissed her warmly, lingeringly, full on the mouth. Her lips clung to his passionately and he felt her body vibrate in his arms. He suddenly drew away and sat rigidly upright.

"Forgive me, I'm mad. I don't know what I'm doing to-night." There was a slight pause. "Oh, Cynthia, you shouldn't be here like this, you shouldn't. It isn't right."

"I had to come." Her voice was low and tense. "I saw you play this afternoon. I saw those thousands and thousands of girls watching, watching, with bright eyes and flushed cheeks. I had to come."

"Don't talk so loud." He glanced around nervously but the card players were still oblivious to all but their game.

"I feel like shouting from the housetops to all the world: 'The football season's over. He's won. Now I can tell him.'"

"Tell me,—what?" His eyes clung to her, dwelling on the pale loveliness of her animated face.

She leaned softly against him. "Don't you know?"

He caught her in his arms again and held her body against his. His lips brushed her neck caressingly. "You are making me mad, Cynthia. You mustn't. I'm not myself to-night anyway. It's the let-down at the end of the season."

They sat apart again now but her white hand rested on his thigh. "Suppose I want you to be mad, even if you consider me as an end-of-the-season let-down."

"I didn't mean that," he whispered passionately. "I mean I want to get away from the crudeness, the hardness, the brutality. I want gentleness, and softness, and your voice in my ear and your fingers in my hair. I—"

He stood up quickly with parted lips and flaming eyes. "Forgive me. I told you I am mad to-night. I'm talking to you like a street-girl. Why did you come here to-night of all nights?"

"Are you really, Dale?" She sat with her head tilted back, her glorious brown eyes glowing up to him. "Lucky street-girl! Why must only she know your fire, your ardor, the real you?" She rose slowly. "We're wasting time, aren't we?"

His eyes met hers and then slowly fell. "I— What do you mean?" He felt he didn't dare trust himself to think.

Her strange laugh rippled softly in the hush of the room. "Why are you trying to be stupid, Dale? It isn't like you."

He hesitated, then cried, "I have to go back to the banquet. They'll be waiting for me and I have to make a speech. I don't know what to say,—now," he finished lamely.

"How nice," she laughed, then went on seriously, "You're not going back, you can't go back. I need you, I—I'm here alone and I have to get back to the city. You have to take me, in your car. That's why I sent for you. Don't you see?"

"Where are the others?"

"Gone! I sneaked away to be able to see you. Dale, do you realize what I've done to see you? I've come here to this hotel and it took so long to bribe people to get a note to you. Now you're here and you leave me. You have to make a speech you say. A speech! Good God! have you no sense? Do you have to hear yourself praised and touted by the numbskulls? You won their games for them, isn't that enough? Must they look at you and paw you and say stupid, boring things as a reward? I need you to help me, to get me back to the city in your car. I'm not feeling well." She added the last thought limply, as if pity might move where passion failed.

He took one of her hands softly in his. He was oblivious now to the bridge players who had finally looked up from their cards during the girl's passionate outburst and were frankly staring. "I'm sorry, Cynthia. We'll go at once. I have the car near here and you can wait while I change my clothes at the Frat House. It'll be deserted to-night at this time. Come quickly, we can go out the side entrance."

She looked at him steadily. Aren't you going to kiss me?" The words crept from her throat huskily.

For answer he gathered her again in his arms. A man and woman paused at the door of the room about to enter, and on seeing the embrace walked slowly away, embarrassed. The bridge players resumed their game with a scornful sniff from one of the women whose hatchet face and dirty gray hair proclaimed her innocence of passion. Arm in arm Cynthia and Dale walked out of the room and toward the side entrance. Just as they reached it some one called, "Hey, Dale!" but he paid no attention. He felt he was walking in a dream, a golden dream, an impossible dream.

As they slipped out of the side door of the hotel the coach rose slowly to explain the hero's disappearance. "It's a little hard to explain, fellers, but maybe when you're a great enough athlete you got a big, wide bashful streak along with what it takes to win. Eustis ain't afraid of nothin' on earth but a compliment and I guess he knew how much we think of him here to-night. I guess he figured he just had to run away."

He sat down and mopped his head amidst roars of applause. He was damned glad that was over. Where the Hell was Eustis anyway?

CHAPTER SEVEN

CYNTHIA opened her eyes to find the pale autumn sun
streaming thinly in at the east window and laying a wraith-
like patina on the dark, old furniture and dull red carpet.
A faint chill breeze crept in at the open window, just
enough to lift the thin curtains languidly and give percep-
tible movement to a silk stocking hanging limply over
the back of a chair. As much of the room as she could see
without turning her head had a nice, tumbled look, and she
was glad; especially glad about that wayward stocking
faintly swinging on the back of the straight little chair so
obviously intended for no such wanton use. In all probability it was intended to be used in conjunction with the
small, inane writing desk she had noticed last night when
gaily undressing. One was supposed to sit and write letters
to "dear mother" or else send picture post cards of the
hotel to one's friends with a cross marking the location
of one's room. One felt certain nothing more important
had ever been written on it.

How absurd it all was and yet it might be amusing to
send such a card to May-May. Just what would the dear
prim soul do with it, because there was no doubt she would
understand; it would be quite impossible for her not to do
so after the memorable walk through the park just a few
weeks ago. It was interesting, almost amusing, to lie in
bed in this particular sensuously luxurious way, and specu-
late on May-May's reactions to such a brazen, public
announcement that her worst fears had been realized; an
announcement on an open post card that the letter carrier

might read, and the butler or footman who received it and brought it to her room, to say nothing of the butcher, the baker, and the candlestick maker. She just managed to resist in time the temptation to sing the words to a silly little tune she had learned long, long ago, and then forgotten completely only to remember it again now when she was so very happy. Because she was so happy it seemed too bad that May-May was so much occupied with the opinions of the butcher, the baker, and the candlestick maker, while on their side they were probably utterly indifferent to May-May's opinion of them and thus were infinitely better off and could be carelessly happy. Wasn't that the ultimate goal of life to be carelessly happy; to be so gay as to be utterly indifferent to any one's opinion of your gayety? But poor May-May could never possibly be that; her sense of duty would not allow it. It would make her miserable if she were too happy, especially if others might see her happiness. It just wouldn't be moral.

A soft smile clung to the girl's lips. It was rather strange how her thoughts kept turning to May-May now when she was radiantly happy for the first time in her life, happy enough to make up for all the thin, gray, meaningless years. If she tried to think of her mother it was an effort, and a useless one at that. Her mother was Mrs. Bronson, no more than that, and equally no less. Certainly that lady could not complain since she had made herself a stranger to her own daughter. So often Cynthia had tried to conceive of her as mother, as Mrs. Thorpe, how strange and absurd the name sounded, but it was impossible. In the words of religion she was the fruit of her mother's womb, flesh of her flesh, life of her life. How ridiculous that seemed. It was easier to imagine herself stirring within the womb of the virginal May-May, an immaculate conception, if you please. May-May would not be such a

bad Madonna after all if she could only be convinced such
was her duty.

It was strange how she wanted May-May to see her here
in bed naked, shameless, happy, indescribably happy. She
would probably just walk from the room quietly and
never so much as slam the door behind her; because that
would indicate lack of composure and such was sin to her.
And then what could she do? She couldn't go to pray
because Duty is a stern god and you can't pray to him,
and equally she couldn't go to Mrs. Bronson who refused
to bow the knee to Duty and who was lost as long as she
had Jane Talbot. Assuredly it was best that May-May
should not see her, that Mrs. Bronson shouldn't, that Jane
Talbot shouldn't.

Cynthia's thoughts swung to a new consideration of herself and Dale. Jane had brought them together as a little
joke, a test. Who knew why? Was it merely a whim to
play goddess and see what would happen to Cynthia and
Dale; the sensitive, repressed girl and the virile, athletic
man? Or was there a streak of glorious, good-hearted
understanding in Jane which she, Cynthia, could least of all
credit to the woman who had finally taken her mother
completely, irrevocably away from her? Perhaps that was
the best explanation of all and yet it did not make Jane a
person to whom she might cry, "Come in; look at me now;
see how happy I can be, after being a gloomy girl for so
long." No, Jane would not be shocked but she would
smile cynically, shrug her bony expressive shoulders and
say, "How ridiculous." Jane was as constitutionally incapable of appreciating as May-May, and there was no
one else.

But what did it matter anyway? That was the beauty
of it. Turning over a little she snuggled closer to Dale's
warm, smooth body and lifting her head from his en-

circling arm kissed his eyelids softly, tenderly, as one might those of a sleeping baby. She felt the delicate skin quiver slightly under the faint pressure of her lips, and as she drew back smilingly the eyes fluttered open, wide and wondering. His lips parted slowly as if to speak, but bending swiftly she kissed away whatever words of surprise might be forming there while her soft fluffy hair drew its perfumed veil across his eyes lest he see too suddenly the harsh outlines of the grim reality of a hotel room, he who had come from dreamland at the sensuous summons of her lips.

Instinctively his powerful arms clasped her tight, and his muscled legs held her flowing limbs in firmer embrace. Slowly, languorously, ecstasy flowed through his flesh-caressed body and hung on his lips drinking the kindred glory from the mouth pressed upon his own. He wanted to wonder, to speak, to cry out, but all wants, all needs, all desires were engulfed in the overwhelming insuperable glory of this being whose body breathed, moved, desired in passionate rhythm with his own.

"Dale, are you happy?" she murmured.

"Oh, oh my darling." His eyes were closed as his lips traced the silken contour of her throat. The husky, half-breathed words flowed like incense over her body, his hands like a sculptor's molding reality, which is always a dream. She locked her fingers in his yellow, curly hair and closed her eyes.

An hour later they were dressing gayly and their mirth had a strange unaccustomed ring in the dull, impersonal room. He held her firmly while he finished rubbing her body dry with the rough towel.

"Goodness that's enough, Dale. I feel all bruises now." She stood up before him stretching luxuriously, arms high over her head.

"That's good for you after a cold shower. That's what makes football players strong. That's what makes 'em win." He grinned.

"Well, I'm not a football player," she cried, then ruefully pointed to a red spot on one of her thighs. "Look at that."

He bent forward swiftly and held her leg firmly while his lips pressed the spot tenderly. They seemed to cling to the soft, glowing flesh. Cynthia pulled his crisp hair uselessly, crying, "Dale, stop it, I think you're terrible. Really this is very improper." But the gay sound of her voice denied and twisted the import of her words.

He looked roguishly up at her but without releasing his encircling arms. "Oh, darling, you don't really think that, do you? Tell the truth, and cross your heart."

She laughed aloud at his lugubrious tone. "Yes, I certainly do. You'd think this was a football game, now I know how those men felt yesterday when you tackled them."

He shook his head slowly. "Oh, you're wrong. Football games aren't like this, not *exactly*. I wish they were."

She slapped his grinning face lightly. "And how long does this lingering tackle last?" she mocked.

"Forever and ever, Amen."

She bent over and caught his big, serious face in her hands, her heart strangely stirred by the deep glow in his eyes and the rich fervor of his tones. He was on his knees now and suddenly as she lifted a hand to ruffle his thick hair he rubbed his cheek against her thigh murmuring so softly, "Forever and ever."

She turned her head slowly until she could look out of the south window. The sun was just reaching in now, its pale gold splashing vaguely on the dusty window sill and spilling over on to the bare floor. Outside one looked

away over the bare autumn hills, lifeless save for a tree
near the window in which several gorgeous blue-jays with
cocky crests screamed lustily and capered about among
the naked branches. Nothing alive but the crested joy
of· life. She turned her thoughts back into the room and
touched Dale lightly on the forehead with a dainty finger
tip.

"And must it be forever on your knees?" She laughed
as she said the words which suddenly seemed ridiculous
and strained like something out of an absurd novel. He
raised his eyes to hers appealingly.

"Forever on my knees to you? Yes! forever!"

"And what if I get tired of so much adoration?"

He loosed his hold on her lingeringly so that his fingers
drew slowly along her skin as if loathe to draw away
from what they caressed. Then he stood up slowly, very
slowly like a figure in a dream until he was standing erect
before her with his arms limp at his sides, the palms of
the hands turned forward.

"I'm sorry, Cynthia."

She shook her head slowly and extended her arms wide.
As he still stood quietly she walked to him until her body
touched his. Her voice was low.

"Don't you want me, Dale?"

His hands leapt into life and caught her forcibly against
his breast. "Oh, God, how much!"

She held her arms still wide, and out, and back, until
she hung in the fervor of his embrace, her bare toes barely
touching the floor. Slowly, carefully he drew her up to
him until his lips caressed her throat. He mumbled,

"Cynthia, tell me you won't get tired of me, ever."

She laughed lightly. "Not when you love me like this,
Dale. But never, never kneel to me. I would get tired
soon then, so very soon."

He laughed huskily. "Well, what do you want of one poor young man who has been visited by a goddess, a goddess of love? Cynthia, say you'll never leave me now."

She drew away gently. "Dale, I can't promise anything until I've eaten, and I'm sure it's lunch time."

He was instantly contrite and a minute later they were convulsed with laughter as they raced to see who could be first dressed. He pulled on his coat, crying, "I win."

"No you don't." With a swift gesture she mussed his curly, yellow hair. "There now you have to comb your hair." As he reached for his comb she snatched it up herself and ran it quickly through her rippling brown hair. He stood watching her with a gleam in his eyes.

"I win, always," she said and passed the comb to him with a mocking bow.

He caught her extended hand and raised it to his lips. "I never knew it could be so nice to lose."

He flung open the door and they danced happily down the hall. Downstairs they had lunch on a glass enclosed porch which made the most of the pale sunlight. A very yellow canary sang brilliantly in a cage that hung above some massed ferns, his throat almost bursting with the power and beauty of his song. The air was flooded with the golden shower of notes as if one breathed music. Then suddenly it stopped.

Cynthia glanced carelessly about the room after giving their order to a little waitress with a vague crushed look. Three or four small groups were eating the Sunday midday dinner with all the stolid seriousness of middle class Sunday motorists. There was no laughing, no joking, no lightness, but only the careful business of getting full value out of the table d'hôte. The only touch of gayety rose from the heart of the imprisoned bird hanging in a ridiculous gilded cage above a dull funereal bank of

ferns. Dale touched her delicate hand resting softly on
the heavily starched cotton cloth.

"Darling, what are you thinking about?"

She caught his brown sturdy fingers in her soft clasp.
"I'm thinking how love can be happy even here, where
there is nothing of beauty but the wild song of a bird that
was forced to sing by being kept a long time in a dark,
stuffy cage. I feel like that bird. I've been kept so long
in a dark, stuffy cage, and now I see the sun and feel its
warmth and I want to sing too; I want to dissolve my
heart and soul in song and pour it out on the world."

"And won't you leave a little of your heart for me?
I need it so much, and it must be such a beautiful heart."

"Poor boy, I am all yours, don't you know that? Last
night I put myself into your arms and said 'here I am.'
Now, what are you going to do with me?"

"Just hold you tight, and tighter every day, because
every day I'll want you more and more."

"Won't you give me time to eat and sleep?" she mocked,
her lips curved provokingly. "I love to eat, you know."

"Just to eat when you are holding my hand like now.
And you shall always sleep in my arms,—as you did last
night," he added very softly.

She sighed. "I won't ever be able to eat steak because
it takes two hands to eat it, so I'll have to be content
with hash."

He gave her hand a happy squeeze but she went on
nimbly: "And I'll have to stop sleeping on your pitching
arm or you'll never make the baseball team this spring.
Wouldn't that be awful to contemplate?"

"What a little goose you are. There won't be any baseball team this spring or ever again. There is only you
from now on."

" 'Thank you, kind sir, she said.' Oh, Dale, how glib

you've become since last night when your only object in life was a football dinner. What price football now?"

His smile slowly faded. "I've learned so much since last night. I know a world now I didn't even dream of before, and now all the other things seem so silly, so purposeless. I wonder if you meant to teach me all of that, so soon. I wonder if you'll believe this is my first time,—like this."

"Dale, you're going to strain my credulity. You were a very ardent and proficient lover once I made you understand. Did you learn it all in the physiology class?"

"And you?" he queried.

She waved a hand lightly. "I have just lived waiting for love. There has never been any distraction in my life. I've had no friends, no fame, no football or baseball, no adulation, no shouts and cheers and excitement, no mother, or father, or sister, or brother, nothing but my dream of love with all the world trying to tear it away from me. And lately there was that terrible fear."

She trembled a little as she spoke but the fire in his clear blue eyes burnt away the strange mist of her thoughts and memories.

"What terrible fear, Cynthia? Tell me and I'll drive it away from you." He was very serious.

"It's gone already, lover, so we'll not talk about it. I'm afraid you wouldn't understand but you needn't now because it's gone, never to return. The strange fear died last night when I lay in your arms; when I kissed your heavy eyes to sleep; when I woke this morning and found you holding me close to you. Then I wanted the whole world to come in and look at me lying happily in your arms, our bodies clinging to each other even in sleep. It was so beautiful to be there and laugh at the terrible fear which was suddenly so ridiculous, and dead."

"Won't you tell me what it is?"

She sat back in her chair and laughed. "I can't tell you what it is because it isn't any more. It's dead, I tell you. And don't think it was somebody else I cared for because there has never been any one; I want you to believe that completely. I never even loved my mother. I tried to and she wouldn't let me. I left school because of the girls and mother didn't even care or bother to wonder why. She simply said girls didn't really need any fancy education anyhow, and that's where the whole thing remained, just there. I understand now, but then I was shocked."

"You poor kid, Cynthia, I want to make up for everything to you. When I saw you that first night I loved and wanted you so much. When I stayed over that night after I'd promised the coach to go back I didn't dream I'd see you so soon again but I wanted to be near you. I thought maybe I might dare to telephone from the station. Why didn't you tell me something was worrying you?"

"I had to tell you finally, didn't I, Dale? I thought I never would succeed in letting you know how much I loved you. I was afraid to tell you until your precious football season was over. I was afraid to ask you to choose between my love and the adulation of a whole university. Don't tell me how you would have chosen because in my heart I know, and I'm not flattered by that uncompromising truth. I'm too proud to be willing to be classed as 'breaking training' along with drunken orgies and girls in bad houses."

"Cynthia!" he cried passionately. "How can you say such things when you know they hurt me? What is the terrible thing which makes you think such horrible thoughts? Even if it is dead won't you tell me?"

She leaned her chin on her clasped hands resting her

elbows on the table. "Dale, now tell me the truth. Did you ever kiss that coach of yours?"

"Good Lord, no. Why Cynthia, of all the crazy questions I ever—"

"Then don't worry about me any more," she interrupted. "Now don't look flabbergasted but get ready to eat your lunch. We've had enough seriousness to last a week." She greeted the little waitress with a happy smile. She was hungry and even the dreary food looked good.

During the meal a little hurt look clung to Dale's eyes though he joined in her gay laughter easily enough, but when they went walking later he again became his jolly self and they ran gayly along a deserted dirt road hand in hand, singing their exuberance to the pale November skies. They returned to the little hotel in the lingering dusk, their faces flushed with exertion and the chill kiss of the keen wind which sprang up as the sun went down. As they were walking across the little lounge the proprietor leaned over the registration desk.

"Will you be here again, to-night, Mr. Smith?"

Cynthia nudged Dale who had paid no attention. "You're John Smith," she whispered; "he's talking to you," and turning she cast her brightest smile on the gaunt questioner staring with drooping tobacco-stained mouth. She walked in the opposite direction across the room.

Dale sauntered up to the desk. "What is it?"

"I was just wonderin' if you'd be with us again to-night," the man drawled insinuatingly.

"Yes, I think so, we were quite comfortable."

"Well," he turned and spit dexterously into a spittoon behind the counter, "we don't have much style here but I guess we have 'bout as good beds as any o' them swell places, and a bed's the main thing after all, ain't it?"

He fastened his yellowish eyes full on Dale and rubbed his bony nose with a still bonier finger. The young man shifted uneasily from one foot to the other and agreed mildly as to the importance of hotel beds. Out of the corner of his eye he noticed Cynthia had strolled across the room and was staring at a very large old print of Landseer's famous dog picture, "Dignity and Impudence." The man lowered his voice.

"I read as how you played a great game o' football yesterday. I almost went myself but last minute found I couldn't get away. It must o' been grand and there sure was a lot o' pictures o' you. Kind o' hero, ain't ya?" He swiftly produced a leading New York Sunday paper opened at the appropriate rotogravure section. Dale stared down at himself, at the pictures taken the week before for use in this issue. A vague wonder crossed his mind if he really was that heavy-jawed, tousle-headed fellow who grinned up at him in mockery. Was he two different men or what? He saw the gaunt man was watching him closely while a vacuous grin disclosed yellow, fang-like teeth.

"It's a good picture, ain't it?" the man said.

"Yes." He waited anxiously for what was to come.

"I thought so." There was a strained little pause. "Well, I guess it ain't any o' my business why you're callin' yourself John Smith, 'ceptin' it's my hotel and the wife is just a bit fussy,—you know how women are."

Dale agreed monosyllabically as to how women are but his brain was in a whirl and he was only too glad Cynthia was out of earshot across the room. The proprietor went on significantly: "I'm a regular guy, I am, an' I know how it is, 'specially after a long, hard season and you workin' so hard and winnin' an' all that, but,—" he spread his hands in a crude deprecating gesture. "You see how it is, the missus don't mind you bein' here but it's—" he jerked a thumb toward the girl now giving meticulous attention to a huge print of "The Roman Forum." "You know how wimmen are. The wife says she's got to go, you can stay if you want to."

"Damn you," Dale cried. "How dare you—"

"Hold yer hosses, young feller. I told you 'tain't none of my doin'. It's the missus as allus acts that way." He lowered his voice still further. "You see she says as how them kind is my perticular weakness and maybe she's right. We been married over thirty years and I s'pose she ought to know."

Dale drew away from the desk, his feelings confused between a desire to smash the leering face before him, and a desire to laugh at the vulgar stupidity of the beast. Maybe running a little hotel especially along the highway made people like that. The man watched him warily as if ready to duck behind the counter if Dale leaped at him.

Cynthia turned toward the desk saying, "Dale, I think we'd better be getting back to town to-night instead of in the morning."

The young man turned swiftly to meet her. "Just as you say, darling." Then he faced the proprietor with his arm about the girl's waist in a gesture of boyish protection.

"We'll be leaving at once."

"Just as you say," the man drawled and turning again spit deliberately into the ever-ready cuspidor. There was a little plop.

Ten minutes later the motor roared as Cynthia and Dale sped away in his car. The man waved a hand vaguely in farewell then turned back into the lounge closing the door carefully behind him. He shook his gaunt head slowly when he saw his wife was waiting for him arms akimbo.

"Well?"

"Gosh, he's sure a great football player. 'Tis a pity I ain't never seen him play or never seen him at all afore now."

"That's got nothin' to do with it at all, Hiram Streeter. He was here with a woman stayin' in sin, that's all I know."

"Gosh, Emly, so's most everyone stops here, ain't they?"

"Mebbe so, but when I don't know it I don't know it, an' when I do know it that's a different thing, 'cause I do know it. When I peeped through the keyhole this mornin' he was on his knees and kissin' her on the leg and them both as naked as the day they was born. It's just plain disgustin' I say. How can people carry on so? I'm sure you wouldn't ever kiss my leg like that."

The man rubbed his bony nose reflectively. "Mebbe so, but I sez you jest robbed us outa five dollars fer to-night. That's what you get fer lookin' in keyholes."

"Thank God I'm a clean Christian woman, that's all I have to say to you, Hiram Streeter. So long as I live we'll walk in the way of the Lord. After I'm gone you can have all the loose women you want." She burst into tears, pulling out a large, very rumpled handkerchief.

He comforted her with a vague pat on the back. "There now, Emly, don't cry. You're right just like always. An' anyway we're only losin' five dollars an' outa that ya gotta figger sheets an' towels an' things. Don't cry no more."

CHAPTER EIGHT

CYNTHIA admired the graceful assured way in which Dale drove his car. She lay back in her seat and watched him with dreaming, half-closed eyes, her hands resting quietly in her lap. How strong and good he was, and almost timidly gentle, with the half awkward gentleness of one who for the first time fears his strength and virility in contact with something he only half understands. How good it would be to go on and on to the end of the world with such a lover, but instead they were driving swiftly back to New York where the stupid sham of living would have to be taken up again, where there was no simple, honest, shameless love to be found. By the time it was thrust and crammed down into conventional molds it was no longer quite simple, or honest, or shameless love.

"Do you want to have dinner somewhere along the road?" Dale asked softly.

She caught the hint of trouble in his voice and rested a hand on his knee. How sturdy and solid and real he was beneath the light touch of her fingers, a rock of stability in an uncertain world of dark and troubled thoughts. "No, Dale, the dream is broken, I had better go straight home. I ought to be there in time for dinner. There will be some explaining to do, you know."

"I'm so sorry, darling. It's all my fault."

She laughed softly in her throat. "If you mean my happiness, yes, that is all your fault. But you can hardly be blamed because you are a celebrity, an 'idol of the hour' as the newspapers so pithily say it, and so are apt to be recognized all over the country. I should have picked out a lesser man for my lover, someone as inconspicuous and useless as myself."

"Cynthia, don't talk like that even in a joke," he cried, half turning his agonized face toward her. "Why do you torment me by talking about me as a lover, as if it just happened to be me and might have been any one?"

"Well, why not? Isn't it true? I might never have met you, or you might have returned to your foolish banquet."

"No! No!" his voice rose passionately. "I won't have you talk like that. You are just doing it to torment me because you know I love you so much; because you know we can't be together again to-night."

She leaned her head far back and closed her eyes. The rush of the car excited her and soothed her inexplicably at the same time. "Can't," she murmured softly. "Can't is such a silly, useless word. If you want to you can do anything; you can *have* anything if only you desire it enough. I wanted you and I have you. Don't shout, Dale, and don't jump around. My hand is still on your leg and I can feel you all quivering to cry out something without giving me time to speak. You see I am really answering your question, telling you what you want to know. I wanted you, Dale, and only you. I wanted you shamelessly, openly, as I told you last night when I had to try so hard to overcome your silly scruples about how you should act toward a girl to whom you had been properly introduced, in whose house you had visited. How silly, and proper, and lovable you were, and all the while I suppose you were burning up inside; at least I hope you were, and later you certainly gave a pretty good imitation. Dale, I wanted you so much, I wanted you even if you didn't want me. Isn't that a crooked, stupid sentence, but it says what I mean? Now are you satisfied? Is that your answer?"

He brought the car to a quick stop and gathered her in his arms ecstatically. "Oh my darling, my darling."

She looked up into his blue eyes gleaming softly, his strong features and crisp yellow hair faintly touched by the tiny light on the dashboard of the car. "This morning you said that when we were together and I love it because it means nothing and at the same time it means everything. Oh Dale, don't take me home! I don't want to go home to shams, and explanations, and lies. Let's just go away, far, far away, where there is nothing but our good clean love and blue sky as blue as your eyes, and the vastness of the ocean, as limitless as my desire for you and my need of you. I want to lie with you all night on the warm sands, just you and I in our glorious nakedness, alone under the moon and stars. Dale, take me away from New York, down to where it's warm, and lonely, and beautiful."

Her voice ended on a high note and broke in a half sob. He soothed her gently as one might a child. "My poor, hysterical little girl, what a gentle, poetical soul you have, and I love you for it, but we can't just drive away and disappear like that. There are things to consider. We have connections, responsibilities."

"No!" she cried fiercely. "There is nothing to consider but our love, our happiness! Nothing else matters, nothing in the whole wide world."

He kissed her very tenderly. "Cynthia, you must listen to me now. I'm a little older than you, not very much I know, but I've been around a little more and I know how foolish it is to escape from life even if you want to. I don't want to, darling, and neither do you when you stop to think things over very quietly. Our love is more than all the rest of the world but we can keep it and keep the other things, too."

He held her closer to him and his cheek rested against hers, the velvet skin sending the blood racing through his veins. "Darling, I'm so crazy for you I want you just to lie in my arms forever, but we can't live like that, nobody can. And then there's mother. I love my mother. I haven't had a chance to tell you about her, but I shall, and then you'll love her, and she'll love you. She'll be able to make up to you for so much you've missed because as soon as we're married she'll be your mother, too." He laughed a little awkwardly. "You see how simple it is when you stop to think quietly and it is so hard to think quietly when you are in my arms and I can feel your heart talking to my heart, whispering to each other very softly as they did last night. Are you listening, darling?" He asked the question anxiously.

The girl was staring fixedly across the road which was lined by tall dark trees. Now and then a car whirled past with a blinding flash of lights, and once a motorcycle swished past, its single finger of light pointing jauntily ahead into the mysterious darkness where lay enthusiasm and ecstasy or perhaps accident and death. Who knows? So therefore let us whirl on to the discovery. Wherever one is can only be disillusion, and ahead lies the unknowable which is happiness. Far away across the road one could just see the lights burning in the windows of a little house. The house itself was invisible but from the lights one judged it to be small, and snug, and cozy. The lights seemed to blink, if one watched them steadily, and say, "Come, come see how happy we are. Out there on the cold road is unhappiness, and darkness, and disillusion. Come be with us here, for we are warm, and golden, and being so far from the city we are lamps. The family is gathered around us for we are lamps and we attract and gather men and women into the golden circle of illumination. They must gather close and be friendly and loving for our light is soft and mellow and we attract and draw people together even as electricity forces them apart. Electricity is glaring and white and cold. Lamps are mellow and golden and warm. Come, come to see us."

The girl became conscious that Dale was shaking her gently. When she looked up to him he kissed her eyes softly, laughing way down in his throat. "Darling, what are you staring at? I'm sure you haven't heard a word I've been saying to you and I've been trying so hard to be very intellectual and think very clearly." He kissed her again.

"I've heard every word. You were talking about your mother." She sighed a little as she spoke.

He smiled at her then ran on earnestly. "Yes, I know you'll love mother, every one does. I used to think I never could love any one as much as I loved mother, but that was before I met you. Now I know mother's got to take second place with me from now on. It'll hurt her a lot, I suppose, but she'll understand. Mother always does."

"Did you find that out last night?"

"Yes, darling, last night and again this morning when you kissed me awake. Oh, my darling, darling Cynthia," and he crushed her in his powerful embrace.

"How nice," she muttered.

"What did you say, darling?" he queried anxiously.

"I said 'how nice.' But really you'll have to drive quickly now if you want to get me home for dinner, even as late as we have that meal."

With a jovial apology he released her and a moment later they were once more riding along swiftly. Cynthia opened a window beside her to feel the cool rush of air brushing against her flushed cheek. It smelt good and

clean, with the power to drive the dust and cobwebs out
of her mind.

"Cynthia, better close the window, you'll catch cold."

"Do you mind it?" There was a touch of surprise in
her interrogation.

"Lord no, not with this heavy fur coat on."

"And I love it." She looked out steadily for a few
minutes. Lights and cars were much more frequent now.
"Is it far? We seem to have come such a long, long way."

"Not very far, darling. But why the tired voice; are
you sick of me already? I might have known you'd find
out what a dull fellow I really am."

She rested a hand once more on his knee. "Silly Dale,
what a question. Unfortunately, I love you."

He shouted with laughter. "Unfortunately! What an
awful word, darling. I'm beginning to think you're just
a witch who likes to tease me."

"Who knows?"

Then suddenly he was serious again. "Cynthia, darling,
do you want me to go in with you to tell your mother
about us?"

She sat up very straight with shining eyes. "To tell
mother what?"

"Why about our engagement, you little goose. You'll
have to tell her I brought you home. Maybe you'd better
tell her you were sick so we had to stop over-night on
the road."

"You think of everything, don't you?" she said. "I
suppose you're used to it, and know just what is the best
kind of alibi. There's nothing like experience in emer-
gencies."

He steered dexterously between two trucks. "I'm used
to nothing. I only know I love you."

The girl smiled softly. "Then you'd better not come

in with me and I'll do my own lying. I'm quite an expert at it. It would seem funny not to lie."

"And you'll tell her we're engaged?"

"Of course." The simple words fell dully.

They were held up by a traffic signal in the little town they were passing through. He turned toward her. "Cynthia, aren't you happy? What's the matter? Am I being a dreadful bore?"

She raised up in her seat and kissed him lightly on the lips. "You are a perfect lover, so you musn't expect me to be very happy when you're going away. Will you go right back to the university?"

"Yes, to-night. I can't afford to miss any classes if I'm going to get through creditably." He paused while getting the car into speed again. "You see I want to graduate with decency if not with honor, so we can be married in June. Darling, I hate the thought of waiting but I'll be with you every minute I can. It really isn't long until June."

"Why wait, Dale? Who knows what will happen in six months. Now is the time for love, as some one said."

"I know I'll love you just so much more."

She patted his knee. "What a dear boy you are."

During the rest of the drive they were both quiet, occupied with their thoughts. When he let her out on Fifth Avenue in front of her door he caught her once more in his arms while he swallowed a lump in his throat.

"Darling, I hate to see you leave me."

She laughed and held wide her arms oblivious of the stares of passers-by. "Here I am to take. It still isn't too late to laugh at the world and run away."

He smiled. "Yes, it is too late, by several centuries." She looked at him steadily for a moment then with a wave of her hand she ran up the steps and rang the bell. A strange haunted look was in his eyes as he watched the door open and then close behind her. A massive door of wrought iron and plate glass and draped lace to shut him away from the vision of beauty that had played havoc with his heart. His hands on the wheel of the car trembled as he remembered her flowing limbs clinging to him, her body pressed against his, and her lips moist and fragrant on his mouth.

Then with a shake of his head he pulled himself together and drove away slowly. Before starting on the drive back he had better go somewhere for dinner; some place where he could write a letter to his mother telling her his happiness.

CHAPTER NINE

GREENLEAF, the butler, beamed as he admitted the young girl. "Good evening, Miss Cynthia."

"Hello, Greenleaf. Shall I be in time for dinner?" She pulled off her hat and shook out her soft, fluffy hair. The butler noted her unusual flush of color. He glanced at his watch with pompous dignity.

"Dinner will not be served until eight-thirty to-night, Miss Cynthia. You have half an hour to dress."

"Thank you. Is any one special coming?"

"Mr. and Mrs. Ventnor, Mr. and Mrs. Ramsgate, and Prince Ladislov."

Cynthia smiled. "Mrs. Ventnor coming? That's very good. It couldn't be better."

"May I say, Miss Cynthia, that Mrs. Ventnor called up twice to-day asking for you. She seemed very anxious both times. I merely said you were not in."

"Thank you, Greenleaf. Did any one talk to her?"

"Yes. Miss May-May talked the second time when Mrs. Ventnor insisted on speaking to your mother. Mrs. Bronson was resting so I couldn't disturb her. I said she was out."

The girl walked slowly up to him and rested a slim hand on his coat sleeve. "Greenleaf, you're a peach and I won't forget it. A few more like you and the whole world might be so very different. Instead—well, you needn't worry about me; I was quite all right." With a nod she turned toward the stairs. Greenleaf stood quite motionless.

"Thank you, Miss." There was a depth of concealed emotion underlying the commonplace words.

Cynthia ran quickly up the stairs and was gone. The butler turned and stared a moment out into the avenue, splotched with lights which gleamed softly on the dark asphalt. He had seen Dale Eustis bring her home and had seen their kiss of farewell. He tried to think what he knew about the young man beyond his wealth, his high social position, and his football prowess. These things told you nothing of how he would act toward a beautiful, impulsive young girl. The girl looked radiantly happy but that might mean anything or nothing, one couldn't be sure. The only reassurance was in her words and manner.

A few minutes later Cynthia was slipping into her simplest evening gown when a faint rap at her door startled her into attention. How well she knew the peculiar delicate firmness of that rap. In answer to her cheery "Come in" May-May entered and closed the door quietly behind her. The precise training of generations underlay even her manner of closing a door.

"Hello, May-May." Cynthia was very cheery.

"Good evening, child." There was a little pause. "Can I help you with your frock?"

"No, thanks. This is a real easy one. I just got in a few minutes ago and I had to jump into the simplest thing I had. Besides I feel simple and happy to-night. I couldn't bear the thoughts of frills and complications."

"You look very beautiful, I must say."

The girl slipped an arm through hers and they sat down on a little stuffed sofa. "Come, May-May, don't look so prim and proper. You know you're dying to ask me where I've been and what and why. Greenleaf told me you'd talked to Mrs. Ventnor, so I suppose you're just bursting

with questions. Well, fire away. You can see the whites
of my eyes now."

The woman shook her head. "Cynthia, why can't you
be serious? Don't you see this is a serious matter?"

"Yes, but I should say serious only for me and I don't
want to be serious about anything now that I'm so happy."

"I don't know whether you're trying to tell me to mind
my business, but you must see I am only doing this for
your sake. We were worried when you didn't come home
last night." May-May's tone left no shadow of doubt as
to the truth of the statement.

"We?" the girl mocked. "Just whom do you mean by
we? I suppose you and Mrs. Ventnor, since I'm sure
mother is out of this. She probably never knew I wasn't
home, much less did any worrying about it."

"Child, be reasonable. Suppose Mrs. Ventnor had talked
to your mother on the phone this afternoon. You must
see how difficult that would have made things."

"All right, suppose she had? What of it? I've done
nothing I'm ashamed of, nothing I'm afraid to tell the
whole world about. May-May, you are the one who is
not reasonable. You don't seem half so much interested
in what I did as whether I'll be found out or not. On
that score you needn't worry. As soon as we finish talking
here I am going straight to mother to tell her just what
I did and with whom. Now are you satisfied? Far from
wanting to hide anything, I want mother to know all
about it."

"Cynthia. You are forcing me to express myself badly;
you are twisting my meanings into something I do not
wish to say. The trouble is I feel too strongly about you.
I was almost a second mother to you. It was a mistake
when I came back here this time. I was very foolish."

The girl patted her strangely white hand. "Don't be

foolish, May-May. Your coming back here to me was a Godsend and you helped me to understand myself. I tried so hard to explain it all to you that one night and you were only horrified, but I did succeed in clearing things up in my own mind."

"Cynthia, you're wrong when you say I was horrified. I was only worried because I could not quite see what was my duty."

"Duty! I am sick of the word Duty! Happiness is the word that counts and last night I proved it to myself. I've found out what I am made for and what you are made for. I've found out why the world goes round, and the birds sing, and the flowers bloom, and the trees burst forth in fruit. I found out what happiness really is all about."

"Cynthia!" The woman's voice rang out in accents of warning but the girl only leaped to her feet and faced her squarely, head thrown back, eyes ablaze.

"You wanted to know about last night and now you shall know. You taught me to tell the truth always even in the smallest thing and now you are having it in the biggest thing. I spent last night with Dale Eustis. I took him away from his football banquet and we started home. We went to a little hotel along the way and registered as Mr. and Mrs. John Smith. I learned the fire and depth and beauty of the love I had dreamed about, and finally we slept in each other's arms. Now there you have the whole story. You thought it would be something terrible and instead it's something beautiful—beautiful like surging organ music in a cathedral, a cathedral with a million glowing stained glass windows."

"Cynthia!"

The woman had leaped to her feet with cheeks afire and horror in her eyes. Then suddenly she pulled herself together with a vast effort and held out her arms gently. "Cynthia, you poor child, what are we to do now? I'm proud you've come to me for help."

The girl's laugh rippled out happily. "Do? I'm going to tell mother. Maybe she'll only be amused, and in any case she can't be horrified. Oh I'm so happy, May-May. Look at me! Do you see how happy I am? Do you see how the scales of fear have fallen from my eyes and I dare to be myself? I have felt terror growing on me, creeping up and up until I could sense the cold fingers of agony reaching, groping toward my heart. I lived in dread, dread of myself and what I might be, what I might become." She caught one of the woman's hands swiftly and held it tightly. "You are shocked at Dale Eustis are you; well, suppose it had been Jane Talbot? What then?"

"No! No!" the woman cried leaping back.

"Thank God, no! But it might have been, yes. Am I finally making myself clear to you, as you wouldn't let me the night we walked through the park? Have I finally shocked you into understanding me? Are you ready to grasp the extent of my happiness, now?"

Miss Downer sank back on the little sofa with staring eyes, her hands limp at her sides. "My little Cynthia, I can't, I can't believe it."

The girl sat beside her and put an arm about the trembling form. "That's all right, May-May, don't worry about it for everything comes out right. Now I am going to talk to mother. Do you want to come with me?"

"Yes, I'd better." The woman rose slowly, laboriously, as if ten years had somehow fallen on her shoulders in as many minutes. Together they left the room but it was the girl who led now and the woman who followed almost as if walking in a dream. When they reached Mrs. Bronson's room they found the maids just leaving. Mrs. Bronson stood giving herself a final glance in her full length triple-mirror before descending to the drawing room. She swung round.

"Why, Cynthia, this is indeed a surprise, and May-May, too." She gave a final glance into the glass before sweeping toward them. "May-May, you look ghastly and Cynthia looks positively radiant. What is it?"

"Mother, I want to talk to you and I wanted May-May to hear what I have to say. There's a good reason."

Mrs. Bronson looked up a little surprised at the firm tone of voice. "Certainly, Cynthia, but why the dramatic voice? What's happened? And why don't you both sit down a minute? No one has come yet, so we can talk. It isn't very often you deign to call on me."

"I prefer to talk standing up," the girl announced.

Mrs. Bronson laughed. "Very well, child, be dramatic to the end. But I haven't seen you all day."

"That's what I want to talk about. I haven't been here all day. I just got back a few minutes ago. I was just brought back from the football game."

"But the football game was yesterday." Mrs. Bronson was clearly puzzled if not annoyed.

"Exactly. I'm trying to tell you I wasn't here last night. I, or rather we, started back in a car and it got too late so we went to a hotel. I thought you should know."

"What of it, Cynthia? Whatever Mrs. Ventnor decided was quite all right of course. You're not a baby any more."

"That's just it. I wasn't with Mrs. Ventnor. I left them yesterday after the game. Now Mrs. Ventnor is coming here to dinner to-night so I want you to know what happened. I think it's best if you're prepared a little."

"Don't listen to her," cried May-May suddenly. "She's just playing some silly game and trying to tease us."

"What a glorious game," the girl laughed, while May-May suddenly began to wring her hands and sob.

Mrs. Bronson looked from one to the other in amazement. "What is all this about? I can't make head or tail of it. Cynthia, what are you trying to tell me? Do be quick because we must go down to dinner at once."

The girl stood watching her as she spoke lightly, carelessly, rubbing the glittering nails of one perfectly manicured hand along the edge of the palm of the other. Then Cynthia took a step to May-May and caught her agonized hands firmly while she whispered, "Steady." She turned to her mother who was now watching her with wide eyes. She chuckled a little. What use was there explaining your soul to a woman intent on manicuring her nails?

"I am just being silly and dramatic, mother, but I am excited, of course. I'm engaged."

"Engaged!" Mrs. Bronson spoke the word so softly that Cynthia barely heard it though she was so near her. The woman's chest rose high with a deep intake of breath and then subsided slowly. Her arms were rigid at her sides, the extended fingers trembling with the strain upon them. The silence was deathlike in the little room, touched only by faint breathing.

"Who to?" The words fell from her motionless lips.

"Dale Eustis. I thought you'd be rather glad," the girl added as she watched her mother's obvious emotion in astonishment. Mrs. Bronson managed a smile.

"I am, Cynthia. So very, very glad and I'm sure you'll be happy." With a wild gesture she flung wide her arms. "Cynthia, now that you're engaged will you kiss your mother. We can be so terribly happy,—now."

Slowly, half mechanically, the girl walked to her mother and the beautiful arms closed about her warmly, strongly.

Mrs. Bronson kissed the soft, gleaming cheek very gently. "You're not afraid of me now, are you?"

"No, mother." She whispered the words. It was all so strange, so unexpected, especially that her mother's arms were around her and there was a strange thrill of happiness in their touch. She glanced at May-May who had retreated to a corner and was crying silently. All three were startled by a faint tap on the door.

"Mr. and Mrs. Ventnor have come." The butler's voice, flat and expressionless, broke the spell. Mrs. Bronson dropped her arms slowly and raised her head high again. Once more she was the radiant Aurelia Bronson.

"Come, Cynthia, we shall announce your engagement to-night. You want me to, don't you?"

The girl ran to May-May. "Why are you crying when everything is all right? I told you it would be. I'm not a child anymore, May-May. You must learn to trust me."

"I'm just happy, that's all." She dried her eyes furtively.

The girl faced her mother. "Yes, mother, let's tell the world about it. I want every one to know and be happy with me. Dale and I love each other. Sing it from the housetops."

CHAPTER TEN

DURING the next few weeks Cynthia often wondered about that one strange moment when her mother had taken her in her arms and kissed her, and for an instant they had clung to each other as mother and daughter might in any romantic story book. How strange a moment it had been and how beautiful. Even May-May crying in the corner had been part of the beauty of it because one knew instinctively they were tears of relief and happiness. And then in a moment the spell was broken and nothing remained but a strange inexplicable memory.

Just why, the girl wondered. Why had her mother seemed overwhelmed with happiness over the realization that she was engaged, and it had not seemed to matter particularly to whom? She had seemed to care nothing where Cynthia had spent the night away from home, or how, and the lack of caring was not from indifference as the warm embrace, the first she had ever known, had so clearly proved. And May-May's peculiar, unprecedented crying. Could it be that her mother had sent for May-May because—? She pushed the idea from her resolutely. It was preposterous.

It was much better to think of Dale in spite of the rather ridiculous formal way in which their engagement was proceeding. It had been informally announced the first night to the Ventnors, the Ramsgates, and Prince Ladislov. Only the Prince had congratulated her in a way which showed he was sincere in his wishes for her happiness. There was always something kind, and tender and dis-

turbing about Prince Ladislov even though it might spring
so largely from a knowledge of his romantic history. Mrs.
Ventnor merely raised her eyes a little at the news of the
sudden engagement, and then was platitudinous, while the
Ramsgates were obviously completely buried in calculation
as to the probable wealth of both sides and how large the
united fortune would be. It was all so ridiculous and sordid, too.

Dale came down two week-ends and on one of them
there was a very elaborate dinner and dance at Pierre's to
make the formal announcement. It seemed altogether non-
sensical to Cynthia as she lay sprawling back in her huge
Charles of London chair and thought about it. The cere-
moniousness of it, the inane congratulations, the stupid
dancing afterward were on a par with the silly double-
meaning jokes of the young girls she knew, who all seemed
to take a ridiculous amount of interest in the coming marriage. Only Gloria Glendale had embraced her warmly as
she whispered, "I guessed it, Cynthia, and I'm really glad
for you." She alone had seemed sincere.

But it would all not have been so bad if Dale had seen
the fun of the thing. Instead he went through his part with
perfect seriousness, as if the whole thing were of real
importance, even chiding her once for grinning at him
during one of the absurd speeches by a fossilized old
banker over ninety years old. It had all been so childish
when she remembered him on his knees in the hotel bedroom clinging to her naked body, his lips caressing the
faint bruise on her thigh. Only when he held her in his
arms as they danced was there any happiness for her and
even then it seemed rather an echo of what had been then
a prophecy of delights to come. With the taste of the fruit
in her mouth what did the first leaf matter?

When he came to say good-by at the end of the second week-end she had clung to him passionately with all the fervor of her frustrated desire.

"Dale, how long will this foolishness last? I want to really be with you now, all the time."

She had felt his powerful arms tremble as they held her tight and his lips crushed warm on her own, but he kept his voice very quiet.

"You mustn't talk so, Cynthia. I'm not going to see you now until you come to see mother in Tuxedo for Christmas holidays. I know you'll love it out there."

"You know what I love, Dale. Why be a prude?"

He had kissed her softly again and then held her off at arm's length to look at her, his blue eyes glowing.

"Cynthia, true love was never lost for waiting."

"It sounds like a copy book platitude."

He had laughed. "I dare say it is. Then let's prove the truth of it. Surely you don't doubt my love?"

"I had proof of it—once."

And that had been all there was to it. He wrote her every day, warm, beautiful love letters, but even as she read them the paper seemed to stand between her and him. Only words remained, words, words, words. It seemed wrong that any one so powerful and beautiful in body, with swelling muscles that rolled and rippled under the satiny skin, should write so quietly, with such simple restrained beauty. To be sure Dale Eustis not only played games at the university but actually studied as well, yet it still seemed wrong, as wrong as when he had knelt worshiping her body. It was all just one of those things you couldn't express in words and yet there it was.

And Dale was always referring to her coming visit to Tuxedo. That was the worst part of it and yet it would be a change for her and she would be with him constantly for two weeks, so her unhappy anticipations seemed utterly groundless. She had only met Mrs. Eustis once, as Dale's mother was not very well and walked with the aid of an ivory-headed stick which almost seemed part of her. Mrs. Eustis had come in from Tuxedo to attend the engagement dinner at Pierre's and the girl could certainly not complain of her treatment. The lady, somehow she seemed ridiculously old to be Dale's mother, had been very kind and considerate, and had not asked a single one of the embarrassing questions Cynthia had feared. In fact she had only been insistent that Cynthia should spend the holidays in Tuxedo with her and Dale and while the girl had had far different plans she had been unable to think up a good reason for refusing, especially as Dale had seemed as keen about the idea as his mother. Yet now that the time was at hand she was sorry to have to go. She had wanted Dale to be with her in the city.

Cynthia squirmed into a more comfortable position in her chair pulling her legs up under her. There was no doubt the days had just dragged along uselessly except for her visits to Jane Talbot. Jane had been her gayest, most amusing self and the only one who seemed to have any comprehension of the happiness Dale and she looked forward to together. Mrs. Bronson now knew that Cynthia saw a great deal of Jane but merely smiled and said how awfully nice it was of Jane to amuse her exuberant daughter. Mrs. Bronson was exceedingly kind to Cynthia whenever she happened to think of it.

One day Jane said, "Do you know, Cynthia, I think I ought to wrangle an invitation to Tuxedo so as to be up there when you visit the high and mighty Clorinda Eustis. It would absolutely make her boil inside, and, anyhow, I'm not so sure it won't be just as well for you to have an understanding friend within reach."

"Oh, Jane, I wish you would do it." Then she stopped a second and added contritely: "Not that I wish to annoy Dale's mother but if she accepts me she'll just have to accept my friends. I can stand up to any one now, you know."

The woman rose swiftly and took a dozen steps back and forth in the bright room. Then she turned to the girl impulsively. "Do you mean to say you would insist on her entertaining me? I think you noticed she looked right through me at the engagement dance."

"I mean just that. You are my friend and Dale's friend and you really brought us together. We almost owe our love to you. We might never have found each other."

"Hmm!" Jane snorted as she reseated herself. "I've been thinking of that myself, though not quite in the same way. Anyhow it doesn't matter. I wouldn't think of having you annoy the dear old lady on my account, aside from which such people bore me to extinction. One week in Tuxedo nowadays would drive me to suicide."

And then Cynthia laughed as her memory shifted to Mr. Bronson. How typical he had been as he expressed his happiness in her engagement very much as if they had just been introduced. He had *attended* her engagement party but it had been just that and no more. She had been tempted to ask him if he wouldn't like to have Olive Smith come but the minute she thought it over she realized that wouldn't be a joke at all.

It was strange, but since her one night of love she had thought a great deal about Olive Smith and in a different way from the coldly indifferent pity which had once summed up her feelings. What did she really know about

Olive beyond the fact that she was beautiful, and quiet, dressed perfectly and had been on the stage? According to Jane Talbot she had been a rather good actress with a real future. Then she had met Thor Bronson, just how or when nobody seemed to know, and had quietly slipped into her strange niche in life as the mistress of a very rich man. All the newspapers knew about it and almost everybody in the streets, it seemed. Cynthia had overheard the servants talking about it for years, she remembered, without any trace of bitterness. To them the woman was simply lucky and wore beautiful jewels and had a grand apartment and a Rolls-Royce.

Now that she knew the extent of her own emotion Cynthia wondered what she would have done under the same circumstances. She laughed at all the tomfoolery of the engagement, and the marriage would be worse, but it was Dale who wanted all this and she who was quite willing to throw her hat over the mill and go off with him. Maybe with Olive it had been the same. Maybe Thor Bronson had meant as much to her even if he didn't have a great, powerful body and crisp yellow hair and laughing eyes. Perhaps all men were the same sticklers for some code, some convention which they blamed on women and which they secretly adored. Suppose Dale had been married and had refused to give up the ridiculous outward sham of his marriage? Suppose he had refused to go away from his conventions, his stock market, clubs, theaters? What would she, Cynthia Thorpe, have done? She hardly needed to ask herself that. She had given herself to Dale openly and without restraint and would have thought it no shame to continue to do so. It put Olive in a different light.

But when the time actually came to start for Tuxedo a few days before Christmas Cynthia climbed into her car with a happy heart intent now on seeing Dale again and firm in her determination to take matters into her own hands. She had won him by decided action and she would keep him the same way. She was sure of herself.

CHAPTER ELEVEN

MEANWHILE Dale was talking seriously to his mother in that lady's small sitting room in which she spent most of the time in her great, wide-spreading house. Indeed it was only when her son was at home that the soft tap of her rubber tipped stick was heard in the spacious drawing rooms and reception halls of this so much too large house. When he was away at school she retired to her compact suite upstairs and lived like any lonely old woman in a three or four room apartment. When she went out riding in her big old-fashioned car she rode down in the lift with quiet dignity and walked through the wide hall as if it were the entrance of an apartment house and nothing in which her interest was any more personal. She had her meals on a little folding table which was opened carefully in her small sitting room and placed before the easy chair in which she sat. Evangeline, her maid who had been with her ever since she could remember and whom she had always called "Vangey," served her and cared for her. Bridget, the cook, often came up ostensibly to help serve the little dinner, in reality anxious to see some little tid-bit eaten which she had culled from long memory as to just what appealed most to a tired small appetite. The two old servants fussed over their mistress and fussed with each other just as if they were indeed the only servants in an old woman's modest little flat. And Mrs. Eustis never interfered. It was their privilege, a reward for their faithfulness.

Yet the life of the great, spreading house went on under

the capable supervision of Mrs. Mellick who almost forgot at times that she had ever been anything else except house-keeper at Gateways and for so many years now, since Mr. Eustis had died, custodian of its splendors. Mrs. Mellick lived on a far more spacious scale than her mistress, with an army of servants at her beck and call. It was she who engaged them and discharged them at will, and it was she from whom all favors came far more than the quiet old woman who sat all day in her suite alone, thinking, read-ing, and writing. It was writing especially which occupied Mrs. Eustis' time for she kept up a large correspondence with all the various branches of her own family and her husband's as well. That she conceived as her duty and she was a woman who never shirked a duty once recognized.

She wrote her son every day whenever he was away from home and she had "crept back into her shell," as she expressed it. That took up a great deal of her time but the letters were not necessarily long. Sometimes they were very short, just a little joke or a funny recollection, or a brief quotation from her quiet, systematic reading. For him she racked her brain to be clever, and gay, and light of touch. For him she ridiculed and laughed at the old Tux-edo ladies who insisted on forcing their way in to see her because she *was* on the visiting lists, and always had been, and always would be. Sometimes she wiped away a tear as she mocked at them and everybody and everything of her own deeply cherished generation just so Dale might smile and wait happily for the next letter. Her household gods must be held up to ridicule so he could laugh.

She cherished some of his letters. One began,

"Darling Mother,
"The minute I get out of class I run to get the mail because there is always a letter from you. And such

jolly letters too, the kind I think people used to write
when they were happier and gayer than we are now."

Another began a little more abruptly.

"Sweetheart!
    "I woke up this morning laughing at your descrip-
tion of old Mrs. Lorimer and her silly Victorian
clothes. How can I ever repay you for teaching me to
laugh at ugliness instead of being angry, which is far
nearer my true nature? I lack your young mind—"

Yes, that was a treasured letter in spite of the fact that
she had cried over it. She was really very fond of Mrs.
Lorimer whom she looked up to as a fine type of real
gentlewoman. Yet she had ridiculed her to make Dale
laugh and was not ashamed of her treachery.

Such was the Eustis household with Dale away at
school. But on his return lights blazed in every window
and the prodigal entertainment at Gateways was proverbial.
The lofty paneled dining-room so long empty echoed with
the sound of gay feasting and Clorinda Eustis blazing with
her historic jewels smiled triumphantly at the head of the
table. Of late years she didn't mind how many came to
dinner, or luncheon, or breakfast, if they cared to, so long
as she could look over the low banks of flowers and see her
boy sitting at the other end of the table. How gracefully
he sat and how well his beautifully tailored clothes set off
his deep chest and powerful body, his crisp yellow hair
catching the soft candle-light and glowing above the som-
ber black and trim white linen. What did it matter if
sometimes she felt very tired so long as his happy laughter
rolled along the table to her, or he ran gayly up to her
during the dancing and cried, "Mother, darling, only you

could think up such a grand party." It made everything worth while. She couldn't afford to be tired.

So as Cynthia was being driven out to make her first visit the house was flung open and in its gayest mood, but Dale and his mother were in her private sitting room because Mrs. Eustis felt she wanted a last talk with her boy before this strange girl came to monopolize his time and attention. She felt weary but it would never do to give away now and be a tired old woman just when Dale would want her to do the honors of the house to the girl he had picked out to some day be its mistress. It really was Dale's house, now he was of age, though he had never mentioned it or even given any indication that he knew it to be so. He had signed all the papers and gone through all the formalities gracefully enough without ever again referring to the occasion. Dale would probably let her live in her few rooms no matter whom he married and that would be appropriate since he would be away. He might be living in the same house, but if he married he would be away, far more away than when he was at school, because she wouldn't be able to write to him and be sure he was thinking of her as he read the letter. They would live in different worlds.

She was interrupted in her thoughts by Dale rubbing his cheek softly against her knee as he sat on the padded stool at her feet, just as he had always sat, as she wished, somehow, he might always sit. She rested her stick against the side of the chair and caught his strong, happy face in her heavy-knuckled, heavily veined hands.

"Dale, it is good to have you with me like this just for an hour, for the last time."

He laughed boyishly. "Mother darling, how gloomy you sound and just when I want you to be so very happy. How can you speak of the last time when I've only just come home for a nice vacation? Have you forgotten that?"

She smoothed his crisp yellow hair tenderly without answering for a minute. Then she spoke very softly. "Just what time are you expecting Miss Thorpe?"

"*Miss* Thorpe? Mother, how prim and proper you are. He hesitated a moment then went on very seriously. "You know I'm afraid you don't seem to look forward to Cynthia being here. I wish I knew why."

"Don't be silly, Dale. If you want—Cynthia," she hesitated perceptibly before the name, "here, I am only too glad you should be happy."

He shook his head slowly. "It won't do, it's got to be something more than that. Mother, I really am afraid you don't quite realize I'm not a little boy any more for whom you're just giving an amusing party. Now it's serious, the most serious thing in my life."

She continued stroking his hair quietly. "Of course I know you're not a little boy any more though I'm afraid you'll always seem like a little boy to me. Dale," she cried passionately, "you've meant so much to me, everything in all the world. I've had no life outside of you,—"

She ceased abruptly as he caught both her hands in his and kissed them tenderly. "Mother, how can you say that? I do know how good you've been, how you've devoted yourself to me. Sometimes I almost wish you hadn't, it's made me too dependent, and humble, and afraid. Mother, that's why I started to play football first because I was afraid. The boys used to tease me because I got so many presents from you and a letter every day, and I was always so anxious to get home to see you. You never knew that, did you? They called me sissy because I loved you so much and that only made me love you the more. Can you understand how that was? Sometimes I'm not sure I know myself or ever shall know. Then I started to play football and baseball and every kind of game, and they started to cheer for me instead of jeering at me. You see I was afraid to just stand up to the world and care nothing what they said. I became an athlete because I was afraid."

He paused breathlessly and once more the woman rested her hands on his head. "I never knew it was so hard for you, Dale. I'm so awfully sorry."

"Oh, but you mustn't be, mother. You just gave me too much, more than I was worthy of. You see I'm telling you all this so you'll try to understand Cynthia better. She's had such a lonely life, mother, with no one to really care for her. You know how her mother is."

"Yes, I know," the woman muttered grimly.

"She needs so much love, mother, so much more than I can give her, so much more than I am worthy to give her. I want you to make up to her for so much she hasn't had, so much she has never known. Mother, I love her so much I can't tell you, or her, or any one. When she is near me I feel as if my heart were on fire; my brain melts when I think about her. I wonder if you can understand."

She smiled grimly. "I was married, Dale."

"I'm afraid that isn't going to be enough to understand us, mother. They all used to rave about spiritual unions but this is so much more important because it is going to be real physical union, bodies perfectly mated."

"Dale!" Her voice was a little sharp. "I have never attempted to interfere in your life. I have sat back and taken what affection came from you, much or little. But I insist I will not listen to your crude modern marriage ideas. It's not right to bring such disgusting things home to your mother."

"Disgusting!" He rose quietly to his feet. "I might have known you couldn't understand. Now I'm sorry Cynthia's coming. I wish there were some way of stopping her. You lived shut up here so long you don't know life."

The woman leaned back and faced him steadily. "I may have sat shut up in this little room but I may know more about modern life than you think. If we are going to be frank or disgusting, whichever one calls it, let's be so. A wife is one thing and a mistress is another. Which is it you want? Which is this girl to be? Do you want a girl to satisfy your body or grace the head of your table?"

Her voice was quivering as she finished, her face unnaturally flushed. She shot her last bolt viciously, with all the pent up fury of a mother who sees her son slipping from her; the anger of a woman who is ruining her own cause, knows she is ruining it, and can't help it. She expected him to flash back at her but he merely shook his head very slowly as if he couldn't quite believe what he heard. When he spoke finally his voice was quiet, dangerously quiet.

"Mother, for the first time you have failed me, failed me completely. I suppose it had to be but I'm sorry. I love Cynthia so much I'm afraid you just can't understand it. If you had hoped I would make a nice marriage of convenience and have a few chorus girls on the side you are doomed to disappointment. Cynthia will be mistress, wife, everything I need or hope for. Now shall I go with her back to town? Maybe it would be best."

The woman rose slowly, so slowly that her son leaped to aid her. She had quite recovered her composure, at least outwardly, and she took her time in replying. Words were important now. She realized the danger of a single slip.

"My dear Dale, I'm sorry. I may have failed you as a mother but I hope I won't fail you in my social duty. I apologize for—"

"Mother," he cried, suddenly contrite, "I didn't mean—"

She touched his cheek lightly with her finger-tips. "Let's not be foolish, Dale. We have been bickering like silly children. Now you've told me how much you love Cynthia—well, she will be my daughter from now on. Can I say more? Remember I haven't had your chance to know and appreciate her."

Dale caught her lightly in his arms, his eyes shining. "That's more like my wonderful mother. I'm so happy now." He set her on her feet again and rested his cheek against hers. "Mother, we'll all be so happy together, you wait and see."

Before his mother could speak the interruption came. He raised his head sharply as the faint sound of a motor horn penetrated the room.

"Mother, she's come!" He dashed wildly out of the room leaving the door open behind him. The old woman followed slowly, leaning heavily on her stick with its beautifully carved ivory handle and rubber tip. She was thinking very fast now, faster than she had ever had to in her life before. Unless she were very careful she was going to lose her son, and she must not let that happen whatever else had to be. She had almost lost him just now through a few angry words, and the single glance into the black lonely abyss had terrified her.

CHAPTER TWELVE

CYNTHIA leaped from the steps of the car into the firm shelter of Dale's outstretched arms. Her arm circled his neck tenderly and she brushed her cheek softly against his crisp hair, reveling in the rough feel of it; the firm masculinity of his hands on her body.

"Dale, it's so good to see you again," she breathed softly. She felt she wanted to say a million things for which there was no time now.

"Cynthia," the word trembled a little in his throat in a way that made her heart beat quicker. "We must never be apart so long again. I just can't bear it."

She laughed happily. "All right, lover, but put me down. I'm sure every one is looking."

"I want them to. I want all the world to look and see how much I love you. Now I'm going to carry you into the house like a Chinese bride."

"No, no," she remonstrated as he started up the steps with her. "I don't want to be a Chinese bride. I'm not a bride anyway."

"Oh yes you are. You're the bride of my heart." And so holding her warmly, he entered the house while Waggoner, the butler, held the door wide with serene composure as if such a method of entry had been the custom of all the Eustis family from earliest times.

When Dale put her down on the floor with a short happy laugh Cynthia found herself face to face with Mrs. Eustis who was standing with quiet dignity at the foot of the stairs. The woman held out her arms.

"Welcome to Gateways." Then while the girl hesitated a second, "My dear girl, how beautiful you are. Won't you give a poor, lonely old woman one kiss?"

Cynthia stood still an instant, a little breathless with Dale's fervid welcome and now this warm greeting from his mother. Then she threw caution to the winds and kissed the lady's wrinkled cheek happily.

"Oh, Mrs. Eustis, you are so very kind. I'm just swept off my feet by such a welcome. Is it a custom to greet visitors so merrily? Are all the Eustis men so romantic?"

Mrs. Eustis slipped her arm about the girl's shoulders. "My dear girl, we do most for those we love most, and—well, you see I've never had a daughter,—until now."

Cynthia felt the tears brim into her eyes. "Please don't say anything more. I'm afraid I'll wake up and find I'm dreaming. I'm not used to happy dreams, either."

Dale caught her hand. "Darling, now you see what I told you. Mother and I between us are going to make you happy for always. You believe me now, don't you?"

"How could I help it?" She laughed up at him.

The three crossed to the lift and soon were laughing and joking together as they made sure Cynthia was comfortable in her room. Finally they left her to change her traveling dress.

"We'll have tea in the sun room," said Mrs. Eustis. "Come down as soon as you can, Cynthia, or I'll have trouble with my impatient son. We can't spare you for longer than we have to."

"You'll just see how quick I can be," cried the girl.

As they walked slowly along the hall, mother and son, Dale's open face fairly exuded happiness.

"Mother, darling, you're wonderful. I knew you could do it and I knew you'd really love Cynthia once we had her to ourselves away from such a mob as there was at Pierre's

the night of the engagement ball. She's the sweetest girl in
the world, just all beauty and love. That's what I meant a
little while ago when we were talking."

"You're right, son; I can see that now. I think the years
seemed to drop away when she kissed me. Maybe with
both a son and a daughter I can throw away the old stick,
and forget the full tide of my years."

"Yes, throw it away, mother, and just let me carry you
through life. Anyway how foolish you are. I think, sometimes, you try to see how old you can possibly make yourself. You know, mother, it would never occur to me to ask
your age or try to find it out, but at the same time I have
a good head for simple arithmetic."

She laughed softly and pulled his ear playfully with her
wrinkled hand. "Don't be too sure of your mathematics,
my boy. I may be fooling you and many others. Maybe I
love you so much because you came to me when I had
begun to despair of your coming."

Dale took her hand tenderly. "Mother, you almost em-
barrass me."

"How could I after our little talk of this afternoon?
Anyway I promise to be no older than necessary. But
though you say you want to carry me as you carried Cynthia into the house, I'm afraid you'd soon tire of that with
an old woman. Very old and heavy."

He paused thoughtfully. "It's funny, mother, but I really
don't know why I picked her up and carried her into the
house like that. I'm sure I didn't intend to do anything so
sort of silly, but the minute she was in my arms I couldn't
help myself. It was as if some power were making me do
it, and making me want to do it, without any active thought
on my side at all. Something seemed to flow out of her
body and into mine."

She pulled his head down to her level and kissed him

very gently. "You are such a dear, sweet, romantic boy that you don't even know the strength of your love. I know your heart better than you think, and that's why I've been afraid for you. But you can smooth away your puzzled frown because that's all over now that I've really seen Cynthia. I'm not afraid any more even for myself, much less for you and her."

He held her tight. "Mother, how could you ever be afraid for any of us when you know how much I love you? I shall always be the same to you, always, always. My love for Cynthia can only increase my love for you."

"I know that, now. I think I had to see her in your arms, held against your heart, to quite realize. And, Dale, how proud you can be of her beauty. I don't think I've ever seen a girl so radiantly lovely."

"Mother, darling, I'm so happy now. I'm afraid I don't deserve it. I'm sorry we've arranged for all the entertainments you've planned. Wouldn't it be much nicer if we three were together, just we three, with all the world of pretense locked outside and far away?"

"Dale, don't be like that," she admonished with a smile. "We must show every one how proud of Cynthia we are. She must see the social group in which she will take her place as soon as you're married, because Cynthia must lead things here, as becomes the youngest and most beautiful Eustis bride Tuxedo has ever known. She is a young girl and wants gayety."

"Yes, I suppose so, but sometimes I think she really wants quiet and simplicity. I don't think she looks forward to living in Tuxedo. It worries me more than I dare confess."

The woman laughed gayly. "Oh, you silly boy, all girls are like that when they first find love and are swept off their feet by the glory and fervor of it. They always want to go to a South Sea Island or some tropic beach and lie all night in the moonlight—"

"Mother!" he interrupted with wide eyes. "How did you know that; how could you know she said that?"

"It's all so simple, Dale. Every woman, at least every mother knows that. We've all been through the same experience and it always seems so original and new in spite of that." She hesitated a second. "I went through it myself. That's why there are honeymoons so lovers can adjust themselves to the real problems of life. You'll both learn that Tuxedo is far more comfortable than Tahiti."

"It sounds almost too calm and settled for Cynthia. Somehow I can't imagine her entertaining formally. Do you think I'm being very silly?"

"Of course not. You'd be a very unromantic lover if you thought of her merely as a hostess. But we won't worry about silly things like that. Trust mother, Dale. Leave stupid details to me and you'll find everything will come out all right."

He kissed her. "Yes, mother, you're always right. I should know that by this time."

Meanwhile Cynthia had sent the maid away and was dressing quickly. She chose a simple frock whose lines accentuated her strange beauty. She had refused to bring a maid with her and she sent away the maid here, because she enjoyed dressing herself and the opportunity it gave her to think things over. What true woman does not know that a large part of the pleasure of fine clothes lies in the happy thoughts while putting them on. Every garment brings a gentle flood of memory, association, and anticipation. She glanced at herself in the mirror and smiled happily at the elegant reflection.

How ridiculous it was of her to have looked forward with dread to coming to Tuxedo. Her reception had been thrilling to say the least; so much different from her expectation as to make those expectations seem utterly absurd. To be sure Dale was deeply in love with his mother but if this was a sample of her way of acting one could hardly blame him and there was certainly no reason why she should fear that dominion over him. Wasn't there an old saying that a man who loved his mother before marriage was the one who really loved his wife after marriage? It was a funny saying, but how often such things were true. With a happy laugh she ran out of her room and down the stairs. Her feet were as light on the piled carpet as her hand on the smooth oak balustrade.

Tea was a happy affair at which Mrs. Eustis poured with dignity and good humor, sending away the butler so the three of them might be alone together. They laughed at anything or nothing at all with equal ease, and Cynthia was quite captivated by her hostess' charm and variety of humor. Dale made her repeat many of her funniest re marks about the Tuxedo celebrities and they rocked with laughter.

"You'd never think how devoted mother is to these people to hear her make jokes about them," he cried, wiping the tears from his eyes.

"Why not? They are really very nice and very kind when you get to know them as well as I do. You see I think you can only laugh perfectly at some one you like very much, otherwise your laughter is unkind."

Cynthia looked up quickly. "You make me feel so very guilty because I've been having such a good time laughing at people whom I don't know. But you do make it all sound so irresistibly funny."

Mrs. Eustis shook her head with a broad smile. "How sweet and good you are! You see you are really laughing now because you are so very happy you find the whole world gay. And even if you don't know these people now you soon will and because of me you are really taking my friends for granted. In England they sing a silly song which expresses it perfectly. 'For your friends are my friends and my friends are your friends.' "

"Why mother, that's nothing but a drinking song they sing in the English pubs. I'm quite shocked at you."

"I know that, and why not? If drinking makes them feel that way why I say they should drink. What this country needs is good beer and a song to go with it."

Dale kissed his mother rapturously. "Mother, darling, you sound wicked if not quite Rabelaisian and I don't dare to consider what Cynthia must think of you. This begins to sound like a political convention."

The woman patted his cheek. "My dear boy, what I am really doing is making a martyr of myself to distract our Cynthia's attention from the fact that you've already eaten three large pieces of cake and *you're* probably using this argument as a strategic move to divert our attention while you take a fourth. See that nice oozy chocolaty one."

"Not a bit of it," he cried. "I'm taking a fourth piece quite openly even if you and Cynthia are still struggling with the first. I got Bridget to make this cake especially for me because I've got so many weeks of training to make up for." He took a huge bite and mumbled: "I certainly do love this breaking of training rules. Nothing else is half so much fun."

"Why I thought the football season ended on the last Saturday before Thanksgiving," remarked Cynthia, "and that's four weeks ago." There was a faint question in her tone.

He leaned toward her with glowing eyes. "So many things ended that day and so many began I'm not quite sure of anything, except one thing, and I can't say what that is. Isn't that a lovely muddled sentence?"

"Why not?" Mrs. Eustis smiled as she poured another cup of tea and added a gauze-thin slice of lemon. "Surely Cynthia knows, and I think I do. That was the day you found how much you loved each other, wasn't it dear?" She turned to Cynthia with a quizzical smile.

"Yes, and I'm afraid I'm like Dale; nothing else seems to matter but that."

"Naturally, my child, and you're not half as secretive as my stalwart son. No, Dale, don't try to be indignant with a mouth full of cake, it simply can't be done. I know because I've tried," she added with a chuckle.

"Am I supposed to bow my head in shame?" he grinned, a little red in the face from bolting the mouthful.

"Certainly. I'm sure you haven't told Cynthia that you are playing on the basketball team when you ought to be spending all your time just thinking of her."

The girl looked up quickly. "Dale, are you playing on the team? You know you said you were not going in for any more athletics. It was almost a promise, wasn't it?"

"They needed me," he responded sheepishly. "I didn't intend to but—" his voice trailed off. Mrs. Eustis turned commiseratingly to the girl with an expressive gesture.

"There it is and you'll have to get used to it, I suppose. Dale simply can't resist the roar of the crowd and a mob shouting 'Eustis! Eustis!', you know the way they do. And he's so bashful at home you'd never think he was at all like that. Just look how he's blushing now," she added with a sly smile. "You see any comment by less than ten thousand people embarrasses him."

"Mother, how can you!" he cried, but Cynthia rose very slowly and strolling to one of the great glass sides of the room stared out into the darkness of the wintry garden.

The night was touched with white gleams of falling snow-flakes.

"It's beginning to snow," she said, "heavy, wet snow. I wish it wouldn't. I don't want it to snow to-day."

In an instant he was at her side, his voice anxious. "That's only a covering remark, Cynthia. What are you really thinking underneath? I'm sure it isn't about snow."

She swung round to face him. "I'm just thinking how nice it is to know the real reason why you could not come to New York to see me over the week-ends. Dale, why didn't you invent some really good excuse and say you couldn't afford it or something of the sort?" Her voice was heavy with sarcasm. "I might have saved up my pennies to send you the fare."

"Cynthia." Dale stared at her in astonishment, but Mrs. Eustis rose quietly. Her voice rolled smoothly into the caustic silence, charming it away.

"Come, children, we mustn't forget we have a long evening ahead of us. Cynthia, we're having a houseful for dinner and dancing afterward so I dare say you'll want a chance to rest before dressing. Eight o'clock is the time. And the white tie is necessary," she explained turning to Dale who still stood bewildered. Then she passed out of the room and across the spacious drawing room toward the lift with Cynthia on her arm. When they were out of earshot Mrs. Eustis patted the girl's hand gently, her voice was very low.

"Don't be too severe on Dale. I'm afraid it's hard for him to tell you how much he loves you, the very best men are often like that. Try to think that perhaps Dale is playing basketball not because he loves you too little but because he loves you too much. You are very young and sweet but you know what I mean, I'm sure of that. With some tremendously virile men control is not so easy. You will excuse my blunt way of blurting things out. After all I'm a lonely old woman far more used to talking to myself than to any one else, and I always talk plainly."

Impulsively the young girl touched her lips to the sagging, faded cheeks. "I think I do understand, Mrs. Eustis, and I'm so sorry I was stupid just now. It only goes to show what a selfish little beast I am. I'm sorry you've found me out so soon."

"On the contrary, you are a darling girl, and I'm sure we're all going to be very happy."

Back in her room again the girl sat down to think things over very quietly. Dale had disappointed her by going back into athletics and so depriving her of his company. But if his mother's implication was true there was a little thrill in the very denial. Her flooding memory assured her it was quite logical.

CHAPTER THIRTEEN

THE next few days were a continual round of entertainment after the rather stodgy, formal manner of Tuxedo, and Cynthia found herself with little enough time on her hands. It was especially bewildering after the long, long neglected life she had led at home. Her mother had left her rather definitely alone after her début and Cynthia had by that time become tangled in her morbid thoughts, and was rather grateful for the neglect. Until she met Dale there had been nothing to draw her out of the dread quicksand of introspection into which she had begun to sink slowly but surely. There had been long weary weeks when she feared she would never have the courage to escape.

So she entered gayly enough into the spirit of Mrs. Eustis' entertainments and those to which she was at once showered with invitations. With Dale by her side everything was good. After the first day it turned cold and she bravely decided to learn to skate, a sport which had never attracted her in any way before. But Dale skated beautifully, as indeed he excelled in every sport, and under his tender tutelage she felt she was enjoying her progress, however little it might be when viewed quite dispassionately. She loved his arm clasped about her; there was ecstasy in the sudden pressure of reassurance of those muscles which caught her so securely when she began to fall, as she seemed to do regularly. Under the tight wool of his skating costume she could sense the clean satiny skin with the muscles crawling under it, and remember her cheek resting on its relaxed softness. Her own body quivered with the ecstasy of remembrance.

With a laugh he caught her arms and pulled her to him, his eyes sparkling, his face glowing in the clean, cold air. "Cynthia, I don't think you're even trying to skate alone. You just want me to hold you up. Now be a good little girl and 'fess up."

"Of course," she answered blithely. "Any one can skate, but I just want your arm around me. Haven't you noticed how well I fall so you can catch me? Anyway if you were very polite you'd at least pretend to like it."

He kissed her swiftly. "What an adorable child you are. When will you ever grow up and be dignified?"

"Never! I'm Miss Peter Pan, so to remain until I become Mrs. Dale Eustis. So you must accept the idea."

"And after you're Mrs. Eustis, then what?" He grinned at her. "Sometimes that seems pretty far off, but when I have you in my arms Time skips merrily through the months and it seems near enough."

She shook her head. "I don't know. I think I'll be so happy then it won't really matter any more. I'm afraid I can't even think about it then. There won't ever be any thinking in our lives, just feeling, and love and happiness."

"Cynthia, there are times when I feel I can't wait; when the days, the weeks, the months seem so long, so much too long. Like a greedy boy I want everything now." His voice shook with suppressed emotion.

"And I, too, Dale. What are we waiting for? Why are we waiting when we are supposed to be above stupidities and conventions, when we have ridden over their drear dead forms so happily once? There are times I think you don't want me at all; that I was only an amusing night in your life, one of so many perhaps, an alternative to black coffee, a cigar and a speech. Something tangible instead of a circulating bottle and dirty stories."

"Cynthia, stop it! Why are you trying to hurt me again,

trying to make me seem hateful to myself, all because I want to enshrine you in my heart; because I want to leave no stone unturned for our happiness?" He tightened his grip on her in his earnestness.

"Dale, listen to me carefully." There was an eager, bounding quality in her voice which held him silent. "I don't want to be enshrined not even in your heart. Don't you understand that? You always say I'm trying to hurt you and I'm only trying to make you see things clearly. You are not a child or a fool, but you won't see that you are killing our love, tearing down our palace of dreams. Your training, your family, your books, your religion, everything has taught you of women who want men because of what men can give them. I am trying to show you the clean, decent love that wants nothing but completion of itself and culmination in itself. I don't want anything in the world, but you."

He stood facing her, staring at her as if trying to comprehend fully what she was saying. When she finished her voice was still low and inaudible to others skating a distance away, others whose shouts and laughter were like vague erratic punctuation to her words. They were silent a moment, then quite suddenly one foot slipped and she would have fallen had he not sprung to her side like a flash and caught her. As he steadied her again gently a whirl of passionate protest ran through her mind. Why must his body move so swiftly, so accurately, so beautifully while his mind stumbled along after hers? Why couldn't his thought flash out to support her thought even as his body supported her body? Why didn't his ideas close round her and thrill her as his arm could? She shivered a little. There suddenly seemed to be a bitter, acid quality in the breeze blowing fitfully over the sheltered lake. In her earnestness she had forgotten the ice under

her feet, the gray, heavy skies, and the dark pine trees
that marched down the long slopes to the very ice-edge.
The gay laughter down the lake suddenly became a thing
apart, a mockery of her thoughts. Again a shiver passed
over her, this time a little more prolonged than before.

"You're cold, Cynthia. Let's go in." His gentle voice
had a touch of fear in it.

"Am I cold, Dale, or are you?" She laughed shortly.
But she submitted without a further word to having her
skates removed solicitously and a few minutes later they
ran into the house together. Mrs. Eustis was just coming
into the hall as they entered. She stood leaning on her
stick watching their glowing faces.

"Well, children, you must be half frozen after skating
on a morning like this. Come into the library now. I have
a big log fire, and you can warm your toes before going
up to change." She slipped an arm about Cynthia.

"That's fine, mother," Dale agreed heartily. "It takes
you to realize a log fire warms you up better than all the
steam heat in the world. You know I had to bring Cynthia
in, she was shivering." His assurance of manner was once
more in the ascendancy.

"Of course she was!" the woman cried. "Dale, you'll
have to be more considerate and thoughtful for Cynthia.
You seem to forget a girl needs more protection than a
chum."

Cynthia laughed dutifully. "Oh, the shiver was nothing
but a piece of acting, I assure you. I got tired of arguing
on skates because whenever I made a good point I'd slip
and Dale would catch me very gallantly instead of answering. By the time I'd get solidly upright again the
effect would be gone."

"Arguing? Why what were you children arguing
about?"

Cynthia danced across and caressed Dale's flushed cheek. "See how bashful he is, Mrs. Eustis, just like a little boy. I'm sure the football coach would never believe it, or the basketball coach either. Shall I tell your mother about our discussion, Dale? Remember you mustn't have a secret from mother."

"Cynthia!" There was pleading in his voice. The girl shrugged her shoulders and turned again to her hostess.

"You see how modest he is, Mrs. Eustis. I'm sure he'd never go swimming at all if he lived in Russia. Glorious Russia with one hundred and eighty million people and not a single bathing suit. At least Will Rogers said so."

"But this isn't Russia," cried the bewildered man.

"Oh, wouldn't it be grand if it only were? Dale, don't you dare say you wouldn't enjoy it, because you know you would. I have a grand idea. Let's set out for Russia at once. We can live on tea and caviar and vodka and study Russian dancing. I think I'll call myself Cynthuska. We'll buy high boots and dance about waving red silk scarves."

She finished breathlessly and the others joined in her laugh. "Now just think, Mrs. Eustis, I couldn't convince him at all, so do you wonder I had to invent a shiver to get him to bring me in? If I couldn't get a glass of hot tea in Russia I could at least get a cup of hot tea here. After an hour of trying to skate I feel I need something to brace me up, ankles or stomach but preferably both."

Mrs. Eustis sat down in her easy chair before the sparkling log fire. "Cynthia, I'm glad you're so happy here."

"Of course I am and to-night will be happiest of all."

"Why, child?"

"Why every one knows on Christmas Eve Santa Claus comes down the chimney to bring us our heart's desire. I know what I want most of all. Dale, do you know what you want?"

"Yes, a ticket to Russia," he mocked with a sweeping ironic bow.

"All right, you asked for it, so don't be surprised if you get it. To-night then hang up your stocking and wait for the giver of all good things."

At that moment a footman entered with the tea which Mrs. Eustis had ordered and the conversation changed to discussing plans for the evening. During the rest of the day Cynthia at intervals would cry, "Don't forget about your ticket to Russia," and he would laugh and say, "All right, I'll sit up waiting for Santa Claus." Mrs. Eustis watched them both with her quiet eyes, a little puzzled line appearing on her forehead only to vanish quickly when they spoke to her or looked directly at her. Then she smiled quickly and joined in the conversation lightly or went on with her careful preparations for the evening. Since Cynthia's arrival she was really directing her household and the housekeeper was for the moment merely a recipient of orders, greatly to that worthy woman's astonishment. Mrs. Mellick vowed to Waggoner in strict confidence that she had never seen her mistress so animated, so keen in her desire that every order be carried out to the letter. Waggoner agreed that she looked ten years younger, while the whole staff listened and took heed. The Christmas Eve ball was to be a never-to-be-forgotten occasion.

CHAPTER FOURTEEN

DALE undressed slowly in his room unwilling to move quickly and so destroy the happy languor which lay upon him so lightly, making his heart want to sing very softly. What a lovely evening it had been with every one jolly and simple and the fun of the best, quietest kind. It had been a beautiful thought of his mother to have the gayly illuminated Christmas tree just as he used to remember it as a child and to lead them all in like children to receive their presents, her little tokens of love and affection. How marvelous mother was to have remembered so cleverly just the little things every one had a fancy for, the little things that in the ordinary way they were so unlikely to get. The tears had started in dear old Mrs. Humphreys' eyes as she received a quaint old Paisley shawl which probably carried her memory back to some golden page of her youth. He was sure there was something, something which his mother knew, some memory which the old ladies treasured deep down in their hearts. No one else knew what it was for Mr. Humphreys was dead, had always been dead it seemed to Dale, just like his own father whom he couldn't remember at all. Yet he could remember a line from one of his mother's wonderful letters: "Old Mrs. Humphreys was in to see me to-day dressed in the height of fashion for old ladies and looking utterly miserable. I'm sure that if she were braver she'd be much happier. Then she'd wear a bonnet with violets on it, and a Paisley shawl."

He remembered how he had laughed about it; and all the while his mother had meant it not as a joke but in

149

all seriousness. He had seen the shawl given not as a sarcastic joke, but in loving memory of some secret, beautiful and fine, which they both shared. And there had been other gifts as gracefully sentimental he was sure, even if not so obvious to him. It had all been so unexpected by every one, especially those who thought they knew Mrs. Eustis best as a very stately rather cold old woman completely wrapped up in her son. Dale was sure of that and the thought warmed his heart all the more. Sometimes he, too, had been tempted to think of his mother as a stately cold old woman, but after to-night he could never be guilty again of harboring such a thought. To-night he had seen her in a new way and in a new rôle. He would never forget.

And Cynthia. He stripped off his undershirt and drawers and stretched luxuriously. How strange and wonderful Cynthia had been, and, all in a way he had scarcely deemed possible. He paused on his way to the bathroom and stood irresolute a moment with his hand on the door knob. How little he really knew about Cynthia when he stopped to think about it. Beyond her love for him, which he could not for an instant doubt, what were her desires, her dreams, her aspirations? She had told him that she wanted nothing but himself; told him so in a way that made his heart throb, the blood race in his veins, and his breath almost choked him. But in spite of what his body desired and his senses felt, his brain would not allow him to accept any such flaming statement at its literal value. It was unreasonable, so it couldn't be and his mind clung to the solace of those dogmatic words. His college training had given him at least so much armor with which to face a world of rapidly shifting ideas, ideals, and concepts. It was mad to suppose, in pure reason, that he was the culmination of all desire in any one's life, much less a bril-

liant, talented girl like Cynthia. But what else were her
needs, her aspirations? He was forced to confess he didn't
know.

Men always wanted many things of life and women
must be the same. For himself he knew, when he was
quiet and calm as he was now, that he wanted her more
than anything else in life, but he wanted other things too,
so many other things. Human nature could not be otherwise.

The realization made him pause. He knew little or
nothing of Cynthia except as a lover, a dryad creature all
beauty, and passion and ecstasy. Yet there must be so
much more than that. To-night he had seen her stand
quietly beside the Christmas tree and sing carols, the simple centuries old carols of childhood and faith. Her voice
was low and warm and a little husky, one of those voices
which sing from the heart to the heart. The sophisticated
gathering had been astonished at first and listened carelessly, but as she went on they gathered around with
growing amazement. Every one joined in the carols which
they knew; the others Cynthia sang through alone, with
all the simple unabashed fervor of a dreaming child.
Where had she ever learned them and how had she managed to remember them? She told him early in the evening
she hadn't even had a Christmas tree since she was very
little and she had never hung up a stocking at all. Then
whence the songs and the simple beauty of their singing?
Out of what strange corner of memory had come the
long series of carols, the songs of simple, childlike faith?
Where had she learned them, so many of them, in the
drear spaces of her lonely childhood of which she had
given him just a glimpse that night when they drove back
to the city after their night of love? And why had she

remembered them? The thought worried him. He wished
he had found time to ask her.

He passed into the bathroom and soon was standing
under a gentle warm shower. He wanted to relax every
muscle and fall to sleep quickly. It was very late and he
wanted to be up bright and early. It was Christmas morning and there would not be long to sleep. He must go to
church with mother and Cynthia. Was he wrong about it
or had Cynthia been a little vague on that subject when
he tenderly kissed her good night, full of the wonder of
his glimpse into one of the strange secret places of her
heart? He remembered his mother's words to her, "My
dear girl, I think you have given us all something to-night
which we can never forget. I don't think I shall ever see
anything so beautiful again." He couldn't remember what
Cynthia had said then but he was sure she would join
them anyway. It couldn't be otherwise.

He rubbed his body with a big soft towel. No hard
rubbing to-night to bring the blood coursing to the surface
and wake him up. And he must wake up in plenty of time
to give Cynthia the present he had chosen for her so carefully, a carved jade necklace resting in a box of lovely
green mutton-fat jade, the kind the old Empress of China
used to love, the kind she collected joyously with the
money she was supposed to use for guns and ammunition
to protect herself against foreign devils. Only stones
worthy of such blind devotion and sacrifice were worthy
of Cynthia. To-night, if never before, he fully realized
it. He had been tempted to give the necklace to her as she
stood transfigured, singing beside the Christmas tree, the
glow of its hundred tiny lights mellow on her face and
throat and arms, pearling the fragrant velvet of her skin.
But he didn't want to give her anything so precious when
every one was around. He wanted no comments, no fatu-

ous "Ohs" and "Ahs," nothing but the happiness in her eyes, a memory to treasure through the weary weeks to come. He didn't even want his mother to see, not just at first. It would be a moment too precious for that. There must be just the two of them and his hands linking about her throat the stones that were the symbol of their perfect love for each other.

He switched out the bathroom light and turned back into his room again. It was rather dark after the bright glare of the other lights, the little bed lamp casting only a soft glow over the heavy furniture. He walked toward the chair on which his pajamas lay waiting to be slipped on.

"Merry Christmas, Dale."

The words reached him softly, almost like a perfumed thought in the stillness of the room. He looked up startled at the sound and instinctively clutched the pajamas to him to cover his nakedness. For an instant he stared, then whispered softly, "Cynthia, where are you?"

A low chuckle drew his eyes to the big, wide old-fashioned bed. "Dale, you silly boy, where would I be but in bed? I've been lying here and waiting for you so long; it began to seem as if you'd never come. In a few minutes I'd have had to go look if you weren't drowned in your bath like all the wives of that English murderer whose name I can never remember."

She paused and eased herself up on the cushion. He saw her more clearly now, a rounded shadow in the duskiness of the big bed. She held out her arms to him longingly while he stood dumbly, still clutching the gayly colored sleeping garments against him.

"I must say, darling, your greeting isn't very cordial. You haven't even said 'Merry Christmas' to me, and I thought you would be fairly bubbling over with the need of saying it properly, just we two, alone with all the world safely barred outside. Oh, I was very careful when I came in, and I've locked the door safely enough. Now come kiss me and tell me you're sorry you lost your tongue. I feel just in the mood to forgive you everything so long as you love me enough. But be quick. My arms are getting so weary."

He stared at her with fascinated eyes. When he spoke the words seemed to gasp from his choking throat. "Cynthia, what are you doing here—at this time of night?"

"Night?" She repeated the word with a mocking laugh. "Dale, darling, it isn't night any more. It's Christmas, the day of all days in the weary round of our lives." She suddenly reached out her hand and switched on the bright reading light on the bed. "See, it's almost four o'clock."

He shrank back out of the range of the light, crying, "Cynthia, turn off that light. I'm not dressed."

"Of course you're not, foolish. I didn't suppose you took showers with your clothes on. I was watching you all evening and I knew you didn't drink a quarter enough for that. I want to see you now as you really are, my Dale, my man as God made him."

"Cynthia, you're mad. You must go to your room at once. Please look the other way until I get these pajamas on."

"Certainly not. I like you much better without them. And I'm not going to my room. Every night since I've been here I've lain awake waiting, waiting until morning for you to come to me, to prove your love. But you never came. Didn't you realize I was lying awake aching for you? Well, now Mohammed has gone to the mountain. Here I am."

He spoke from the side of the room. "Cynthia, please go. I can't talk to you now."

She laughed softly. "Who wants to talk, you big baby?

Come here this minute so I can teach you some sense. Dale, darling, I've brought you your Russian Christmas present. Aren't you even interested in it?"

For an instant his mind swung back to his thoughts under the shower. How far away they seemed now, how stupid and meaningless in his present predicament. "Cynthia, won't you listen to me? You're breaking up our happiness." His voice broke in its appeal.

She flung back the bedclothes and sprang to the floor. The lights glowed on the soft roundness of her white flesh, the pointed firmness of her breasts, the tapering flow of her limbs. Her head was flung back a little in proud exultance.

"Dale, don't you see I am giving us both happiness? If you will not be brave and tear down the barriers to our love I must. I am here to give myself to you, not as a little gift, but as the greatest thing I own. Have you so soon forgotten our night of love; our triumph over convention and stupidity? Can you dare to say you have forgotten?"

"Cynthia, how could I forget? But we're fighting for something more than a night, a mere few hours. We can't do this here in mother's house; while you're mother's guest."

"Why not? I love you and you love me. Your mother knows it and that is all there is to know." She walked swiftly to him and drew herself against him, her arms about his neck. Her hands clung to his flesh, she could feel his muscles quiver under the pressure of her embrace.

"Cynthia!" He gasped the single word.

"Dale, why are you fighting against happiness, our happiness? Can you have me clinging to you like this and say you don't want me, don't need me as I need you? I can feel your body trembling, your great arms holding a rag of convention between us, between your body and mine. Must all men be conventional fools to deny themselves what life holds out to them, Dale?"

She buried her face against his throat, her cheek against the swell of his shoulder. Her hair was like a cloud before his eyes, brushing against his cheek, blinding him to all the world but she who thus clung to him. Slowly his limp hands relaxed and the pajamas slid to the floor. His hungry hands freed of their flimsy burden moved over the soft contour of her swelling hips, drawing her closer to him. Their bodies seemed to melt into each other even as his haunted eyes rose to the ceiling in desperation.

"Cynthia, I beg you——"

She drew back her head to look at him. "Dale, don't you see? We must have each other. Nothing else matters now. Tell me that."

His arms tightened on her body, crushing her until she felt she could hardly bear the exquisite agony without crying out her pain and exultation. At last here was the man she needed, as willing as she to laugh at the world, secure in their happiness.

He bent his lips suddenly on hers and the burning ecstasy of his touch coursed wildly through her veins. Exalted she clung to him, her lips trembling under the quivering passion of his mouth. Then with a sob of rapture she sank forward limply, her legs sagging under the spell of her transport. His arms caught her anew and he swung her up off the floor, holding her lightly as one might a sleeping child. She opened her eyes to look at him. His head was flung back passionately and his tousled blond hair gleamed crisply under the light.

"Dale, tell me now."

She murmured the words softly as he held her out before him, his blazing blue eyes following the sensuous curves of her body. His feet were wide apart, bracing him easily for all his burden. "Cynthia!" The single word fell passionately from his lips. Then with swift steps he started across the room. She closed her eyes ecstatically.

A light tap on the door of the room froze them both into statues. It was repeated impatiently, a little louder, and the knob was turned vainly.

"Dale! Dale! Are you awake?"

Cynthia's eyes were startled now. Instinctively she reached out and circled his neck with her arm. He held her tight, frozen in the midst of a stride. Only a muscle in the arm encircling her body quivered nervously. The silence hung heavily, cloyingly a moment, then that knock was repeated still more firmly.

"Get up, lazy boy, I must talk to you. It's mother. Now don't pretend. I'm sure you're not asleep because I can see your light is on."

Dale slowly set his burden down on the heavy rug, then straightened up again. Cynthia remained frozen on the spot he had placed her, lifeless save for her eyes which clung to him appealingly. They both trembled slightly as the knocking was repeated a third time more firmly than before.

"Dale! Wake up! Why have you locked your door?"

The voice was still quiet but the last sentence seemed suddenly pointed with meaning. The young man took a slow hesitating step toward the door and at the same instant Cynthia's whisper fluttered in the silence. "Dale, be still."

He half turned to face her and whispered, "But it's mother. She wants me."

"Dale!" Cynthia's word contained an agony of appeal. For an instant he stood irresolute, then threw back his head nervously.

"Yes, mother." His voice was not loud but it seemed literally to shatter the tense silence. Cynthia caught her hands together before her to still their sudden trembling as Mrs. Eustis' voice came through the locked door preceded by a little light laugh.

"There now, I knew you couldn't be asleep. Now be a good boy and open the door. Mother wants to talk to you about something important."

His agonized blue eyes turned toward Cynthia a swift instant, then swung back toward the door.

"I can't, mother. I'll talk to you to-morrow."

The knob rattled in time to the answer. "Lazy, lazy, lazy. I never knew you to be so. Come on now, it's really important."

"Mother," there was a strained pleading note in his voice. "I haven't any clothes on."

"Well, put on some pajamas, child. Come now, mother's getting tired."

He snatched up his pajamas from the floor and slid into the bottom half deftly even while he said, "All right, I'll come to your room in a minute. Please go, mother."

He pulled on the jacket while the girl watched him with fascinated eyes. There was a moment's silence and they fancied the old woman walking slowly away down the long hall. But an instant later her voice came again, more firmly, more sharply now.

"Dale, stop being silly. I must talk to you about Cynthia. She isn't in her room and I've looked everywhere for her. I'm afraid. You must help me search for her. Have you any idea where she is?"

"No, mother." The words were almost a gasp.

He turned to face the girl who suddenly swept him with a glance of withering scorn, her body trembling with excitement now. She threw back her head and called

loudly, "Yes, Mrs. Eustis, I am here with Dale. I locked
the door and I'll open it."

"Cynthia!" He held out a hand in an agony of appeal,
but she swept it aside and caught up her robe from a
near-by chair. She walked firmly to the door and turned
the key. Dale caught her hand.

"Cynthia, what are you doing?"

She laughed a bit hysterically. "Going to my room, of
course. I dare say you can explain to your mother whatever she cares to know."

She flung the door wide. Mrs. Eustis stood there, still
in the glittering splendor of her lace gown and bands of
diamonds. The girl faced her a moment scornfully.

"I came to give Dale a Christmas present, but I changed
my mind. I don't think he's capable of appreciating it.
You two probably have so much to say to each other; I
won't intrude. Good night."

She swept away as they stared after her. The faint
gleam of the hall light touched her soft brown hair, and
the trailing velvet of her golden robe. Her beautiful bare
feet made no sound on the soft carpet.

CHAPTER FIFTEEN

DALE stood in the doorway, motionless, staring with haggard eyes after the slim retreating figure. Even when the door of her room slammed behind her his body was still tense in a vain attitude of expectation. For a full minute the dull silence held, broken only by his heavy breathing as if he had been running in a long race.

But Mrs. Eustis paid no attention to the figure which had retreated so swiftly down the long hall. Her eyes were only for her son; her mind fascinated only by what he was thinking. During the long minute of silence her eyes never left his face, she was waiting for the precise moment at which to speak, to call him to a consciousness of himself and of her. Finally her low voice broke the silence.

"Dale!"

He turned his head slowly until his eyes met hers with a staring look as if she were some one far removed from his life and thoughts. She took two steps forward swiftly, lightly, and rested both her hands on his broad shoulders. The soft sure touch brought him to realization. He wrapped an arm about her and drew her slowly into the room, closing the door after him with quiet precision. Once the door was safely shut he shook his head a little as if to drive away some bad thought, some vague ghost of the shadowland of memory. Mechanically his fingers began to button the loose pajama jacket, and his mother smiled faintly as she saw the gesture. To her it meant that he was once more her son, obedient to those fine conventions of which she so strongly approved.

"May I sit down, Dale?"

"Of course, mother." He was instantly solicitous, helping her into a comfortable chair and taking her omnipresent ivory headed stick. For a moment he stood holding it in his hands as if it was a symbol of the love which existed between them, a symbol of the domination of her mother love over his thoughts and actions. Finally he put the stick on the bed, noticing as he did so how the bedclothes were tumbled. His face flushed and he turned to his mother with an outstretched hand of appeal.

"Mother, what must you think of me?"

"Why, what should I think of you?" Somehow the old woman made those few simple words contain all her thoughts. She made them mean so much more than they would if spoken by any other person. In them was understanding, extenuation, forgiveness, realization, everything that a mother could say to her son to make him comprehend her idea that no matter what he did he still remained the idol of her heart. Dale had been sufficiently long under her control to know all this. He fell on one knee beside her chair and lifting her hand placed it on his head as one might kneel to a saint for benediction.

"Mother, how can I ever explain it to you?"

"But, my dear boy, there is nothing to explain. I think Cynthia gave all the explanation that was necessary to make me understand completely, even if I had not understood before."

He jumped to his feet with a faint cry. "Mother, you must not misunderstand Cynthia."

She threw back her head and looked up at him with loving eyes. "I don't misunderstand Cynthia. I'm beginning to wonder if I don't understand her far better than you do."

He took a step or two up and down the room nerv-

ously. Her eyes dropped to his bare feet which seemed so
white and sculptural against the dark carpet of the room.
She said softly, "Hadn't you better put on your slippers,
Dale? It seems very warm in here but you might catch
cold."

He crossed the room and pulled on a pair of bedroom
slippers without a word. When he faced round again he
saw that his mother was standing and he ran to give her
her stick. She accepted it with a little pat of affection
on his cheek and turned toward the door. "It's very late,
Dale, so I think I had better be getting some sleep if I
am to do justice to all the Christmas gaieties to-morrow.
I'm not like you young people who can stay up all night
and show no sign of it the next day."

A minute more and she was gone, refusing his escort
to her room, insisting he must go to bed at once. He
stood in the doorway until she had turned a corner and
was out of sight, then he began to walk slowly in the
direction of Cynthia's room. When he reached her door
he stopped for a moment, listening, but there was no
sound loud enough to reach his ears. The dead stillness
of the house seemed to close over his head and he
could hear the heavy thumping of his heart. It seemed
so loud that he imagined she must hear it too, if she
was awake; that she must know he was standing there
torn by his conflicting emotions, wanting her and yet
unable to go to her. He never knew how long he stood
there with his hand raised to knock but with no will
power to cause the knuckles to perform the necessary
duty. It seemed hours later, though it was probably only
a matter of minutes, that he dragged his feet slowly
down the hall again into his own room, closing the door
carefully behind him. His fingers trembled a little as he
turned the key though he couldn't have explained why

or even why he was locking the door. Who was there to lock out now? Surely not his mother, and still more surely not Cynthia. By no stretch of imagination could he imagine her coming back to him again to-night. There had been something so definite, so coldly final about her manner as she had flung open the door to walk out, defiant of whatever his mother might think. He couldn't lock out his unhappy thoughts either, for they were in the room with him, deep buried in his heart.

He walked swiftly to the windows and flung them all wide open. The cold, biting air rushed in as if eager to devour the warmth and security his room had always held for him until now. Now it was better that the wind should blow in keenly and clutch at his body with its icy fingers of reality. He climbed wearily into bed after putting out the lights and lay there wondering in the darkness. He was not thinking of Cynthia alone so much as of Cynthia in relation to himself, to his mother, and to the whole scheme of life in which he was inextricably bound. The dreary winter dawn was creeping into the room before he finally fell into a troubled sleep.

He woke up with a start several hours later to the realization that some one was knocking persistently on the door. It was several moments before he could gain complete control of his senses, and then as he jumped out of bed he noticed it was after ten o'clock. He stood for a second in the middle of the room wondering just why any one should knock so persistently instead of entering, before he remembered he had locked the door e'er going to sleep. He ran to open it now and found Waggoner standing in the hall, deferentially.

"Merry Christmas, Mr. Dale."

The simple words of greeting were startling but he managed to mumble an equivalent reply. Then the butler delivered his message. Mrs. Eustis was waiting for him in the breakfast room. Would he please come down as soon as convenient.

He said "Yes" and turned back into the room to dress. As he pulled on his clothes quickly he wondered just why his mother was sending for him in this way. It was so much more logical that she should either come herself, as she always had in the past when he overslept, or else allow him to sleep until he awoke naturally. The thought bothered him all the while he was shaving. He wondered a little why he thought much more about his mother's message than about the happenings of the night before. On that score he had merely reached a determination to see Cynthia as soon as possible and clear up the unfortunate mix-up. He felt sure he could do so.

When he entered the breakfast room his mother greeted him cheerfully and laughed just a little as he kissed her cheek lightly in his customary greeting. He seated himself at his place at the table.

"Where's Cynthia, mother? Has she come down yet?"

His mother leaned back in her chair and fixed him with her steady glance. "Would you rather know now or after breakfast?"

The words startled him. "What do you mean, mother?"

The old lady drew forth a small envelope that had rested out of sight on her lap and held it toward him, somehow not so much as if to give it to him as to merely show him it was there. "Cynthia has gone. She returned to town early this morning and left this note for me offering her excuses. She doesn't feel very well and thinks she will be better off at home with her mother."

"Gone!" The single word fell turgidly from Dale's lips while his eyes opened wide in astonishment. His mother thought she had never seen them look so startlingly blue before.

"Yes, Dale, she has gone. And do you know the poor dear girl actually had to get herself off all alone merely because she was afraid of waking us too early."

There was a strange lightness in Mrs. Eustis' voice as she spoke, but the intonation was lost on her son. He still sat staring at her as if she had uttered some strange incomprehensible statement. "Gone!" The word sounded still more incredible as he repeated it. "But that's impossible!"

She smiled. "Nothing is impossible, Dale, and as for Cynthia's going you may be sure it is a fact. You know I would not have told you under the circumstances until I had made sure of it. She packed her bags and ordered a car about eight o'clock. Wilkins took her to the station and made sure she got safely off on the train. She told him her mother was ill and he offered to drive her directly to New York but she said she preferred to go by train."

Dale shook his head slowly from side to side. "But mother, we can't let her go like that. Don't you see it's impossible after what happened last night?"

The old woman tapped her polished finger nails softly on the white linen tablecloth. "Well, son, just what did happen last night? I was under the impression that nothing occurred beyond Cynthia's perfectly logical explanation. She came to offer you a Christmas present and you were probably very sleepy and very rude, so she was annoyed, as she well might be. That's all there was to it—isn't it?"

Their glances met and crossed like the swords of two fencers but Dale's plodding thoughts were no match for his mother's rapier-like skill. He opened his mouth to speak but no words came forth; indeed what was there to say when the question was put so bluntly by one's own mother? For a moment they both sat looking intently into each other's eyes, then he was the first to drop his glance and shift restlessly in his chair.

"We must do something, and I don't know what."

"I don't exactly know what you mean by 'must do something.' Cynthia has felt obligated to return to New York, so I don't see there is anything we can do about it. I think she is old enough to know exactly what she wants to do under the circumstances."

"Oh, mother. I don't know how to explain myself; I don't know how to put in words what I am trying to say. I know that she's hurt, suffering, and I must do something. I must go after her and try to explain."

The old lady rose slowly to her feet and her son followed her action as if under the spell of her steady, quiet gaze. "Dale, are you trying to tell me there is something which needs explaining, something as serious as all that? Why should there be anything which you can't easily put in words to me, your mother?"

She held him with her steady glance while she took a deep breath as a person does about to plunge into deep cold water. "Are you trying to tell me you've done something to be ashamed of, something unworthy of any Eustis gentleman? Have you forgotten yourself so far as to insult the woman you wanted to marry and so broken every tradition of your family?"

"Mother!" Dale's single word rang out in the small room.

"Well, you want to be candid, don't you, and it seems to me nothing else is possible under these circumstances. You are either at fault in your behavior to Cynthia last night or she is guilty of forgetting herself and her position as guest in my house." Dale opened his mouth to speak but she stopped him with an imperious gesture of her hand. "Please don't interrupt, Dale. I understand how willing you are to protest every remark I make, but if we are to see things clearly you must allow me to finish what I have to say. I'm not asking you for any explanation of what happened in your room last night. That would be unworthy of my trust in you and, I dare say, unnecessary. I have not had the benefit of your psychology courses but I do have the good common sense with which the Lord used to endow us. I can't say just why you are acting so nervous now, still I do think it can only indicate your conduct last night was such that you are ashamed."

Dale passed his hand over his face as if to brush away something unpleasant clinging there. When he spoke his voice had a weary sound. "I can't explain anything to you. I only know I've failed Cynthia. That's why she's gone away."

"Failed Cynthia!" The old woman's rising inflection was keen-edged as a razor. "Just in what way can you have failed her unless it be that you remembered you were a gentleman? Even if you didn't remember then, at least understand now that you have certain obligations to yourself and to me. We have guests coming here to-day that are to be entertained. Whatever your private feelings may be it is absolutely essential for you to be here to receive them and to offer them the open-hearted hospitality for which your father in his time was noted. It is your duty."

"But that's impossible," Dale cried, brokenly. "I must get the car and go after Cynthia at once. You don't understand how much I love her and how much her love means to me. It doesn't matter a bit what happened last night or who was right or who was wrong. Her love for

me is the most tremendous thing in my life. If you must
know she came to me last night because her heart cried
out for me and because I represented the need of her life.
What else could I ever mean to any one comparable to
that? What can Christmas parties and social gestures and
stupid conventions mean to me now when I've lost her
love. That's all that really matters. I'm going after her
now to plead with her to forgive me for my weakness
and indecision."

He paused, gasping for breath, his blue eyes blazing
with the fervor of his emotion. His mother stood before
him leaning a little more heavily on her stick than usual,
her attitude clearly showing the weight of the long years,
but in her voice there was a quiet intensity which seemed
to cut through and render futile the wild ecstasy of his
words. "That all sounds very pretty, my boy, but you
forget there are other things to be considered. For example, I am here. What about my position? I don't know
how much you have changed under this girl's influence
but there was a time when you would not have wished
my home to be reduced to the level of a house of assig-
nation."

"Mother!" There was the tragic stridency of agony in
his tone now but his mother did not allow him to say
any more, pressing her point home firmly, relentlessly.

"That seems to you a little callous and hard, but I am
one of those people who recognize and abide by the moral
standards and conventions of the world. I try not to allow
my own selfish whims and desires to lead me into forget-
fulness of my responsibilities and duties. I am beyond the
age of passion myself but for that very reason I can see
so much more clearly. You are fascinated with a woman
who has chosen to fling herself at you, with a woman
whom I must stay up at nights to watch, lest she disgrace

the decency of my home. You may call that whatever you
choose but to me it has only one name which I would not
insult my own son's intelligence by using in his presence.
This sort of thing cannot go on. I refuse to yield my
place as head of this house to such a woman. I refuse
to have her enter these doors again even if you choose
to bring her. I command you to remember your self-
respect, your pride, your upbringing, all those things
which have made Eustis men respected for hundreds of
years. She has chosen to leave us, so there is nothing to
do but be thankful for it."

Dale stood shifting irresolutely from one foot to the
other. No one who had ever known his prowess and
lion-like courage on the football field would have suspected him of this sudden irresolution, this sudden capit-
ulation before his mother's majestic onslaught. "Mother,
you are unkind and unreasonable." The words sounded
so futile, so useless that any one could at once sense his
outburst of passion had failed him and he was once more
submitting himself to her domination. Mrs. Eustis sighed
a little even as a faint smile of triumph curled her lips.
She realized she had won but also she had taken the
greatest chance of her whole life. She had staked everything on a single throw of the dice, knowing full well
that had Dale insisted on going after Cynthia there was
nothing she could do about it. His wealth was his already;
the house which she said she would bar against Cynthia
was his and not hers. She had taken a desperate chance—
and had won. She turned slowly toward the door, which
Dale sprang to open for her, his solicitous gesture indicating the more clearly the completeness of her triumph.
She faced him squarely on the threshold.

"Dale, there is no further use in our talking about anything so unpleasant. I'm sure you realize now I am only

doing what is necessary for our happiness. Your happiness and mine are so closely linked together we can't tear them apart and it goes even further than that. My happiness only exists in and as a result of your happiness, so maybe I'm a little selfish when I try so hard to keep you from making mistakes which can only result in misery for both of us. You are making the mistake that men have made down through all the long ages of history; especially men who have been carefully nurtured in high traditions as you have. You are mistaking physical passion, the needs of the fleeting moment, for love, which is not a thing of the moment but something which must last down through the long, long years. Your idealism has been so implanted in you that you find yourself completely enveloped in a woman who is nothing more than the object for carnal desire. I know what I'm talking about. I'm an old woman who has sat a long time on the sidelines of life watching the game, and like your football coach I know more about the game than the players themselves. That's why I'm telling you that your happiness, our happiness, lies here in the path of social obligation and duty.

"About Cynthia, make no mistake in my feelings toward her. I don't hate her or even dislike her. To me Cynthia is not so much a person as a force, an undisciplined force, which has been let loose to trouble our modern world. Try to understand that if I thought she loved you truly and simply in the way which means love to me and all the people of my generation, I would be the first to say 'Go, and bring her back; we both need her.' But she is not the girl to carry on the Eustis tradition, she is just a flame in the wind blown hither and thither by mad gusts of passion which she can neither understand nor control.

I am your mother and I am a very proud woman. I will not have you destroyed for her amusement."

Slowly she held out her arms in the deep, maternal gesture which seemed to envelop her son like endless veils of soft, clinging chiffon. A moment later he was in her arms with his head on her shoulder, his body racked by heavy sobs. She brushed his crisp yellow hair with a gentle hand. "Dale, you must trust me. You must realize mother knows best."

CHAPTER SIXTEEN

JANE TALBOT was eating her breakfast in rather gloomy silence when the doorbell rang and her faithful colored maid left the room to answer it. Jane felt rather weary this Christmas morning, not at all up to planning any gaieties for the day. She was sorry it was Christmas as she was nearly always sorry when it was Christmas, or Thanksgiving, or New Year, or any of those holidays on which one was supposed to be unthinkingly gay. Such days were all annoying; your friends went away to visit stupidly remote relatives whom they ignored the rest of the year and even the restaurants seemed to be full of those same out-of-town relatives who had no friends from the city to come to visit them, so they in their turn came to New York to eat in unaccustomed splendor and titillate their souls with the *Jewish renaissance* magnificence of Roxy's. Christmas was invariably the worst of all. People sent you meaningless presents and you gave them presents in return because they had given you presents first, because you had given *them* presents the year before. At any rate it was all a ridiculous muddle and Jane found herself left high and dry even by those who most admired her.

She was particularly annoyed because Aurelia Bronson of all people had accompanied her husband to visit his mother at her lonely estate out on the far end of Long Island. It was a visit of ceremony only, it goes without saying, and happened each year at Christmas time. Old Mrs. Bronson, though monstrously fat and almost crippled by rheumatism, knew perfectly well of the state of affairs between her son and daughter. She had no intention of interfering in any way with their lives, being quite content to devote her energies entirely to prolonging her days upon the earth which she loved so well. She was confessedly selfish, quite willing that every one should do as he or she pleased so long as she, Mrs. Thor Bronson, Senior, was not interrupted in the orderly procedure of her quiet life. She did not even insist on the Christmas visit which had become so much a tradition but it did make her happy because she felt that traditions should play a part in all wealthy families and because in her heart she had a strange liking for her daughter-in-law whose loneliness she sensed even if she was quite incapable of fully comprehending the complete cause of it.

Now all this might help any one to understand why the Bronsons had gone for the day to visit his mother, but to Jane such considerations meant nothing whatsoever. She had no family either to come to her or to whom she could go and all such feelings of kinship she classified bitingly as intellectual bosh. Jane was a pure individualist who felt her own needs far more than she valued any social concepts, so she was correspondingly delighted when Cynthia dashed into the room a moment later like a small but very determined whirlwind.

"Cynthia, I thought you were to stay in Tuxedo for ever so long yet." She clapped the girl familiarly on the shoulder as one man might greet a lifelong chum. Cynthia pulled her hat from her head with a twist of the hand and flung it in the direction of a chair. It missed its objective and fell limply on the floor but she paid no attention, and sat down on a corner of the table swinging one leg nervously. There was a moment's silence while the two women sat very quietly with no sign of life between them but the strange glitter of Jane's monocle which even at this early hour was safely screwed in her eye. A quizzical smile played about the older woman's thinly cut lips and she waited in patience for her guest to acquire complete control of herself which for the moment she seemed to lack.

Finally Cynthia blurted out, "Don't ever mention the word 'Tuxedo' to me again! I hate it! I hate everything about it, the houses, the people, the skating, everything and everybody in it."

Miss Talbot took a sip of her delicate Formosa tea without for an instant letting her steady gaze wander from the girl's excited features. "That's just a little strong, isn't it, Cynthia? I know Mrs. Eustis is more than trying with her queen-mother ideas, and her friends are all bores, but I had hoped you would find them amusing bores at least. The place is really a museum."

Cynthia sniffed and dragging off her gloves threw them in the general direction of the hat. "Amusing? How can you use such a word in connection with a place like Tuxedo? Every one is mean, contemptible, vicious, I can't think up enough words to express my feelings for them. I'm only sure of one thing and that is I'll never see that terrible place again. Never. Never."

Jane pushed back her chair with the sudden vigorous gesture which so astonished those people who met her for the first time. She crossed her legs determinedly. "Isn't that a rather strong statement for the future Mrs. Eustis?"

Cynthia jumped to her feet with a cry and began pacing swiftly up and down the room while she talked very rapidly. "Future Mrs. Eustis! That is a good joke! I can't ever imagine anything else half so funny." As she spoke there was that in her voice which rendered doubly bitter the biting mockery of her words. "When I said I hated

everything and everybody in Tuxedo, I meant Dale Eustis
in particular. I'm fed up with convention, sick to death
of people whose petty little lives are ground out day by
day exactly to measure according to the dictates of Mrs.
Grundy.—Oh, Jane, I've had such a perfectly horrible
time." Her voice broke in a strange little sob. "I've found
out what Dale is really like. He's a coward, the most
horrible kind of a coward just because he's just that much
stronger physically than the average coward. I was a fool
to think that he loved me while as a matter of fact he
only loves his mother. She's his whole world, all he does
is sit looking at her, kow-towing to her, hanging around
her, as if she were some saint before whose shrine he had
sworn perpetual adoration. It was funny at first and then
it became horrible, and cruel, and vicious. His mother
comes first in everything that he does, and thinks, and
says. You don't understand how terrible it can be. He is
at her beck and call, her slave, morning, noon and night.
He does everything except sleep with her."

Jane raised her rather heavy eyebrows mockingly. "You
are bitter, aren't you? It's only a few days ago that your
pet Dale was the living embodiment of all unquestionable
masculine virtues. How has he failed now?"

Cynthia stopped her pacing and swung round to face
her friend. There was a quiet determination in her voice
now which was infinitely more impressive than her rant-
ing of a moment before. "I don't know just how to tell
you what happened, Jane. I don't know whether I ought
to tell you, whether I have any right to burden you with
the sordid, disgusting story."

Jane shrugged her lean, expressive shoulders and picked
up a cigarette from the open box on the table beside her.
She paused with the flaming lighter in her long hand
before touching it to the end. "I hope you understand,

Cynthia, that I am not trying to pry into your secrets but just reminding you I am always here to be of any help I can."

The girl gave her a swift glance of thanks. "I'm afraid there's nobody can help me and I don't think I want to be helped to any further understanding of Dale Eustis. My pride is a very peculiar thing because it's the pride of a person who has tried to eliminate all pride in its ordinary sense. When I give myself to a man such as Dale I expect nothing more than normal reciprocation but I think I have a right to that. When I am lying naked in a man's arms in his bedroom and his mother knocks at the door for a little bedtime gossip, I think I come first."

Jane puffed her cigarette placidly. So that was why Cynthia had returned so precipitously from her visit. All her raging against Tuxedo and everything connected with it was merely frustration at Dale's failure to reciprocate her passion. She smiled faintly. What an ardent girl Cynthia was, and at the same time how strange it was that a man like Dale had failed her in the one way which she had felt he was not likely to fail any woman. It was amusing and at the same time it was all rather sad. She had hoped Dale and Cynthia would really hit it off together because she liked them both and felt they were both worth saving in a world that had gone mad and lost sight of its normal aims in life in a veritable forest of distorted notions. She was fond of the deep-rooted passion in Cynthia's nature which no one but she had sensed, and she had been very sure it was sufficiently strong to rouse her lover to a completed viewpoint of life. She had evidently been wrong. She had failed to take into sufficient consideration the tremendous dominance of a woman like Clorinda Eustis, the practiced skill of a shrewd tactician whose very life depended on maintaining her ascendancy over her son.

But all of this she could not express to the girl who had lit a cigarette and was now puffing at it nervously, sunk in a deep chair into which she had flung herself after her last outburst. Jane stood up slowly. "I'm awfully glad you came to me first of all, Cynthia. You know I'm always ready to do whatever I can. Now just what can I do to help?"

The girl looked up at her with tired eyes. The long, lonely vigil of the night during which she had turned over and over in her mind the minute details of every moment of the time spent in Dale's room, was finally having its effect, and she felt weary, inexpressibly weary. She wanted to talk to some one, to explain the reasons for her act, and yet there was no one to whom she could speak. She had gone first to her own home forgetting in her excitement that her mother would not be there. She didn't know exactly why she had rushed home to her own mother while under the spell of resentment toward her erstwhile lover for his obvious mother fixation. Perhaps it was because her mother could have no possible control over her and she wished to strengthen her normal point of view by contact with some one whose ideas were as far removed from those of Mrs. Eustis as possible. But no one had been there, so she had turned to Jane; Jane who had brought her and Dale together but who was always understanding and always sympathetic. She sighed a little as she thought of the first luncheon with Dale in this very room. And now Jane had once more understood without the necessity of any long explanation. It was comforting and at the same time it was a little annoying because she wanted to talk the whole thing over with some one and now that Jane understood so completely without explanation all attempts at explanation could be only superfluous if not ridiculous.

She leaned her head back against the chair and stared up at the ceiling. She was glad of the knock at the door and the silent entrance of Jane's maid who began to clear away the breakfast dishes with swift precision. Jane stood for a moment looking out of the window, then turned slowly. "Just what are you going to do, Cynthia?"

The girl shook her head slowly. "I don't know. I feel I haven't energy to decide. Won't you decide for me? I feel like that to-day. I'm tired of trying to force the issue, trying to force people to see things as I see them. I'm utterly weary of the obtuseness of the world. I want some one to decide for me at least for a few hours, to tell me what to do and just let me obey mechanically, without thinking, or planning, fighting, or even reasoning at all."

The older woman drew her gleaming monocle from her eye and began to polish it quietly on a large white silk handkerchief which she drew from the pocket of her snugly tailored jacket. "Well, if I must, I suppose I must. Suppose you lie down then and get a little rest for I'm sure you had little or no sleep last night. I'll call you in a couple of hours and we'll go some place sufficiently gaudy and stupid and watch the country bumpkins solemnly eating their prescribed turkey. I know several places where we may be able to get a good laugh. Then I'll drive you out to your grandmother's on Long Island. We'll dash in with a loud cry of 'Here we are for Christmas dinner,' and dear old Mrs. Thor Bronson, Senior, will be so surprised and glad to see *you* that she'll forget she cut *me* off her visiting list years ago."

The girl looked up in astonishment. "Do you really mean it, Jane? Do you seriously mean we should go out to grandmother Bronson's for her interminably dull Christmas dinner?" She shivered. "I remember last year."

"Exactly." Miss Talbot nodded sagely. "After all, my dear Cynthia, you can't exactly dash up and down in a chariot shouting to the world that you ran away from Tuxedo because of Dale's impotence. Even in this year of careless morality one can't go quite that far. But such is the stupidity of the world that all the dear old tabby-cats will be overjoyed to learn that you felt you could not be apart from your family on this festive occasion." She laughed cynically. "You see, you want me to arrange it all for you, so I'm doing it with great thoroughness even at the risk of being ordered out of the house by the ultra-dowager Mrs. Bronson or having bolts of filial lightning flung at me by the redoubtable Thor."

Cynthia jumped up all animation now. "Jane, you are certainly the cleverest person. I'm ready to confess now I really didn't quite know what I should have said to mother, much less to the virginal May-May who luckily was out when I dashed into the house a little while ago. I dare say she was bruising her knees at her favorite Very High Church where the soul is thrilled by a symphonic orchestra in conjunction with the organ, which is so much more important than a mere organ alone. Can't you just see May-May singing 'Hark, the Herald Angels Sing,' and believing every word of it?"

Miss Talbot's short laugh was almost a grunt. "At any rate I can see that you've recovered a little of your usual spirit. It will be a sad day when all the Dale Eustises in the world can keep us from getting a little laugh out of May-May."

Arm in arm the two women passed into the drawing room where the pale wintry sun was now flooding in, and five minutes later Cynthia was fast asleep on the piled-up cushions of the couch, while Jane sat in her deep easy chair, feet stretched far out before her, trousered legs comfortably crossed, smoking cigarette after cigarette and wondering about many things in her own strange, silent way.

.   .   .   .

Late that afternoon Thor Bronson was sitting with his wife in his mother's rather old-fashioned drawing room. They both felt constrained being there alone together, yet it, too, was one of those rites of Christmas-time which neither would have thought of breaking. The dowager Mrs. Bronson had left the room a few minutes before rustling out to answer the telephone in her stiff, black satin dress which had been her habitual attire for so many years. With her out of the room the silence was painful, for what was there that Thor and his wife might have to discuss? Except for this one day in the year their orbits of life crossed so seldom outside of the formal dinner parties which she gave to his associates at his behest or he attended as a matter of obligation to convince the world that in spite of the long years of ugly rumor they were still living together. Their life had come to be as formal, as regulated, as that. Now they sat facing each other in silence, he with his cigar, she with her cigarette, and they were far enough apart so that even the rising smoke did not mingle in the still air of the room.

A moment later they both rose to their feet in surprise as the drawing room doors were flung wide open and old Mrs. Bronson entered with Cynthia on her arm, closely followed by Jane, now conventionally attired in customary semi-evening clothes. The old woman was radiant as she faced her son and daughter-in-law.

"Now dare to say you're not surprised. Cynthia called up several hours ago to say that she and Miss Talbot were coming to dinner but I thought it best to wait till they got here so I could surprise you both."

Jane moved forward from her position behind the two others and bowed ironically to Thor. "How do you do, Mr. Bronson?"

He bowed frigidly in return, yet in his eyes there was a sudden gleam of determination as if the insolence of her action had suddenly brought him to a consciousness of some neglected duty. He opened his mouth to speak but before he could do so his wife gushed forward to her daughter's side.

"Cynthia, darling, this is a surprise. When did you leave Tuxedo? It's just too flattering to feel that you have run away from Dale's side to be with us on this occasion."

Cynthia smiled a little nervously but Jane walked coolly into the breach. "Aurelia, if you've ever spent a Christmas in Tuxedo you should know that Cynthia is quite justified in preferring any place else, especially her grandmother's home on Christmas day. Cynthia was so insistent on my coming I had to forego the pleasure of being nicely lonely all by myself and intrude on your happy family gathering. Unlike Cynthia with too many places to go I seem to have had too few."

Old Mrs. Bronson was touched by this statement, and utterly oblivious to its lightly veiled sarcasm which was so apparent to her son and his wife. She took Jane's hand in her own. "My dear Jane Talbot, I am so glad that you did allow Cynthia to over-persuade you. I'm sure I'd have asked you to come myself if I had dreamed there was a single chance of your accepting. I must never allow myself to forget that when I was a little girl your grandfather in Philadelphia gave me the happiest party I have ever known. The Talbots and the Bronsons were inseparable friends once, and should be so again."

Jane returned the squeeze of the hand with perfectly cool equanimity while Thor bit his mustache angrily and swung away to look out of one of the wide windows into the gloomy twilight closing in over the lawns before the house. Suddenly without considering her impulse Cynthia walked over to him swiftly and laid her hand lightly on his arm. "Aren't you going to say you're glad we came?"

"Of course I'm glad you came." The personal pronoun was sufficiently stressed to indicate his feelings with no possibility of doubt even to the most casual listener. His daughter smiled faintly as she looked at him.

"I dare say that means you resent my having brought Jane. I suppose you even wonder why I did it. I'm not going to try to make any explanation. Explanations are always ridiculous, aren't they? But without Jane life to-day would be completely unlivable. I wonder if you understand that."

He looked steadily into her eyes. "Is there anything in particular that requires understanding?" The question was heavy with meaning and the girl instinctively resented it. She laughed shortly.

"I have been taught that understanding is a thing which happens whether there is need for it or not."

He bowed coldly. "You've been taught so many things that are completely beyond the range of my comprehension. I, for one, don't understand why you've run away from your fiancé at Christmas time to come here with Jane Talbot." The way in which he pronounced the woman's name was a sudden startling indication of the intensity of feeling which his ordinary cold, indifferent voice would seem to deny. There was a moment's silence and then he suddenly caught both of Cynthia's hands in his. "I thought you loved Dale Eustis. I thought that was one thing I could be sure of in this damned quicksand of affairs going on around me. What's happened between you two? Why not try telling me for a change instead of the others you've been turning to? Maybe I could understand more than you give me credit for."

The girl's brown eyes opened wide as she allowed her slim hands to remain passive in his firm, vigorous grasp. This was a startling revelation of a new man which she had never even suspected. For a moment she was tempted to throw her arms about his neck and weep out her feelings on his broad chest but even at the same instant memory swept over her like a tide. How could this cold-blooded, sensual man attempt to understand her feelings, her thoughts, her predicament; this man who obeyed every convention so completely that he devoted himself exclusively to the cold accumulation of money and the pampering of an expensive mistress, while he went through the formalities of life with a supposed wife, her mother? How could he understand the significance to her of that final scene in Dale's room, of the importance of her gesture as she had flung wide the bedroom door and walked insolently past her lover's mother who had destroyed the flimsy bubble of her ecstasy? So she merely said, "Nothing has happened between Dale and me beyond the fact that I wouldn't marry him if he were the last man on earth."

She turned as she finished the sentence to find her mother directly behind her watching her with rather startled eyes. "Do you mean that you have broken with Dale?" she cried with startled tones.

"Exactly." Cynthia was quite calm now. She knew exactly what she must do. "I don't want to see him or hear any more about him. The whole affair was a ridiculous mistake."

With a heavy snort Thor Bronson stamped out of the room banging the door behind him. Cynthia was rather startled now by the look of apprehension in her mother's eyes. That look found expression in nervous words. "But what are you going to do now, Cynthia?"

"Do?" She laughed lightly. "Why I suppose I'm going to go on just as before or maybe I'd better say I'm going to go on much differently from before because I've learned so much in the last few days. Don't forget, mother, two or three days in Tuxedo is equivalent to two or three years any place else. In that dismal place I've learned my lesson. I'm going to be very gay now and have all the fun in the world. I'm going to Palm Beach with you the beginning of next month and break a heart every day, or at least as many as I can. For several years I've been a silly little pale-faced stick, but now that's all over. For a few weeks I've been a little romantic fool, and that's all over. From now on I'm going to be Cynthia, the gayest girl in America, and I think Palm Beach is the proper place to begin. Every winter I've been down there with you without causing a single ripple in the turgid puddle, but this time there are going to be waves."

Jane Talbot laughed raucously because the girl's voice had been loud enough so that every word was heard throughout the room. Old Mrs. Bronson stood with a bewildered smile on her face a little unable at once to grasp the thread of these strange, seemingly contradictory emotions which seemed to be swirling suddenly about her head invading the quiet seclusion which she cherished so dearly. Cynthia's mother stood a moment gaping at her suddenly grown-up daughter, then she swung round quickly to Jane whose heavy laughter seemed to echo and re-echo in the silence.

"Jane, how can you laugh when Cynthia says such a thing?"

Miss Talbot fixed her monocle nonchalantly. "Aurelia, f you had any comprehension at all you'd laugh too, be- :ause it's all really very funny. I'm beginning to think I nay find Palm Beach amusing this year for the first time."

CHAPTER SEVENTEEN

MRS. VENTNOR always enjoyed entertaining even though she sometimes sighed publicly when discussing the obligations of her social position. Most of all she enjoyed entertaining in Palm Beach where life was 'so delightfully informal that minor formalities were cherished wholeheartedly. Of course she was not the author of such a rather precious witticism but she made it her own by living up to its concept even while she always gave due credit to Richard Edgar Sperry, the brilliant novelist, who had made Palm Beach so popular in the writings of to-day. Mrs. Ventnor glanced at the clock and was not in the least impatient when she noticed it was already eight-thirty. To be sure, her dinner party had been announced for eight-thirty, but she knew none of her guests would be likely to arrive before nine while her cook, old and experienced in the ways of Palm Beach society, understood that if dinner was ready to be served by nine-thirty or even ten everything would be quite all right.

Mrs. Ventnor rather liked sitting about this way waiting for her guests. Her sense of duty made it necessary that she be ready at eight-thirty herself when she announced the dinner for that hour, while some little imp within herself, far back in that part of her nature which she never acknowledged to the world, delighted in the opportunity of being able to think about her prospective guests and perhaps chat about them with some early arrival. She frankly enjoyed discussing "who is coming."

So she was glad that Gloria Glendale was visiting her

and that in her daughter's absence on a yachting party it was necessary for her to explain what was going on. And Gloria was very anxious to be explained to.

"Oh, Mrs. Ventnor, you simply must tell me all the gossip and what's going on. Coming this late, at the beginning of February. I'm afraid I've missed all the early season scandal."

Mrs. Ventnor's beaming face denied her casual remark. She said, "Oh, there's nothing particular happened so far. It's really been a very quiet season."

"Quiet?" Gloria's voice rose in a rapidly ascending scale of incredulity. "That isn't at all the sort of report I've been hearing in town. I've been rather led to believe that with Cynthia Thorpe on the war-path things have been more than a little hectic."

Mrs. Ventnor waved an elaborately manicured hand nonchalantly. "You know you mustn't believe all you hear, Gloria. Cynthia has been very gay, there's no denying that. But then it's only natural. I must say that I for one felt that giving a party to celebrate the breaking of your engagement was a little bit overly advanced in thought, but then other people seemed to be just amused by it. At any rate, it was done with her mother's approval."

There was something just a little off-color in the last statement, rather as if Mrs. Ventnor was voicing a delicate, oh ever so delicate, criticism of Aurelia Bronson's method of raising her beautiful daughter. It was not lost on Gloria who was the type of young lady who flourishes on nuances and innuendoes. She smiled faintly to herself, secure in her knowledge that there had always been a veil-like jealousy between Mrs. Ventnor and Mrs. Bronson. She said, "I dare say Jane Talbot is down as usual."

"Of course. My dear Gloria, you can't imagine Aurelia

Bronson ever being separated from Jane Talbot by more than a hundred yards."

This time the implied criticism was a little more obvious but Gloria, being a skilled person, refused to make any obvious retort. She had been reading a great many psychological books and felt herself for the moment to be on the side of the scientists if not of the angels, and so somewhat above delicately pointed caustic remarks in regard to Jane Talbot, who had been very friendly to her on one or two occasions and whom one could easily consider in the light of a good pal. But she was interested in Cynthia and in finding out just how much truth there was in the stories which had been galloping gayly up and down Fifth Avenue and even penetrating the rather ginny drawing rooms of Park Avenue penthouses. "But do tell me about Cynthia, Mrs. Ventnor. How many men's heads has she really turned?"

"How many?" Mrs. Ventnor was delicately vague. She loved gossip in a rather good-natured way, as she loved to discuss expected guests with a clever listener in a manner which she considered as character analysis, utterly repudiating any suggestion that her remarks might be interpreted as mere gossip. "My dear Gloria, are you insinuating that people are saying such awful things about Cynthia in New York?"

"Awful?" Gloria's voice ran up the scale lightly again. "I believe the general impression is that she's been stirring things up down here and having a grand time doing it. I suspect horror is running a bad second to admiration."

"How delightfully you children do phrase things," Mrs. Ventnor gushed in her best manner. "Agnes is always saying something clever just like that. Which reminds me every one down here is quoting Cynthia's rather daring remarks, or maybe I should be very frank and say that her remarks are much more than daring. Agnes calls them Rabelaisian. But personally I think they're just vulgar. Of course I've never read Rabelais, have you?"

Gloria was mildly annoyed by the directness of the question and at the same time rather delighted to voice her opinion on the subject. "Now Mrs. Ventnor, you know perfectly well that every young girl reads Rabelais these days. I don't know of a single better read book."

Her hostess emitted a faint shriek of delighted horror. "Why Gloria, you're almost as bad as Cynthia Thorpe. I'm sure it must be positively shocking to read Rabelais in bed. From what I've heard I've never dared to do it."

"That's the advantage of being young," Miss Glendale was a trifle caustic. "Personally I always use it to put me to sleep." There was a moment's pause. "But you haven't yet told me just what Cynthia *has* done."

Mrs. Ventnor sat up a trifle straighter in her chair. It suddenly occurred to her that it might be wise if she did not discuss things too intimately with this girl who, after all, was her daughter's friend and Cynthia's friend far more than her own. So she just said, "Well, report has it that just now Cynthia is leading Richard Sperry around by the nose. Anyway they'll be here to dinner in a few minutes and you'll get a chance to see for yourself."

Gloria's eyes opened very wide. "You don't mean Richard *Edgar* Sperry, the novelist?" The girl's interest was unrestrained now. "Why I always understood he wouldn't even look at any woman. And since when did he get picked up socially?"

" 'Still waters run deep.' " Mrs. Ventnor often had a way of saying equally trite things with all the grandeur of creation. "And we've just had to take him up on account of Cynthia. But she was given no chance to expatiate on her favorite theme which consisted of numerous variations

on the 'you never can tell' idea with a slithering emphasis
on the word 'can.' "

The butler appeared in the broad archway leading to the
entrance hall to announce her first guests.

"Mrs. Bronson, Miss Talbot, Prince Ladislov."

Mrs. Ventnor greeted her first guests with the peculiar
effusiveness which is so customary when greeting some
one who has just been under discussion. Gloria was introduced to the dreamy-eyed Prince Ladislov who bowed over
her hand with quiet dignity, murmuring in the depths of
his fine beard.

"I've heard so much about you, Prince Ladislov. You
know I'm one of Cynthia's best friends, at least I flatter
myself I am, and she used to talk about you so often in
school. I've always thought of you as a kind of prince of
romance."

The Russian's pale cheeks flushed ever so slightly and
he bowed again in his strange way which so captivated
the hearts of young American girls, combining as it did
both the formality and glamour of the Russian court at
which he had been so bright a figure. "You are very kind,
Miss Glendale. Maybe I am a prince of romance, who
knows? Aren't all lost causes romantic; isn't futility the
very essence of romance? The prince in the fairy tale is a
romantic figure because he is of no possible use in a real
work-a-day world, because he is able neither to plow a field
nor run a machine." A faint smile played over his delicately chiseled lips which the trimly cut mustache and
beard could not hide. "You see, Miss Glendale, I make up
definitions to fit myself and the exigencies of the moment."

Gloria laughed a little, her heart strangely warmed by
his mellow voice and distinguished manner. "I think I see
already why Cynthia has always been so fond of you.

Please be good to me, and don't make me lose my head."

She noticed out of the corner of her eye that several other guests had arrived but she ignored them and strolled to one side with this very delightful prince of whom she had heard so much. A moment later they were seated on a couch a little withdrawn to the far end of the room and rather in the shadow of a magnificent Milanese suit of armor.

"You are a very clever flatterer, Miss Glendale, and I think apt to forget that I am a notorious adventurer in search for some beautiful American girl sufficiently wealthy to rehabilitate my fallen fortunes."

Gloria smiled up at him. "And pray who is to blame for that? You are clever enough to make any young girl forget anything you didn't care to have her remember."

"All of which leads up to something, doesn't it?" he remarked seriously. "Why don't you come right out and ask me to tell you about Cynthia and Richard Sperry?"

The young girl's eyes opened very wide. "Now I know you must be a dealer in black magic. You simply couldn't guess a thing like that, but now that you have guessed it there's nothing for me to do but acknowledge the truth, though I must say Cynthia shows rather bad taste in picking on first a football player and then a rather toothless novelist when she has you at her elbow."

He rose swiftly and bowed before her. "I'm afraid you are the dealer in the black arts. Do you always guess people's secrets as swiftly as that?"

In spite of his bantering tone she knew instinctively that she had touched some chord deep down in his nature which vibrated to emotions far more fundamental than those which usually actuated his formal politeness. She rose and stood beside him. "Aren't you going to tell me something about Cynthia? After all you've been down here living in the same house with her for a whole month. Has she really gone mad?"

He shrugged his shoulders expressively, even as he obediently caught his hostess' eye bidding him come be introduced to a new arrival of rather portentous dignity. At the same moment Cynthia and Sperry were announced. "Now you can see for yourself," the prince said, as he moved away.

Gloria ran impulsively to greet the girl and as she did so it flashed through her mind that she had been told to see for herself twice within the last few minutes. She kissed her and then was introduced to her escort of whom she had heard so much, but had never seen before. She couldn't help noticing the change in Cynthia's appearance. Her eyes were too bright, glittering almost where formerly they had lain slumbering in her pale white face like the languid waters of some southern river at sunset. Her pale face was tanned now but managed to look rather drawn in spite of its color where in former times it had merely appeared slim. Her whole body seemed to be pervaded by some inner excitement which would not let her spirit rest.

She thought all this even while she was speaking polite banalities to Sperry, complimenting him on his latest novel, "Flung to the Stars," which had flourished on best-seller lists during the whole winter. He received her rather fulsome praises with perfect equanimity, smiling in a complacent way which revealed the pathetic condition of his stumpy, blackened front teeth. She felt like saying, "My dear fellow, you certainly need the attention of a good dentist, and if I were Cynthia I'd see that you went to one before I ever kissed you even the first time." But instead she said, "It must be wonderful to be so overwhelmingly popular, Mr. Sperry."

"Popularity is a very minor thing." He waved the thought aside with a pudgy hand. "The friendship of Cynthia here, for example, means more than the acclaim of millions."

Cynthia laughed raucously. There was a quality in her voice which Gloria had never noticed before. "Good work, Dick, but you really don't have to be quite so pompous with Gloria. She won't be impressed by it and she doesn't need to be. She manages somehow to be in at the high spot of all my affairs."

He smiled indulgently. "Cynthia, darling, as a writer I must protest against the unnecessary use of the word 'all.' Either my faith or your rhetoric must be at fault, and I prefer to let you take the blame."

The girl shrugged her naked brown shoulders. "Just as you say, Dicky. You know I've given up trying to keep pace with you grammatically though I can outstrip you in other ways."

It was his turn to laugh now. "Hadn't you better be a little more specific in order to allay any suspicions Miss Glendale may have as to the amount of *double entendre* attached to the word 'outstrip'?"

"By all means *don't* be careful," Gloria chimed in quickly. "It would be too stupid living in a world full of careful people."

"Exactly my sentiments," exclaimed Cynthia. "I am glad you've come down finally, Gloria. Every one down here just sees what I do and never gives me a chance to explain the very elegant theories I have made up to account for my misdeeds. I suppose you're aware Dickie is my leading misdeed, at least just at the moment. We're invited everywhere as something to practice frowns on."

Sperry frowned a little. "Cynthia, I do wish you wouldn't call me Dickie."

The girl flashed a bright, quick look at him. "Which is equivalent to saying you acknowledge being a misdeed. Anyway, why shouldn't I call you Dickie? Your wife calls you Richard." She pronounced it very formally.

The man drew himself erect. "I don't care for Richard from you, either. What is becoming for Ethelreda is unworthy of your greater distinction."

"My! My! My! you are being the grand novelist in your grandest way to-night. I think I'd better take you over and leave you with Prince Ladislov so you can talk about the social significance of the fall of the Romanoffs or some other equally flimsy chit-chat."

"I've just been talking with the prince," Gloria burst out. "I don't think I ever was so impressed with any one in my life."

"Well, don't let him run away with you, anyhow," Cynthia remarked. "Besides, as a friend, you ought to leave me my Prince of Glamour. He's all I have to use when I get fed up on life and sick of the sordid everyday world of affairs. When I get thoroughly tired of reading what the Senator from Kansas had to say about the omnipresent farm bill and the like, it's a relief to think about the prince hunting wild boars or some equally impossible animal in one of the innumerable corners of Russia."

Sperry beamed on her through his heavy eye-glasses. "Well, if the prince represents escape through glamour what do I mean in your life?"

"Why, you are intellectual stimulation, of course. Through you I learn about split infinitives, dangling participial clauses, periodic sentences, stylistic bombast and other matters of equal importance."

He smiled. "I'm not quite sure that's meant to be flattering."

She tapped his cheek lightly with her long, slim white
fingers. "Dickie, you know perfectly well it is not flattering. 'I could not love thee, dear, so much loved I not
flatter less.' Isn't there a quotation something like that?"

"Thank God, no."

"Well, if there isn't, there ought to be. Now, Dick, be
a good boy and run over and pay your respects to Mrs.
Ventnor. She's been eying you quizzically ever since we
came. I feel I ought to warn you she's almost as much a
stickler for propriety as you are, and if you can think
of any more pompous platitudes, use them. She loves them
so much. She not only remembers them but quotes them
as well."

He wandered off obediently to greet his hostess. He
was a little thrilled at being here in Mrs. Ventnor's house
at one of her most select dinner parties after she had
snubbed him so consistently for years until Cynthia came
along to remedy that and a thousand other similar social
errors. Meanwhile the girl turned impulsively to Gloria.

"When I said you were always in at the big moments
I really meant it. Do you remember the afternoon in
New Haven when I got the note from Dale? That was
such a thrilling moment and you were grand about it all,
I know. I heard later from Agnes Ventnor how clever
you were. Well, that affair was just a big bust, but Dick
is the real thing. He takes me out of myself in a way I
can't possibly describe. When I'm with him I seem to
be moving in a world where men do things, and think
things, and say things that really matter. I don't suppose
I ever realized I had a brain until he came along to show
me how stupid I was to attempt to find solace in cock-
tails when there are people who are so much more important. To-day, to-night I've decided that nothing in the
world matters except that Dick and we must have each

other no matter who tries to interfere. Tell me what you think of him."

"Do you really want to know what I think of him?" Gloria said cynically. An imp seemed to be at her ear, forcing her to speak.

"Yes." Cynthia's tone managed to give the single short word a vital significance. Gloria shrugged her shoulders eloquently.

"Then the blood be on your own head, as they used to say in melodramas. First, I don't see what there is to be melodramatic about, and second, if you must go off the deep end why not take him to a good dentist first?"

Gloria never was quite sure why she had said anything so bitingly cruel. When she thought it over later it seemed unnecessary in its venom, but at the moment of speaking, the words seemed to spring unbidden from her brain and pass swiftly over her lips before her consciousness had time to censor them.

Cynthia stood for a moment thunderstruck, then said very quietly: "You're quite right. I believe he needs to go to an oculist, too, and his hair is falling out, not to mention that a chiropodist might be of service, and a masseur, and a dietitian. Only those capable of seeing beyond surface and external things could possibly appreciate him."

She turned on her heel and walked slowly toward the other side of the room where Jane Talbot was standing all alone for the moment. Before she could reach her the butler announced dinner was served, and Mrs. Ventnor, who had been gossiping rather gayly with young John Flannagan, began to pair off her guests with the swift dexterity of the perfect hostess.

CHAPTER EIGHTEEN

CYNTHIA lay flat on her back on the sand, allowing the warm sunshine to penetrate her body until the golden rays seemed to reach her very soul and lift it to a higher plane of ecstasy. It was very soothing to lie on the beach between dashes into the crystal clear surf but in spite of the complete repose of her body her mind was working rapidly. Last night had removed all doubts of the completeness of her devotion to Dick Sperry. He represented all those things which she needed, for which her soul cried out. His keen mind made him the exact opposite of the purely physical Dale who had only brought her disillusion. Now she felt she was dealing with a man of sophistication, a real man of the world, whose talent was recognized by the world. Even his luxurious living was supplied by his pen and through association with him she was acquiring a rather profound respect for all those who were not only clever enough to live by the power of their brain but to do it very well no matter what standard you judged by.

Last night at Mrs. Ventnor's dinner she had been seriously annoyed by Gloria Glendale's stupid remark about the condition of Dick's teeth, yet that very annoyance perhaps had brought her to a realization of how much he meant to her in ways that were not physical. He had no power to crush her in his arms as Dale had done on that never-to-be-forgotten night at the Connecticut roadhouse, but he had the power to stir her mind to move vigorously and swiftly with his along the paths of thought.

She was beginning to think about things such as had never entered her consciousness before. She had to be a woman of the world now in order to match his sophistication, his considered, slightly cynical view of life and affairs which had made his novels so popular, so much sought after on both sides of the Atlantic. She ought to be grateful to Gloria for having brought her mind around to a consideration of his physical defects because only when thinking keenly about them had she come to fullest understanding of how far they were outweighed by his mental capacity, by the mental stimulation which he brought into her life. Last night in his motor boat they had floated languidly along the lake, bathed in the glory of moonlight, and there had come to complete realization of their love for each other. She was so sure of that. Dawn had been breaking before they returned and it was full daylight when she had jumped into bed, but there had been no sense of weariness or languor, only a triumphant song in her heart which sang of the fulfillment of desire. Last night in the motor boat with his mouth crushed passionately against hers, her tongue had touched the broken irregularity of his teeth and she had thrilled to the realization of their imperfections. Forever, she felt, they would be the symbols of what he was not, symbols of how much more he was in consequence.

She was rather surprised to see Thor Bronson walking across the sand toward her. It was surprising how little she ever saw of her stepfather, and especially at this hour when he always played golf with two or three of his Wall Street cronies whose company he seemed to find preferable to that of any women. She thought he looked sturdy, more than stolid, as he walked slowly toward her, his heavy figure seeming to belie all the romantic stories she had heard since she could remember about his attachment to his beautiful mistress, Olive Smith. Yet there could be no doubt of that attachment since Olive was always brought down to Palm Beach in open defiance of all gossipers and was at the moment living in a pretty little house on Cocoanut Row. Only yesterday Cynthia had driven her car slowly past the house, shamelessly trying to look into the windows, actually hoping for a glimpse of the beautiful Olive who was so important to her stepfather to whom nothing else on earth seemed important. She had driven past the house purposely because her emotional feelings for Dick were surging high within her and she wanted to see where some one lived who loved completely enough to calmly defy all convention. She thought of it now, now that last night had meant the fulfillment and culmination of her love for Dick.

Mr. Bronson sat down on the sand beside her with a little sigh as if either the weather was too warm for him or else his tangled thoughts needed easing. The girl was frankly surprised. It flashed through her mind that she could never remember him having sat beside her in this way, seemingly anxious to indulge in conversation. His first words surprised her still more.

"I've just been talking to Sperry. He called to see you a few minutes ago looking as flamboyant as a peacock, but I told him I didn't know where you were and he went away."

Cynthia looked up questioningly. "Father, why did you say that? You might have guessed I was down here at this hour."

He drew a circle very slowly in the sand with his stubby forefinger, then blotted it out with a sudden gesture. "I didn't need to guess where you were because I knew you were down here. I saw you from my window and put on my bathing suit to join you. I knew if he

came down here you wouldn't want to talk to me and it
so happens I do want to talk to you."

There was frank wonder in her deep brown eyes now.
"Why, father, you've never paid me such a compliment
in your life before." She smiled rather mockingly. "Since
when have you become the jealously protecting parent?"

"Since about seven o'clock this morning. I saw you
and Sperry come home. I saw you kiss him good-by and
being a very sensible, matter-of-fact person, I drew my
own sensible, matter-of-fact conclusions."

"Which were,—what?" The girl's eyes narrowed just
a little.

"I don't know just how to say what I want to say. I'm
scarcely the person to give you moral lectures even if I
cared to do so or had the right to do so. After all, I'm
not your father and somehow our relations have never
crossed the most frigid barrier between stepfathers and
stepdaughters. You'll forgive me if I happen to be
'sloppy,' as your mother so very kindly remarked this
morning, and I happen to like you. I don't expect you
to believe it or anything else I say. You've been brought
up to doubt everything you hear, to mistrust everything
anybody tells you. But I am worried about you. I don't
like the way you've been running around with Sperry,
and maybe that's because I don't like Sperry. I don't like
his books, or his reputation, either literary or personal.
Even if I do spend most of my time in Wall Street I
hear stories about a man as well known as he is. He has
a bad reputation with women; to him every woman is
just to be used until he gets sick and tired of her. Wherever he lives it's always the same."

The young girl's lip curled cynically and her tone when
she spoke was bitingly sarcastic. "All of which is very
interesting, isn't it? You seem to be positively overflow-

ing with information about Dick. Just who is the source
of your information—Miss Smith?"

He bowed his head ever so little. "Exactly. I would
not bother to interfere unless my source of information
was good."

She laughed flippantly. *"Good* is such a convenient
word, isn't it? But isn't it a little antiquated for you to
protest about my affair with a distinguished novelist
because of your affair with an undistinguished chorus
girl?"

He looked at her a little sadly. "Now I am surprised
at you. I didn't quite think you were the sort of person
who would say that in just that way. I suppose you feel
that now I will withdraw all objections to your carrying-on
with a scamp like Sperry. But I'm not built that way.
I'm not ashamed of my love for Olive, maybe it's the
only thing in my life I'm not ashamed of. In any case, I
wish you wouldn't talk like your mother does when she
tries to show off in front of that disgusting Jane Talbot."

Cynthia got up from her reclining position and faced
him squarely, her feet spread a little apart, the wind
fluttering the ends of her gay beach wrap. "I'm sorry, but
there doesn't seem to be much for us to say to each other.
You're forgetting three very important things. The first
is, you have no right to interfere in my life and even
if you had it would make no difference because I intend
to live absolutely as I please, a free woman of this magnificent twentieth century. The second point is, I happen
to like my mother and admire Jane Talbot, so I am not
interested in whatever you think about either of them.
The third point is the most important of all. I love Dick
Sperry. He means everything to me and I intend to have
him. Now are you satisfied?"

He rose to face her, his head lowered a little trucu-

lently. "No, I'm not satisfied, and I'll stop you making
a fool of yourself if I have to break that damn fool's
jaw. He's just using you so he can get ahead socially.
He's a nobody from nowhere and like all people of his
type, a social climber. That's what he wants you for, to
get him invited all the places he's never been invited
before, to let him force his way in on people who have
never spoken to him and don't want to speak to him."

She laughed loudly. "How silly you are. When you
try to be very calm you're just stupid, and when you ·
start to bellow and shout you're only a fool. Men like
you make women appreciate men like Dick. Good morning, father." With a light gesture of her hand she flung
aside her cloak and ran gayly down into the surf.

Bronson stared after her helplessly. For the first time
in his life he had tried to take an interest in the girl's
affairs because he really did like her and because he was
convinced she was making a fool of herself over some
one who was utterly unworthy of any consideration. And
he had failed, of course, to get any more tangible results
than an insult. Now he had destroyed whatever little feeling of respect and kindliness the girl had had toward
him. She had told him in so many words that she had
given herself to Sperry and that was all there was to it.
Olive had said he would be foolish to try to interfere,
and she had been right. The only hope now was that
she herself might somehow be able to do something where
he had failed so miserably. Even his wife had merely
laughed at him not a half hour before when he tried to
make her understand the situation. She had laughed that
cruel, insinuating way of hers which always made him
feel miserable and useless, and she had merely said, "Well,
what of it?" If there were only something he could do

about it all things would be so much better. If he only
could smash Sperry's jaw, that would be tangible.

A half hour later Cynthia was ringing the doorbell of
Sperry's house on Brazilian Avenue. As soon as her step-
father had left the beach she had rushed back into the
house and dressed quickly. She felt she must talk to Dick
and once more be restored in the completeness of her
faith in him. What Mr. Bronson had said was ridiculous
of course, but at the same time it had destroyed the beautiful calm of her feelings, the glorious aftermath of her
night of love on the boat. Now nothing would do but
that the man who had been reviled should take her in his
arms gently and restore her faith.

The door was opened by one of the four Chinese servants who ran the household. Once more it annoyed her
that she could never tell them apart. He informed her
in his strange high voice that Mr. Sperry was not in.
For a moment Cynthia stood irresolute, stunned by this
break in her scheme which she had not anticipated. She
was just turning slowly to go when a frail, pallid looking woman with streaky gray hair entered the hall from
the drawing room. "How do you do, Miss Thorpe? Did
you wish to see Richard? He isn't in now but I'm expecting him back for luncheon."

"Oh, that's all right, Mrs. Sperry." The girl tried to
make her voice sound very casual but she knew she had
not succeeded. Somehow she could never convince herself
that she did succeed in being really casual with Mrs.
Sperry. Not that she particularly disliked the woman or
even the thought that she was Dick's wife; that was one
of the things which she had taken for granted from the
very beginning. But there was something about Mrs.
Sperry's frail, almost childlike simplicity which disturbed
her, and made her doubt herself and the importance of

her emotions of the moment. She seemed to have the same effect on Dick, too. Cynthia had noticed that even before the man mentioned it to her a few days before during the course of one of their long nocturnal automobile rides when she had sat beside him entranced while he spoke, in his rather high-pitched voice, of the beauties of the full, complete life.

Now above all she didn't want to talk to Mrs. Sperry but she managed to say, "Oh, I just wanted to see him about a book." She knew it was an absurd thing to say even as the words passed her lips.

The novelist's wife smiled ever so faintly and said, "Why don't you come in a little while, or better still, stay and have lunch with us. Richard will be home in a few minutes, I'm sure, and he'll be delighted to see you."

The girl was thankful for the invitation even though she did not relish the thought of an intimate conversation with Mrs. Sperry whom she considered rather dull. Other people had said Mrs. Sperry was very clever and it was a fact that visiting intellectuals did make a fuss over her but Cynthia failed to see why. Mrs. Sperry typed her husband's manuscripts, that every one knew, but she for one refused to believe the malicious gossip which strove to insinuate that she was probably at least half-author of all the Sperry opuses. To Cynthia's mind a single glance at Mrs. Sperry's plain, pale face, tumbling gray hair and almost shabby clothes would be sufficient to show how ridiculous such an idea was. But for the present her main hope was that Sperry would come quickly and so spare her any unpleasantly long conversation. To say the least it was a little difficult to talk quietly to a woman whose husband had sworn eternal devotion to you but a few hours before and whose body had been linked with yours in proof positive of passion.

If she had expected Mrs. Sperry to indulge in any dramatics she was pleasantly disappointed. That lady merely began to discuss different light and easy topics of general interest to all who lived in Palm Beach, and almost against her will the girl was impressed by a certain dry, deep rooted good humor which she had in no way anticipated.

A few minutes later Sperry dashed in rather precipitously and then stopped at sight of his wife and Cynthia sitting near each other conversing. For a single instant his eyes seemed to narrow nervously, but then it was gone and he greeted the girl casually. "Hello, Cynthia, what good wind brings you here?"

The girl jumped up quickly. "I want to talk to you, Dick. I've got something terribly important to say to you."

The novelist laughed, and this time a nervousness caused by the proximity of the three of them was much more apparent. He tried to laugh it off. "Now it surely can't be as important as all that."

"But it is. It's the most important thing in my life." Something in Cynthia's voice made it impossible to doubt her statement, impossible for any one even so skilled in banter as Richard Sperry to ignore her earnestness.

Mrs. Sperry rose quietly. "I must go see how luncheon is getting on, and I know you two have so many things to say to each other." She turned to her husband quietly and in her beautifully modulated voice there was not a shadow of mockery or suspicion. "Cynthia is staying to luncheon with us."

The man's eyes were fastened on the young girl and he seemed oblivious to his wife's remark. Mrs. Sperry left the room quietly and closed the door softly behind her. For a moment the two remaining stood looking at each other, one with glowing eyes of love, the other with apprehension clouding his desires. Finally the man spoke nervously.

"What's the matter, child? Why have you come rushing here?"

She drew herself close to him and put her arms gently about his neck. "Dick, I'm worried this morning as any woman would be after your protestations last night. Now when there's no moon, no glamour, no champagne, no delirium, I want to know if you really love me."

He drew her body swiftly to him and his lips were pressed full on hers. For a moment they clung to each other and the faint irregularity of his imperfect teeth seemed to be reaching from her lips to her heart. He said, "You know I love you, Cynthia. What can I say more than I said last night?"

"Nothing." There was a sigh of content in her voice like the faint evening breeze in heavily-leaved maple trees after a long, hot summer day. Her body swayed slightly with emotion, her eyes closed softly in perfect content.

CHAPTER NINETEEN

Mrs. Bronson lay back on her chaise-longue with her hands clasped behind her head. A gracious breeze floated in through the huge windows of her room and she felt it would be awfully nice just to lie here and do nothing forever. She rather wished Jane would go away and leave her to her half-dreaming meditations but she knew it was ridiculous to suggest such a thing to her. Jane sat on a small wicker chair and the heel of her French slipper tapped the floor impatiently.

"Well, Aurelia, just what are you going to do about it?"

Mrs. Bronson turned her head ever so slightly and opened her lovely violet eyes very wide. "Do about what, Jane? Just what are you hectoring me about on such a drowsy afternoon?"

Jane jumped up impatiently and strode over to the couch. "You know perfectly well what I'm talking about. You know that I'm the last person to interfere in what any one does. I haven't a very savory reputation myself, as I scarcely need remind you, but I do think there's a limit to all things, and the way Cynthia is carrying on with Dick Sperry these last few days is a disgrace. The way they both behaved at your dinner party last night was altogether beyond reason. Why didn't they go the whole hog in front of every one and be done with it?"

"Dear me, you do sound so terribly moral, Jane. Since when have you joined the Mother Grundy Association?"

"I haven't. Moreover, you know you're just saying things like that to befog the issue and try to keep yourself from recognizing that you must do something about the matter. I've known you so long I understand just how your mind works. You're simply too lazy to face the issue squarely."

"Exactly, Jane." Mrs. Bronson stifled a little yawn delicately. "I'm very comfortable down here. I enjoy the bathing, and the breeze, and the gentle ease of life in Palm Beach. I don't intend to worry myself over what Cynthia is or is not doing." She sat up rather suddenly and there was a strange, grim quality in her voice as she continued her thoughts. "I was worried about Cynthia once, but only for one reason. Whatever she does as regards Dale Eustis or Richard Sperry or any other man doesn't come under the head of that worry."

Miss Talbot smiled a little grimly. "I think I understand what you mean, my dear. The greatest fear in life is to be afraid of yourself; to fear in others that which you know so well from your own experience. But you aren't insinuating by chance that I was one of your worries?"

Mrs. Bronson shrugged elaborately and lay back in her former position of languid content. "Who knows, Jane, just how the gods may decide to plague us at any moment?"

Her companion laughed raucously in the hard, harsh way which always annoyed people. "I think I'd better be running along. When you talk about being plagued by the gods it's a little too awful for me to stand." She walked swiftly from the room while her friend merely closed her eyes and inhaled the warm perfume laden air a little more deeply. She couldn't help thinking how silly it was to worry about Cynthia, who was a very clever girl after all and would undoubtedly find herself soon enough. The thought vaguely crossed her mind that she must talk to May-May and let her know it would be quite safe for her to return to England at any time now. There would be a large present, of course, and she would give it gladly enough. Somehow or other May-May had been instrumental in bringing Cynthia to a realization of her womanhood. She was entitled to unending thanks.

But if Mrs. Bronson was quite willing to take her daughter's flagrant conduct as a matter of course Jane was not. She walked swiftly through the house and climbed into her roadster which always stood in the driveway waiting to serve her needs. The car fairly spun down the Ocean Boulevard and five minutes later stopped before a pretty little house on Cocoanut Row which was almost concealed by a glorious bougainvillia vine in the fullest glory of its purple flowering. In answer to her ring the door was opened by a beautiful woman dressed completely in white. She looked very cool standing in the darkened doorway and for a moment the extreme simplicity of her costume left Miss Talbot almost speechless. She might have been a nurse in attendance but the visitor was sure that no nurse had ever been half so ravishing looking.

"May I come in for a moment and talk to you, Miss Smith?"

The woman in white smiled a little and held wide the door. "Yes, Miss Talbot, please do come in." They passed together into the little drawing room. There were flowers and light cool hangings that made the room infinitely restful after the glare of the sunny streets. In the silence one could just hear the strange sound of the cocoanut trees as they twisted and turned in the light breeze. Both women sat down quietly.

"You have a very pretty place here, Miss Smith."

"Thank you so much. It suits my needs and is the sort of thing I like."

Jane looked around her more carefully. "How wise you are to live simply like this. I envy you more than I can possibly say." There was a moment's silence during which it seemed the visitor was waiting for her hostess to speak, but she said nothing, merely sitting with a quiet smile lighting her lovely face, her hands folded softly in her lap. Jane spoke again suddenly. "How did you know I was Jane Talbot?"

Miss Smith smiled a little more. "How did you know I was Olive Smith? Isn't it rather axiomatic that we two should know each other—by sight?"

Jane watched her shrewdly. "Wouldn't it be sensible if we knew each other a little better than that? I rather think so."

"And I'm sure of it." There was a quiet music in the woman's voice which touched her visitor deeply. For a moment again the silence settled coolly over the room, but this time there was in it a new quality, a kind of richness as there always is when two people are interested in each other. Once more Jane seemed to be waiting for this quiet woman to speak, and again it was she who had to take the forward step. She leaned forward earnestly.

"I'm going to assume, then, that we are friends, Miss Smith, at least of a sort. I've come to you to-day because I need your help, because I am in a difficulty and I don't know what to do. No matter how quietly you are living here you must have heard how Cynthia is carrying on with Richard Sperry. I want to do something to stop it and I don't know how. I've talked to her mother and she refuses to budge to prevent her daughter from making herself ridiculous. I can't go to Mr. Bronson. I dare say you know how much he hates me, so I'm forced to come to you. The girl won't listen to me at all. I tried to talk to her last night and she only laughed at me. That never happened before."

"And just how do you expect me to help, Miss Talbot?" There was a quiet earnestness in her voice which was irresistible. "What is there I can say that you failed to say?"

Jane jumped to her feet. "I don't know. I can't explain why I feel that you could accomplish something where I couldn't, but I do feel that way about it."

Miss Smith rose quietly to face her visitor. "Then I suppose I must do what I can. In fact, I confess I was sitting here thinking what there was for me to do at the very moment you rang the bell. Thor talked to me for hours last night insisting I do something. Like you, he talked to her and talked to her mother, both without result. Like you, he feels I can do something to help matters, so I suppose I must try even while I feel helpless and just a little ashamed." She stopped talking and sighed deeply. "Has it occurred to you how difficult it is for me to explain to a girl that she cannot give herself recklessly to a married man, when that is just exactly what I have done and am doing; when I glory in the happiness I've found by so doing? I should think I would be the last person to be able to dissuade her."

Miss Talbot leaned forward swiftly and caught both the woman's beautiful tapering hands in her long, bony fingers. "That's just why I want you to go to her. Will you forgive me for saying that? Cynthia has talked to me about you several times. To her you symbolize the supreme happiness that can be found by defying the world and letting your heart dictate to your body. She will listen to you as she would listen to no one else because you represent happiness found in the way which she is bungling.

If you talk to her and tell her to consider her step before it is too late she will know it is not Mrs. Grundy speaking but the beautiful Olive Smith who has found happiness, complete happiness, dangerously. You represent at the moment what she is trying to be. It is up to you to explain clearly to her the difference between men, the tremendous gulf which separates Thor Bronson from a mere clever social climber like Dick Sperry. Do you understand what I'm trying to say?"

"Yes." The single word carried complete conviction. "I'll go to her to-day and I promise you I'll do my best."

A moment later Jane Talbot drove away swiftly in her car but her mind was no longer bewildered. Against all reason she felt that this woman would accomplish what she set out to do.

Left alone Olive Smith went to her bedroom and put on a large floppy hat of Italian straw. Now that she had promised to do what she could, she was free to consider the difficulties involved in merely meeting Cynthia, much less having a heart to heart talk with her. She glanced at her watch and saw it was almost five o'clock. She couldn't very well call Cynthia on the telephone and ask to talk to her, and still less could she trust to Thor as an intermediary to effect a pleasant meeting. For a moment she stood in deep thought tapping her fingers lightly against the frame of the door, then suddenly an idea came to her. She picked up the telephone and gave a number quietly. A moment later the connection was put through and she asked for Mr. Sperry.

"Mr. Sperry is not in just now. Can I take any message? This is Mrs. Sperry speaking."

She could hardly repress a chuckle at her good fortune but she merely said, "I was wondering if you could tell me where he is. I'm very anxious to reach him at once."

"Who is speaking, please?"

"Miss Smith, Miss Olive Smith. I have a message for Miss Thorpe. I dare say she is with him." She smiled faintly at the curiosity she hoped would be aroused in the breast of the woman at the other end of the wire; but as she anticipated there was no explosion of temper, only a polite answer to her original question.

"How do you do, Miss Smith? I think you'll find Mr. Sperry at the Tea Garden, and I'm rather sure Miss Thorpe is there with him."

Miss Smith thanked her in her sweetest tone and hung up the receiver. Five minutes later her wheel chair was being propelled swiftly along the lake trail past the old houses almost buried under masses of flowering shrubs and trees which had once constituted the most fashionable part of Palm Beach before the great houses were built along the ocean front. When she stepped from her chair at the entrance to the Tea Garden she noticed it was thronged with a gayly dressed crowd and the negro orchestra was playing one of their most pulsating rhythms to which most of the guests were dancing. She passed through the entrance and managed to find a small table under the cocoanut trees a little removed from the dancing platform. As the waiter was taking her order she saw Cynthia dancing with Sperry. The girl was leaning back in his arms, her eyes closed ecstatically and there was a look about her which fairly screamed aloud the abandonment of her passion for this man. Miss Smith felt sure that several others were watching as closely as she and equally certain that as soon as the dancing stopped she, herself, would be the cynosure of many eyes. But that was the sort of thing which must be risked if she was to go ahead and accomplish anything of what was expected of her.

The music stopped and the dancers drifted back to their tables. She noticed that Cynthia and Sperry had a small table to themselves quite a distance from her own. She summoned a waiter, a colored man who approached with a flourish.

"Do you happen to know either Mr. Sperry or the young lady with him, Miss Thorpe?"

"Yes, ma'am. Ah know both o' them verra well. Ah see 'em now sittin' right across the floor there."

She smiled a little. "I dare say one does get to know most of the celebrities."

"Yes, ma'am. Ah know you, too, Miss Smith."

She raised her eyes toward him quizzically. "I dare say that means I'm one of the celebrities. Thank you very much. Now will you do a favor for me? I'm going to give you a little note which I want you to deliver to Miss Thorpe, if possible without attracting Mr. Sperry's attention. Is that clear?"

The darky smiled, disclosing a row of brilliantly white teeth. "Yes, ma'am, Ah understan'. You just leave it t' me. Ah'll have her over here in a jiffy," and he shuffled away just as the orchestra struck swiftly into another dance number.

She noticed him cut swiftly through the first dancers on the floor and reach the table she was watching. He was only there a second when Sperry rose quickly and went toward the entrance. Then she saw him talk earnestly a moment to Cynthia who glanced up in her direction and then came quickly toward her, circling the dance floor past the musicians' platform. The leader of the orchestra bowed to her and Miss Smith noticed the girl smiled happily in return. It was clear enough that every one here knew Cynthia well and liked her. While the thought was still crossing her mind the girl reached her side and stood with outstretched hand.

"I'm awfully glad to meet you at last, Miss Smith." There was a real ring of candor in the girl's voice. "I'm going to ask you this very minute if you won't let me call you Olive. You know that's what I've always called you to myself whenever I've thought of you, and I assure you I've thought about you a great deal."

For a moment the two women stood facing each other their hands clasped cordially. The older woman's face flushed just a little but there was a happy look in her eyes as she spoke.

"You're awfully sweet to say that, Cynthia." There was a slight hesitancy before the name which lent color to the simple words. "But then I always was sure you would be like that. I often used to wonder if I'd ever meet you."

"And I was in the same fix." The girl laughed lightly and they sat down side by side at the little table. "I wonder if you quite realize that ever since I can remember your name has spelled Romance for me. You have always been the symbol of the woman who was brave in her love and whose bravery was richly rewarded. Even when I was a child," she smiled happily, "and that certainly wasn't very long ago, I used to think of you as 'the happy lady.'"

Olive joined in her little laugh. "Cynthia, do you mind my wanting to talk to you now when you're busy dancing? You see I didn't know just how to reach you. I couldn't very well call at your house or ask you to come to see me at mine, could I?"

"Why not?" The girl's eyes opened very wide. "Wherever I am, there you're welcome. I hope you'll never forget that. Only the other day I was terribly worried to know if Dick really loved me as I hoped he did, as every one was trying to force me to believe he did not. I drove past your house very slowly, hoping I'd see you on the porch, or looking out a window, or on the lawn, or somewhere that would give me an excuse to stop and talk to you. I wanted to go into your house, such a pretty little house, and say to you, 'Olive, please tell me that love is the only thing in the world that matters.' But I couldn't see you and I didn't have the courage to just walk in. I don't know who would have."

"Am I really as infamous as all that? Anyway Jane Talbot came to see me a little while ago."

"Jane Talbot?" Cynthia voiced her astonishment.

She bowed. "Yes. It does seem funny when you stop to think of it. I dare say clever writers could make ever so many jokes about Jane Talbot and Olive Smith sitting together talking. Yet it wasn't a joke at all. It was really very serious.—I like her," she added impulsively.

"So do I." Cynthia was positive in this. "But I wonder why she came to see you."

"Do you really wonder? I'm sure that in your heart you know. Because she came to me I'm here talking to you now. I want to talk to you about Richard Sperry."

The girl leaned forward and her elbows rested on the table, her lightly folded hands supporting her chin. There was a touch of mockery, almost insolence, in the casualness of her position. She said, "I think I rather did suspect that and I'm sorry about it. I'm afraid Jane doesn't like Dick any more than my step-father does. Only mother seems to like him."

"I'm glad you said *seems* to like him. Will you believe me if I say your mother doesn't like him except in so far as he is a man, and perhaps because Jane Talbot dislikes him sufficiently? That's rather a funny way of putting things, isn't it? But at least you see I'm talking to you as one woman of the world to another, and then you know

I've been down here a number of winters and even as far removed as I am from the social circles I hear things about a man as conspicuous as Richard Sperry."

"Naturally you do. He's a very prominent novelist."

"Among other things, yes. But his reputation in Palm Beach is more concerned with his ability to turn the heads of foolish young girls who find him fascinating. That's the way in which I know most about him."

Cynthia chuckled. "My dear Olive, are you calling me a foolish girl?"

There was no answering laughter in the older woman's eyes. "Indeed, I am not. I wouldn't think of doing anything so silly. Do you want to know what I really do think deep down in my heart? I think you are in love with Richard Sperry. I think your love for him is a big thing in your life, but I don't imagine it occupies the same place in his. I'm sure his liking for you is too closely tied up with your ability to get him ahead socially, to take him into all those houses from which he has been barred so long. I also believe you sometimes forget just who you are. It was rather simple for a very moderately talented actress named Olive Smith to become the mistress of a distinguished banker; it's a little different when Cynthia Thorpe tries to turn herself into the kept woman of a not too brilliant novelist. In fact, it just can't be done."

The girl looked into her eyes steadily. "That sounds rather insulting, doesn't it? And yet I'm sure you don't mean it that way. You're a clever woman, Olive Smith, clever enough to understand my love for Dick, but not quite shrewd enough to understand his love for me. You're right about one thing, though. It isn't in my nature to be kept by any one in any sense of the word. Dick is going to marry me. Will that satisfy you on that score? Is that what you wanted to know?"

The two women looked deep into each other's eyes and then the older said gravely, "I'm sure that would satisfy any one. I'll be the first to congratulate you, if I may. When are you to be married?"

The girl flushed just a little, then she said, "Of course he must get a divorce first. I'll speak about that to-day." She turned around in her chair to look for her lover. The dancing had ceased again and across the empty floor she could see him sitting at their table. She waved her hand to him gayly and he responded in like manner. With a bright smile she jumped up to go to him. "Good-by, Olive. I know we're going to be real good friends, no matter what happens. And it was a clever trick to get Dick out of the way first."

Their hands clasped again across the little table and in a flash she was gone. Miss Smith sat down again just in time to receive her tea and sandwiches. She took a delicate, appreciative sip of the beverage, then sat back with a smile. It had all seemed impossible to do and yet she was sure she had succeeded. If all that she had heard of Richard Sperry was only partially true the affair was as good as broken up already. Now that she had talked to the girl and their hands had clasped she was glad, terribly glad, she had taken the necessary step. As she looked toward the table which was occupying her thoughts she saw they were already deep in earnest conversation.

CHAPTER TWENTY

THAT evening after dinner Sperry paced up and down the paved terrace beside his house smoking a magnificent Havana cigar, as was his after dinner custom, but even though the fragrant smoke curled enticingly around his head it could not distract him from the problem on his hands and lead his mind into the pleasant realms of My Lady Nicotine. He was more disturbed to-night than he had been in many years, and the deliciousness of his dinner had not soothed his mind as usual. All through the meal he had wanted to speak to his wife, to explain the difficult situation which was facing him and whenever he had raised his eyes to do so he had found her looking at him across the table with a steady, quizzical gaze which stripped him of determination. It was as if she was expecting him to speak, expecting him to say something of far greater import than their usual domestic chatter which scarcely ever penetrated below the surface of social convenience in these days. And just because he felt she was expecting him to broach some unusual subject he felt powerless to do so.

Yet he must go through with it, and there was little time to be lost now. In half an hour Cynthia was calling for him in her car to take him to the Van Schlessingers' ball. He had looked forward to going so much, to entering the beautiful villa as the guest of the haughty hostess for the first time after so many years of planning and scheming had failed to get him across the threshold. How simple it had all been for Cynthia, who was part of the social scheme, so much a part of it that she took him everywhere with her as a matter of course, without realizing how important these things were to him. He had half an hour, even less now, in which to break up the long continuity of his marriage and make Ethelreda agree to divorce him. Too short a time by far for any delicate adjustments or reasonings or discussions, but it must be done. Cynthia had been very definite this afternoon, insisting on immediate action.

He took the fine cigar from his lips and flung it from him. Its glowing tip described a parabola of light in the darkness, and then lay redly on the grass. He passed through the French windows into the drawing room where his wife sat reading a book by the light of a carefully shaded lamp. He walked over to her impulsively.

"Ethelreda, I must talk to you; seriously."

She put her book down carefully on the little table beside her and looked steadily up at him. Her voice was quiet, almost monotonously so, when she spoke. "I know something has been bothering you all evening, Richard. What's the matter?"

He took a step or two backwards and sat down nervously on the edge of a chair. "It's about Cynthia."

He rather expected some sort of outburst, even though she had never made any trouble over his little affairs before, but this was more than a little affair. He knew it and he was sure that she did. For years now he had realized she seemed to understand his emotions in a way that worried him, tortured him. Whenever he confessed anything to her, as sooner or later he seemed to be driven to do, she always said she had known all along about it and made him feel that her words were no braggadocio, but mere, unvarnished truth. Once more she surprised him. She merely said, "About Cynthia? What about Cynthia?"

He squirmed restlessly. "You might as well know, Ethelreda, I love Cynthia." He said it doggedly, firmly now that he knew he had to carry the thing through to a conclusion, but she only smiled at his vehemence.

"I know that. I believe I have known that for some time now, at least since the other day when she was here to luncheon. I suppose it was to be expected."

He jumped to his feet irritably. "I don't see what you mean 'was to be expected.' I have fought against this thing, struggled all I know how, but I can't help myself. Nothing on earth matters now except my love for her. I can't live without her."

"I didn't think you were living without her. I'm not complaining. Now just what more do you want?"

The simple words were said so quietly that they seemed to be so many darts lunged into his mind. He writhed under the impact. "Ethelreda, this time you don't understand at all. This is not an affair, not like the silly flirtations we've discussed before. This is love, the real big thing, the biggest thing in the world."

"Really?" Her voice rose ever so slightly. "You have a way of saying it, Richard, which makes it sound like a quotation from one of your own books, one of the early books, before you were quite as clever as you are now."

"I don't know what you mean." The words leaped angrily from his lips.

"I dare say you don't. You're rather restless and jumpy to-night and when you're that way you always think you've discovered something of vital importance. If you're not careful you'll be too nervous to enjoy the Van Schlessingers' ball. It's quite true I never go to any of these affairs, with you, I never have enjoyed them, and I never could learn to, but I have always gotten a kind of vicarious enjoyment out of your pleasure in them. The higher society you manage to invade, the happier you always are and therefore the happier we both are in our peculiar, quiet way, which is the way I like. Naturally I welcomed Cynthia Thorpe this year. Your affairs heretofore have been such stupid things, things which gave you so little mental stimulation and certainly brought you no social recognition. This girl took you everywhere with her, into the very heart of the social world for which you yearned, and I was grateful for it, especially grateful since I was not forced to accompany you and chaperon your indiscretions. I think she's an awfully nice girl at heart, though too much dominated by her body. She acts like a person who had discovered her physical potentialities after being crippled for long years. I didn't particularly mind when you showered your attentions on her because it's so many years since you have cared for me at all passionately that I have quite forgotten what it was like, and I have no desire to drag your affection out of the limbo of forgotten things. Now what else is there?"

The novelist took several paces up and down the room and then stood squarely before her, his feet wide apart as if to brace him while he lifted a load beyond his strength. "This time, Ethelreda, you don't understand. This is not an affair, this is love. I want this girl for always."

"And what do you want me to do?" The voice was still monotonously quiet.

He stood silent and stolid for a moment, then shot out his two momentous words. "Divorce me."

"Divorce you?" There was a shade more emotion in the voice now, though it was still repressed. Her rather flat chest rose and then sank in a deep sigh. "That *is* a little different, isn't it? You have come a long way since the affair of last year with the cigarette girl in West Palm Beach. You tempt me to unwilling congratulations. I didn't think it possible you could dare to risk so much on the single throw of a die."

"There's nothing I wouldn't do for Cynthia." He held his head high.

His wife rose slowly to her feet and about her at this moment there was a dignity which seemed to lend interest to her small stature. "Richard, I've underestimated you before, but I won't make that mistake again. We've drifted along together for years now and I never suspected what a man you really were. Now is the time for me to be worthy of you. As a sensible woman there is nothing for me to do but agree. I will divorce you at once. I will pack to-night and start in the morning for Reno or Paris, whichever you prefer."

"Do you mean it?" There was incredulity in his tone.

"Yes. Why should I not mean it? We've been rather happy together in our strange way and I've enjoyed working with you. Being a silent partner in your books has brought me more true happiness than I ever hoped to have. Well,—that's all over now. We'll part as good friends as ever."

"Then you will divorce me; you won't stand in the way?" He couldn't seem to grasp her simple acquiescence, but she was very patient.

"I'll do everything possible to facilitate your happiness. I know I'm a strange woman, Richard, but I can't be different. I insist on being true to myself. I like you, and I want you to be happy. I also like Cynthia, and want her to be happy. So you see there is only one thing for me to do and I'm quite willing to do it."

He caught her hand in his impulsively. "You are a

marvelous woman, Ethelreda. I've always said so, and I
always will say so. I don't know what I would have done
without you. It's marvelous of you to be so understanding."

"Thank you, Richard. Maybe it isn't understanding at
all. Maybe it's just pride, or sexual coldness, or a dozen
other things; anyhow I'm glad you find a nice name for
it. Other people are apt to find other names as easy to
say but much harder to hear. Now you can run off to your
ball in perfect contentment. She ought to be here any
minute now. We can say good-by in the morning."

She left the room with a strange smile on her thin
face and slowly mounted the stairs. He stood in the center
of the drawing room looking after her. It didn't seem
possible that after all his perturbation it was going to
be as simple as all that. He had never realized the extent
of his wife's understanding and sympathy so clearly as
now. What other woman on earth could not only divorce
him but also wish him happiness and say she liked the
girl who was usurping her place in his heart? But had she
ever had a place in his heart in that sense of the word?
The question suddenly rose before him with all its startling
implications. What had his feelings for Ethelreda been
from the very first, back in the long, dead days when he
was a struggling novelist and she had first come to him
as a typist who could do justice to what he considered
the importance of his manuscripts? Had he ever loved her
with any fervor, any passion such as he had felt even
for the least important of his long succession of casual
affairs? There had been no children to link them together, no passion or latent memory of passion to hold
them as one through the passing years. They had been
bound together always by his books, his work which they
had done in common. Through the long years he had

dictated to her and discussed with her all his plans and plots and character developments. She had changed things, turned his thoughts and feelings to her way of thinking, completely re-written his first society novel when it came back from the publisher and he was crushed by its rejection. How often since then she had done the same thing; how much of his work was done not only in collaboration with her but actually by her. She had written the last eight chapters of his latest novel alone in order to meet a delivery date while he had gone off philandering to Bermuda, disgusted with his work and regardless of the consequences of delay. And that was only a few months ago.

The thoughts flashed quickly through his mind and he stood aghast at what his reasoning led him to. He bounded out of the room and up the stairs. He dashed wildly into his wife's room and then stopped dead as he saw her with an armful of clothes which she was putting into a trunk already yawning open to receive them. He gasped, "What are you doing, Ethelreda?"

"Doing?" She followed the question with a little dry chuckle. "Packing, of course. It's rather necessary, isn't it?"

He shook his head as a swimmer does to get water out of his eyes. "I don't mean now. I mean what are you going to do after you get the divorce?"

"I dare say settle down somewhere along the French Riviera and join the English widows and governesses. I've worked pretty hard the last few years and it will be nice to just sit on the balcony of my hotel room all day long and look out over the blue Mediterranean. I think I'll like that, and you've always been so generous with money I have plenty for my simple needs."

"You can't do that!" There was a sudden vehemence

in his voice and his hands trembled slightly with emotion. "You can't leave me like that. I need you for my books. You know I can't get along without you. We've just started a new book and I wouldn't be able to finish it without your help; you know that. You've got to stick with me."

She carefully deposited the dresses on the bed and then turned to face him. "Richard, do you really know what you want? You're acting like a child now who wants to have his cake and eat it, too. A few minutes ago you begged me to divorce you so you can have the love which means everything in the world to you. Well, I agree to that. If you want it so much I would only be a fool to try to interfere. Now you come trying to tell me that I mustn't desert you, that I can't leave you." There was a little pause, then she went on slowly, "You must see you make it hard for any one to understand just what you want. I don't see how I can divorce you and let you marry Cynthia without leaving you."

"You must. You know you've never really cared for me, not for myself. You know you've always loved the work we do together. In a way my books have been far more of your mind and soul than of my own. Why can't we go on working together as we always have done? Don't you see if you leave me my career comes to an end? I've got to go on writing, and at the same time I can't go on writing without your help. I've come to depend on you for everything."

She smiled. "A few minutes ago you were telling me nothing mattered in the world but your love for Cynthia. Now you're telling me you can't live unless you go on with your writing and that you can't go on with your writing unless I stay to help you. Richard, I've put up with a great deal from you; I have interfered less in your personal life than any wife I can even imagine; but things have now gone just a bit too far. Are you calmly suggesting that I should divorce you so you can marry Cynthia Thorpe and yet go on working with you on your books, helping you over the rough spots, actually doing your work for you when you are disgruntled or annoyed? Are you suggesting I should cease to be your wife and continue to be your secretary?"

"Yes." The single word fell heavily from his lips and he stood with hanging head like a michievous boy about to be punished for some misdeed.

She laughed a little louder this time and there was a strange, hard note which caused him to raise his head and look suddenly at her. She crossed swiftly to the open window and drew back the light curtains. A big, luxurious car was just stopping before the house and the wail of its caliope horn floated up to them. She turned to face her husband.

"That's the signal, Richard, for you to decide what you want out of life. The day I divorce you you will never see me again as long as we both live. I shall make it a point of always being so far away from you that you can't reach me. All these long years I've really been your secretary, though the world knew me as your wife. Now I refuse to disgrace us both in the eyes of the world by first divorcing you and then continuing to write your books for you. I, too, have my pride. The choice is up to you now. If you cannot live without this girl you must live without me. That's final."

He stood in the center of the room looking at her with gaping eyes. As he did so the horn again wailed out its shrieking cadence. She stood motionless by the window, but her light laugh reached him and seemed to pierce his very soul.

"Think fast, Richard; the young lady you love is getting impatient. She's waiting to take you to the Van Schlessingers' ball. She's waiting to lead you into every drawing room in America and in the Fall your name will appear in the Social Register. She's waiting out there with her ardent eyes, and beautiful young body, to lift you into transports of passion. What are you waiting for here? What have I to offer you to make you hesitate now that you are forced into a choice? Remember, she's rich, overwhelmingly rich. She can give you more money in a single day than you and I working together could earn in a dozen years, and never miss it. What does it matter if your name doesn't appear in any more book reviews, or on news stands, or in book stores, or on magazine covers? You'll be so rich it will be ridiculous for you to even think of writing. Out there are social position, passion, thrills, all the things you have yearned for all your life and are now come to offer themselves to you in the guise of beauty. Why are you hesitating?"

Once more the horn shrilled through the night, this time more impatiently than before. She dropped the window curtain and walked swiftly up to him. Her voice suddenly raised in pitch and volume and she stamped her foot as she fairly shouted at him, "Why don't you go? She's waiting for you. Go! Go! Go!" She emphasized each exclamation with a stamp of her foot, her eyes flashing fire.

For an instant he faced her, then held out his hand in piteous appeal. "Ethelreda, I can't go. I can't give up my books. I can't give you up."

"Spare me the 'you,'" she cried bitterly. "You mean you can't give up the public acclaim and the sight of your name in print. You mean you want me to go on working with you as before, doing all the drudgery that you care to shirk. Very well, then. You said that I really loved your books far more than I did you. Maybe that's the truth."

"Please stick with me, Ethelreda. To-night I've been a fool, because I lost my head. I'll do anything in the world to make it up to you. After all, I am a writer." He added the last thought parenthetically, and a little pathetically, too, as a drunkard lying in the gutter might recall his gentle birth.

"Do you mean that?" There was irony in her voice now.

"Yes! Yes!"

"Then I'll give you a chance to prove it immediately. She's waiting for you out there in the car. Go out and tell her you never want to see her again, that her love means nothing to you beside your books. Tell her you have been forced to choose and you have chosen—me."

"Ethelreda!" There was a sob in his voice now, but she faced him ruthlessly, pointing her hand dramatically out into the night. A shiver ran through the man's body as there was a sharp ring to the house bell and he knew that Cynthia had come to the door for him now. Three times it rang clearly and distinctly in rapid succession. He tried to look squarely at his wife, but she seemed strangely bigger, taller, dominating him with the force of her unguessed inner strength. Slowly, brokenly he turned from the room and walked down the stairs.

Mrs. Sperry stood in the very center of the room listening. She heard the murmur of voices from outside the house and knew her husband was talking to Cynthia, still dominated by the force of her will. She heard the voices move off in the direction of the street and realized they were walking toward the car while talking. It seemed hours, though it was probably a matter of a minute or two before she heard the car drive off toward the Ocean

Boulevard and then she waited breathlessly, drinking in the stillness of the night. Finally there was a step on the porch and she heard the front door close. True to her woman's instinct she knew all that that meant and with a cry flung herself sobbing on the bed, crushing the dresses which would not have to be packed,—now.

CHAPTER TWENTY-ONE

It was late afternoon and Prince Ladislov was enjoying his cigarette in the quiet seclusion of the patio. He liked to sit there after the sun had sunk low enough to give one the benefit of the shade of the house, when the sound of the fountain in the center was most refreshing, the water splashing limpidly in the cool marble basin. The last week or two had been rather hectic and he had been caught up in a round of social obligations which left him little time for quiet contemplation. To-day he had pretended a headache which was one of the things entirely a stranger to him, just so that he might sit alone like this and try to get his bearings. He leaned his head against the high back of the wicker chair and gazed musingly up into the blue sky. It was so vividly blue it reminded him of Algiers where he had spent a winter as a young man with a very beautiful French dancer whom, at the time, he had considered a perfect mistress. How mad had been their passion for each other, day after day, hour after hour. He couldn't bear the thought of having her out of his sight. And how the years had mocked him. Now he couldn't remember exactly what she had looked like, or the color of her hair, or her eyes, or anything beyond the fact that she always drank too much champagne. He couldn't even remember her name. Nothing remained of the beauty of that winter season except the memory of the blueness of the sky and the soothing sound of running water splashing on marble.

He smiled ironically in the depths of his full blond

beard. Life was so often like that, you forgot things you wanted to remember and you remembered things you wanted to forget. It would be nice now if he could remember the dancer intimately and feel some thrill pass through his tired body in recalling ecstasy even of such ancient vintage. But it was impossible. He couldn't remember what his passion must have been like back in those days when passion was so important. Now the word passion meant nothing more than *if, and,* or *but.* It was just another word, one of the words which are so plentiful in the English language, so carelessly, flippantly used. He wished it might be something a little more important to him and at the same time he was glad that he had reached that stage of development where he could be no longer swayed by desires or animated by lust.

That brought him around to the thought of Cynthia. He couldn't help thinking of Cynthia a great deal these days. For the last two weeks she had been acting so strangely he could not understand her, no matter how hard he tried. Only last night she had insisted on taking him for a ride in her car, and later practically insisted on forcing herself physically upon him. She had been acting strangely since the night of the Van Schlessingers' ball when she had arrived very late, all alone and much the worse for drink. He had sensed then that the drink represented an attempt to crush some heartache, but he wasn't quite sure. It wasn't until several days later when he learned that Sperry and his wife had gone to Havana that he sensed the probable cause of her difficulties. He could not help knowing how infatuated she had been with the novelist, though he tried to maintain an air of complete detachment, living apart from all the affairs of his friends, legal or otherwise.

At this point in his meditations he was interrupted by

the object of his thoughts. Cynthia bounded out of the drawing room.

"I rather thought I'd find you here. That's why I came back. I knew I wanted to talk to you much more than I wanted to see horses run around in a circle." The prince rose to his feet and bowed gravely, thanking her for the compliment, but she waved the social gesture aside.

"This is no time for politeness. I want to talk to you seriously. Last night I was awake for hours and hours, going over things with myself and trying to drum a little common sense into my stupid brain." She sat down rather heavily on a marble bench near the fountain. The spray just touched her hand as she leaned on it to support her body. "I've been a stupid little fool long enough now and I need some one who can give me real advice."

"Meaning me?" The prince laughed a little ironically. "Seemingly you insist on saying nice things to-day and I appreciate them. I was having a rather heart to heart talk with myself, too. Should we join forces?"

The girl looked up eagerly. Were you thinking about me by chance?"

He bowed. "My thoughts were very pleasant, so of course I was thinking about you."

She waved her hand in the air as if to brush aside any indications of a formal compliment. When she continued to speak her voice was low in tone, but for that very reason it carried the greater conviction. "We needn't waste any time in complimentary preliminaries. I've confessed that I've been a stupid fool, and I suspect you know to what extent, and with whom. Now I want to find some way of standing quietly on my feet and gaining full control of my emotions. I'm tired of being blown hither and thither like a flame in the wind. Last night I tried to force you to desire me, to rouse in you whatever latent passion there might be so I might be thrilled by having a veritable prince of romance for a lover. Last night I was very stupid, I realize that much to-day. I hope you'll forgive me."

He rose again swiftly and catching her hand in his lifted it lightly to his bearded lips. "My dear child, I'm sure I shall never, as long as I live, forget the compliment you were good enough to pay me last night, or cease to regret my inability to be worthy of you." He sat down again and leaned forward a little, looking steadily at her, one hand lying loosely on each of his knees. "You were kind enough to forget that I am a rather tired old man, if not old in years at least old in experience. My blood runs coldly in my veins and I have no passion to offer Beauty when she knocks at my door. I have only remembrance of what has been, and even that is a little uncertain. I only know that even in the fullness of my youth I was unworthy of the glorious gift you offered me last night. It's rather sad to be forced to say that and at the same time it gives me the power to appreciate your beauty as I do the paintings of Rembrandt or Velasquez, the sculptures of Phidias, or the music of Mozart."

When he ceased speaking Cynthia sat for a full minute looking at him quietly, a strange glow in her beautiful brown eyes. Finally she began to speak in a soft, low voice that barely reached him. It seemed to come from the very depths of her soul. "How I wish I were like you, Boris. How I wish I, too, were beyond the claims of passion and necessity; unable to remember what had been, and a little glad because of it. With me, my memories and fears are a whip to drive me on, and sometimes, like to-day, I am so weary. Do you know what it means to feel like that?"

His long white hand rested for a moment on his full

beard, then he laughed so faintly that the sound was almost lost in the delicate splash of the fountain. "My dear
girl, all of us remember our weariness long after we have
forgotten whatever it was that made us weary. We remember we had a heartache long, long ago, when we must
utterly fail to be able to conjure up a vision of the source
of that heartache." He stopped a moment and a strange,
dreamy look came into his large, gray eyes. "Isn't it
peculiar that you and I should be talking here, two people
separated from each other by a world of emotions and
a lifetime of years? You are at the beginning of passion
and I am at the end. Last night when your head was on
my shoulder I seemed to feel that between us we had
closed the circle of life, that beginning and ending had
come together and for a moment there was a quiet beauty
comparable to that when an old man sits holding his
grandchild on his knee. The cycle of life was somehow
fulfilled."

"Except that you are exaggerating your age and my
youth," the girl demurred. "I am neither so young nor
innocent as you imply, nor are you so helpless and full
of the venerable weight of years. Since coming down
here this winter I've learned what it means to be no longer
young. I sometimes think that a woman has to be repudiated by some man before she becomes fully conscious of
her age, no matter how young she may be. Sperry promised
to divorce his wife and marry me. Ours was going to be
one of those idyllic unions in which wealth and brilliance
and talent and beauty would make life as nearly perfect
as it could be on this earth. Then something happened,
I dare say his wife was far too clever for him, and I was
sent packing. Oh, yes, it was as simple and as plain as
all that. Dick was very candid, as he can be sometimes,
and I am coming to learn that candor is far more effective

as a weapon of hurt than any other in the world. He said he had talked to Ethelreda and they had both come to the conclusion that it would be impossible for them to destroy their union. He said there was nothing for us to do but not see each other again. He said he was going away as soon as he could manage to arrange his affairs."

Her voice had trailed off until it was barely audible, until the words blurred into a faint succession of sounds which carried the thought clearly enough, however, despite their individual indistinctness. Suddenly she sat up very straight. "Well, I'm glad he's gone. I really mean just that. It hasn't taken me very long to begin to sense how much my love for him was merely resentment against some one else and not a little the desire to show off down here. In my heart I think I knew all along how much he craved social recognition and it flattered me to be able to take him casually to places where all his brilliance of mind and literary reputation could not force an entrance. That's all there was to that."

"And I'm glad." There was something in the tone of voice when the prince spoke which added weight to the simple words. "I knew you were making a mistake, Cynthia, but it is one of my creeds never to interfere with a person in love. You would have resented anything I told you in an attempt to change your feelings and it would have merely brought about a change of feeling toward me, which is something I did not care to risk. I have always been proud to think you liked me a little and that some day, when you were old enough, we might be great friends. I may be too old for passion, or too tired for it, whichever you wish to call it, but like many people in such a position I have an infinite capacity for friendship. Sometimes I lie in bed thinking of my friends through the long years and I can remember them, their appearances, their likes and dislikes, their little foibles, their thousand little acts of kindness toward me, even while I fail to recall the name of a single mistress. I know other countries laugh at the rather exorbitant value we Russians place on friendship, but I am a Russian and have no wish to be otherwise. I am one of those men who glory in the bloody, foolish history of my country and who set romance and chivalry far above economic value. I used to feel I wanted to fight the new régime which has filled the stomachs of my poor countrymen and stolen their ideals, but now even that is gone. All I ask now is quietness, and sympathy, and understanding."

"You are a strange man, Boris, and your capacity for friendship does explain so many things. You've actually had a long friendship with mother, and you can be friends with Thor Bronson at the same time. You're the only person I know who can be a friend to both of them and at the same time be liked and admired by both. I covet your peace and calmness."

The man rose from his seat and caught the girl's hands delicately in his. He seated himself beside her on the marble bench and for a moment they were both silent. Finally she looked into his eyes and began to speak very quietly without withdrawing her hands from the gentle firmness of his grasp.

"Boris, why not be a friend to me, too? Why not help me escape from myself and lead me into the quietness and beauty of life which you possess? I need you so much to keep me from being a fool over and over again, to save me from the demon who is forever lashing my body with his whips of desire. Why not take me away with you? Take me away some place where there is all calmness, and reason, and beauty, where we could live so happily together." She paused a little breathlessly, and as she did so his grasp tightened slightly on her hands. "Do I have to tell you I'm proposing to you, Boris? Please marry me and take me away from all the foolishness of my life."

He lifted her hands to his bearded lips and kissed them very gently. Then he released them and held out his arms. An instant later she was lying clasped to his breast, her head pillowed on his broad shoulder, her cheek touching the full blond beard. For a moment they sat thus together, then he said very quietly, "Are you happy now, Cynthia?"

"Yes." The single word was almost a sigh, and then she went on slowly, "It will be so lovely to be peaceful and quiet like this forever."

He unwound his arms from about her and drew back a little. For an instant he sat looking down at her face upturned to his in surprise at his movement, then he rose slowly to his feet. "You're wrong, Cynthia, absolutely wrong. It wouldn't be lovely for more than a day,. or a week, perhaps not even for an hour. Inside of a month you'd hate me for my helplessness, and I'd hate myself because I was helpless. Every hour with me would remind you of your lost youth which I had stolen from you, the beautiful ebulent passion of youth which is the very heart of its being. Gradually I'd come to feel that with your restlessness and desire you had crept into the empty spaces of my heart to mock its false security. At my age, and after my kind of life, one needs rest and quiet, and at your age one needs only love, which is all life, all beauty, all happiness." He bent down a little over her to look closer into her brown eyes. "Cynthia, am I making myself clear?"

She rose quietly to her feet as he drew back and for a moment they stood facing each other before she held out her hand impulsively. "Yes, I do understand what you mean, and I suppose you're right, but there's another side

to it. You have your quietude which you have gained.
What have I? Do you realize you are driving me back into
the mad arena of desire, and that if you fail me there is
nothing left but a world of sensation into which I must
plunge to find excitement? You tell me love is all beauty,
all happiness, everything in the world. But what is love
and of what does it consist? Two men so far have talked
to me of love with glowing eyes and trembling lips, but
love to them was something so different from my conception. One man was devoted to his mother who had him
completely under her subjugation, while the other was a
slave to his vanity and desire for applause. Now you have
refused me, preferring quietude to my love. What is there
for me to do? Where can I go now to find the answer.

He spread his hands wide in a deprecating gesture.
"You see how it is, Cynthia, even now. Where can I tell
you to search for love except in your own heart?"

She laughed a little boisterously and the sound seemed
to shatter the idyllic peace of the patio, her voice was
raised a little in mockery. "Very sound advice, my dear
prince, but like all sound advice thoroughly worthless."
With a half choking sob she turned and ran into the house.

CHAPTER TWENTY-TWO

For several days after her conversation with the prince Cynthia wandered about almost in a daze. All the normal meanings of everyday life seemed suddenly foreign to her and she could not interest herself in anything even for a few minutes. Once again she and the prince fell back into their custom of good-natured banter and she appreciated his admirable restraint and tact more and more as the days went by. But at the same time she could not deny that she had proposed to three men and in each case she had been either refused or dropped. That thought rankled in a strange, impersonal manner. It was not that she resented so much the action of her lovers as that she questioned the motives which caused them to behave as they had. She bore less and less resentment against them for what they had done, and more and more began to question if she herself were not to blame. What was there about the love which she had to offer which caused it to be valued so lightly? She had read and heard much of women who controlled men and their destinies, women who wound them around their fingers, as the saying was. She was in a quite opposite situation and had now been left stranded emotionally. When she thought things over quietly she could realize how wise the prince had been and with what supreme tact and gentleness he had let her down, but nevertheless she now had nowhere to turn emotionally and to her young eyes life seemed to stretch forward interminably, purposelessly.

She went listlessly through the social life, going to

lunches, dinners and dances, but there seemed to be no purpose in it all. The prince was very kind, and Jane Talbot
tried her best to rouse in her an active interest in her daily
life, but without success. One day they were playing
tennis together on the Everglades Club Court when she
ceased suddenly at the end of a game and flung her racquet aside. "Jane, it's simply no use, I can't play at all,
because I simply don't care whether you beat me or not."

And Jane, as always, was immediately understanding.
She merely picked up the fallen racquet and said, "It is a
stupid way to waste time. Let's try some shopping instead."

But shopping even in the delightful Via Mizner was not
amusing, and so with everything else. Mr. Bronson made
one or two rather bear-like attempts to be helpful and
then returned to New York to be gone for a week or two
on matters of business. The same day Cynthia almost without volition found herself calling on Olive Smith at tea
time. She was received warmly and for an hour or so sat
chatting happily with the woman who had engineered the
break-up of her affair with Dick Sperry. When she rose
to go she held out her hand.

"Olive, I feel I should thank you for trying so hard to
help me in the matter of Dick Sperry. Now I know what
a miserable mistake it would have been to have married
such a man, and I realize how clearly every one saw it but
me. I was infatuated, of course, as I suppose dozens of
silly girls have been every year, but you were the only one
clever enough to know just how to bring me to my senses.
I shall be grateful forever for that."

Miss Smith flushed a little. "Seeing you are going to be
so very sensible I dare say I can confess that I deliberately went to see you with the hope of getting you to ask
Sperry to marry you. It was rather mean of me in one

way but I didn't see what else I could do. Maybe the end
does justify the means."

Cynthia smiled. "I can only say that I hope I shall be
half so clever if the emergency should ever arise in which
I could use my influence similarly for good. I feel I'd like
to tell the story to the whole world so that everybody
could know how kind and generous you really are."

And that was all there was to that. It was a rather pleasant interlude in the long succession of dreary days and
Cynthia was glad that she had had the courage to go and
thank the woman to whom she had every reason to be
eternally grateful even as she had said. She shivered a
little as she thought what misery would probably have
awaited her if she either had continued in her stupid affair
with a man so coldly selfish as Dick Sperry, or worse still
become his wife and so been linked to him by those legal
bonds which can sometimes be so annoying. Yet she felt
at the same time she could not make a friend of Olive in
the ordinary sense of the word. She liked her immensely
but they were separated by walls which were not of her
building and which she would not have the strength to
tear down. Perhaps that was why Olive, being such a
clever woman, kept herself almost exclusively to herself
and made no attempt to mingle in any group. It must be a
lonely life, of course, but at least it was a safe one, safe
from insult and misunderstanding.

The next day she awoke with a slight headache after a
night of restless tossing on her bed and wandered about
aimlessly for several hours. There seemed to be nothing
she cared to do, nothing on which she could focus her
attention. She tried reading several books, but without
avail, and finally ordered her car in desperation. She went
out to the garage to speak to Timothy, the chauffeur who
had driven her for the last year or two.

"Timothy, I want you to go to the cook and get a big luncheon basket. Then I want you to drive me up somewhere along near Hobe Sound. I'm going to have a nice picnic on the beach all alone by myself. Get the cook to give you whatever you want for your lunch." Even as she spoke she felt it was a silly idea but anything was worth trying.

So shortly after she sat back in the car enjoying the fine cool breeze as they sped north on the Dixie Highway. In a little more than an hour they reached their destination and the deferential chauffeur spread her lunch on the gleaming white sands. While he was so doing she changed into her bathing suit in the rather limited privacy of the car and was waiting when he came to tell her everything was ready.

She stood on the road leaning against the mud-guard and suddenly it seemed she was really seeing him for the first time as a man. She looked him over slowly from head to foot. He was rather tall and sleek looking with black hair brushed down smoothly on his head. He had a pleasant, rather smiling Irish face, the nose a trifle short and the upper lip a trifle long in that peculiar way which lends a kind of special whimsical good humor to some Irish countenances. He looked very neat in his close fitting uniform with shining puttees and boots.

For a moment she waited, watching him as he stood deferentially in expectance of her next orders. How strange these people were, chauffeurs, butlers and the like. When they were not saying "Yes, ma'am" and "No, sir," what were they really thinking about? Or better still, what were they thinking about when they were saying "Yes ma'am" and "No sir," no matter what you said to them? What lay behind the mask?

"Timothy, what are you going to do while I'm having lunch and swimming?"

"Just wait, Miss Cynthia."

She smiled a little mockingly. It was strange to be called "Miss Cynthia" by a tall, powerful young fellow whom you were thinking about in quite another way. She said, "Did you bring your bathing suit with you?"

"Yes, Miss Cynthia." The man unbent ever so little. "I always carry the suit in the car down here."

"Very clever of you, Timothy. Why don't you put it on now and join me on the beach? We can go swimming together."

The man's jaw dropped just a little. "We can—" He seemed incapable of finishing what he wanted to say, but she nodded briskly.

"Yes, that's it exactly. I'll give you just about two minutes to get undressed." She ran gayly down the road and out on to the sands while the man stood gaping after her with wondering eyes. He felt he didn't quite know what to make of a situation like this, but after a moment's pondering he realized there was nothing to do but obey, so he began to undress speedily. No other cars were in sight and they were at least a quarter of a mile from the nearest house which was invisible.

Timothy was rather proud of the figure he cut in his tight black bathing suit which set off the dark tan he had acquired by persistent sun bathing in the "bull pen" at Gus' Baths. Cynthia eyed him critically as one might an animal about to be purchased. There was a firm leanness about him which appealed to her and she held out her hand impulsively.

"Well, Tim, now for a good old-fashioned swim. By the way, I suppose you're a good swimmer."

The man's embarrassment was wearing off a little.

He took a deep breath and said, "I was life guard for two years."

The girl laughed. "Well, that ought to be some evidence, though I did once hear of a life guard who in an emergency wasn't able to swim a stroke. It seems he'd been hired for his good looks and nothing else. I'll bet you used to break a lot of hearts when you were a life guard, didn't you?"

The man grinned. His confidence in himself which was well known around the various garages was rapidly returning. "Well, maybe one or two, Miss Cynthia, but I was never asked to swim with such a beautiful young lady before."

"Not bad, Tim, but it would be a good deal more effective if you dropped the Miss in front of my name. Now we'd better have a little practice on that before we go into the water. Let me hear you just say, 'Cynthia,' as if we'd just met at Coney Island."

"Cynthia," he breathed obediently, and true to his instincts and training tried to catch her by the arm.

She leaped back lightly and dashed for the waves which were curling in emerald splendor on the sands. About ten feet away she swung round and faced him again, calling, "I'm not quite so easily caught as that, Tim." As he darted toward her she turned and plunged into the surf. With swift, vigorous strokes she swam straight away from the shore, breasting each high wave as it would seem to engulf her. She glanced around once and saw he was directly behind her, swimming a powerful American crawl which excited her admiration instantly. This was the sort of man who went after what he wanted, the sort of a man she had wished for, one who took her at her word instantly and plunged into the sea in swift pursuit.

A minute later he was beside her and had caught her

hand in his firm grip. His eyes were blazing triumphantly. "Now I got you. What's·the reward for catching the mermaid?"

She held her head high, treading water easily. "You are a very domineering young man, aren't you? If you're very good I'll let you have lunch with me in about five minutes. How will that do?"

He cupped his hand and with a swift stroke sent a shower of spray over her. "Is that all I get?"

"What more do you want out here in the middle of the ocean?" she mocked, and began swimming swiftly shoreward.

An hour later they lay side by side on the sand, shading their eyes from the brightness of the sun. She suddenly burst out laughing as she thought what people would say if they could see her now, lying on the sand with her chauffeur, thigh pressed against thigh after their delicious intimate luncheon. Even in this half-wild district they were within a mile or two of at least a dozen houses of her acquaintances where astonishment would reign supreme could anything so absurd have been imagined. She knew how these people looked on such things, and to them her affair with Sperry, even if he was a social climber, was quite understandable. But luncheon with a chauffeur on the beach, and in bathing suits would be utterly incomprehensible. She suddenly nudged him.

"Tim, what are you thinking about now?"

He sat up lithely and brushed his eyes with the back of his hand. "Sure 1 think I must have gone to Heaven, because things like this only happen up there."

She leaned back on her arms looking at him quizzically. "I suppose that's the regular thing you always say under the circumstances, but there is no reason I should expect any particular originality. Are you married, Tim? I suppose I ought to know all about it, seeing you've been driving me for a year or two, but I don't think I ever got a real good look at you until to-day. Now I want to know all about you,—everything there is to know."

He grinned a little sheepishly. "I usually lie when I'm down here, but I couldn't lie to you to-day after you've been so nice to me and all. I got a wife and two kids up in New York."

"How romantic! I don't think I ever realized you were quite human, and here all at once I find out that you are very nicely human, with a wife and two children. Is your wife's name Nora?"

"Yes. How did you know?"

"Timothy O'Flaherty! I just know that when any man has a name like yours he probably has a wife named Nora. It's one of those things that seem fated to be no matter what you try to do to stop it. You don't bring Nora and the two kids down here, do you?"

"Sure I couldn't afford to."

"Yes, I suppose there is something in that. It does cost something and at the same time it's nice to play bachelor for a few months, isn't it? How many sweethearts have you got down here this year, Tim?"

The man flushed. "Sure I don't have sweethearts like that, miss. It wouldn't be right at all."

"Oh, wouldn't it?" she mocked him with a lugubrious shake of her head. "I didn't know we had a kind of young saint driving for us. I dare say you carry the picture of your wife and children in your coat pocket all the time so you won't forget about them. Don't you ever have a good time? Don't you ever just go out and enjoy yourself and say, 'To hell with 'em, they're twelve hundred miles away, and what they don't know doesn't hurt any?'"

He squirmed restlessly in the sand and looked at her

with a puzzled expression. He couldn't quite understand the combination of what she was saying and the peculiar aloof way in which she was saying it, despite the fact that she felt no condescension was discernible in her tone. He finally blurted out, "I don't know what you mean."

She crawled over to him and ran her hand lightly along his brown muscled arm. He quivered at the touch of her delicate fingers and in his face there was a kind of hunted look, but she continued ruthlessly. "Are you sure you don't know what I mean, Tim O'Flaherty? Are you sure some girl who was pretty enough couldn't make you forget whether your wife's name was Nora or Evangeline for a little while?" She swung one of her legs over so it lay across his, and now because of their position her arm was about his body and her leg across his thigh. His flesh was warm and rough with hair, and against her skin she could feel the faint quiver of his muscles. She bent her head slowly down, down until her lips touched his like the kiss of thistledown in a light summer breeze.

For an instant they lay so, an instant in which there was no sound but the man's heavy breathing. Then he caught her in his arms fiercely, with passionate abandon, and swung her back so she lay on the sand with his body crushing hers. His lips were against hers, pressing her head down into the sand while his emboldened hands ran hotly over the soft contour of her form. For a moment they lay thus, drunk with ecstasy, and then he sat up swaying with the stress of emotion, and gasped, "I'm sorry."

The girl lay on her back with her brown eyes glowing up into his, her arms stretched flat on the sand in the luxury of her triumph. Her lips moved faintly to say, "Sorry?" There was a world of mockery in the word as she pronounced it. "How crude it is for you to say that, and yet I expected you to say it, I knew it was coming.

Now kiss me properly this time so that we can both laugh at the world and say, 'We're glad.' "

With a half cry he flung himself upon her body, his hungry lips pressing the velvet slimness of her throat, his eyes half closed in rapture. Her head was flung back so she could see into the interminable blueness of the sky spotted only by a single airplane high overhead. The sound of the motor was so faint it resembled the hum of a drowsy insect in the full silence of an August moon, something far away and almost a part of the dream world that lies beyond reality. On all the long stretch of beach no one to see her abandonment to the joys of the awakening of her heart which she had felt could never spring into rapture again. She murmured softly, "Tim, what's your wife's name now?"

But the man made no answer except to press his mouth hungrily against hers while his brown arms lifted her shoulders from the sand to make the embrace more perfect. She wanted to laugh aloud in her exultation, but what sound could her lips make when they were held prisoner to his ardor?

CHAPTER TWENTY-THREE

THE next two weeks Cynthia lived on a plane of mad ecstasy in which all normal rules of common sense living were flung aside, and she devoted herself whole-heartedly to the pleasures of the moment. Every morning she set out in her car for some trip, sitting boldly on the front seat with Timothy, her left arm casually draped over the back cushion. Her explanation was that she just wanted to ride and ride all the time and be by herself. The fact that this sounded rather ridiculous as the days went by did not disturb her in the least, nor did Jane Talbot's shrewd suggestion that if she wanted to be alone so much she could certainly drive herself in her own roadster. Jane was not a little piqued that Cynthia for the first time rejected her offers of company so unceremoniously.

"Must you always take Timothy with you?" Miss Talbot inquired cynically.

"Of course." The girl was at no pains to conceal her gayety. "I wouldn't have a good time at all if Timothy weren't along. He and I understand each other perfectly."

Jane half closed her eyes in a searching glance. "And just what am I supposed to deduce from that?"

"Anything you please. I make no attempt to control people's deductions. Possibly you might gather the idea that I prefer my chauffeur's company to any one else's— for the moment."

It was Miss Talbot's turn to laugh now. She added, "I wonder if, having made what one might call an intellectual mistake already this season, you aren't now making a physical one. Such things have been, you know."

"And always will be probably until the end of time. But if you knew Timothy as well as I do, you'd know he can't be called a physical mistake no matter what other name one might care to use. Have you any particular objections?"

The woman shrugged her bony shoulders and spread wide her long hands in a deprecating gesture. "Certainly not, my dear Cynthia. I did think you were foolish when you were throwing yourself at the head of a social climber whose only qualification was that he writes bad novels, or rather that his wife does. But outside of that,—well, it's none of my business, is it?"

"I don't mean to be rude, Jane, it's only because I'm so happy and always afraid some one may interfere with my happiness." The girl laid her hand on Miss Talbot's arm with an impulsive movement of contrition. Jane patted it gently then turned away slowly.

"This time I promise not to interfere with your happiness no matter how false I consider it. After all, 'Les affaires sont toujours les affaires.' "

Somehow Cynthia felt her conversation with Jane had done her good, possibly because it showed her that that determined woman was not likely to interfere with her momentary happiness, and also because she so cleverly drew the distinction between her devotion to Sperry and her happiness in the present love of the moment. She evidently dismissed Timothy as a mere affair of the passing moment, but such a misunderstanding did not anger Cynthia in the least. She had deliberately and calmly seduced Timothy from his position as an impeccable chauffeur into that of a lusty lover with no thoughts that there might be any permanency to the unstable relationship. But now, as the days went on and turned into weeks, she was more and more impressed with the simple manliness of this man who had been her paid servant for so long and whose good qualities she had never sensed. He was crude and rough, a little brutal perhaps, as last night, for example, when he had half torn her clothes from her body because she had pretended reluctance in order to tease him. There was a black and blue spot on her arm where he had seized her with his vise-like grip and held her firm against all resistance while he fairly devoured her kisses. But all that was nothing beside the real nature of the man which she was sure she could sense underneath. He ate sloppily with his fingers, gulping his food down with half-savage, wolfish noises, but she didn't care. His speech was crude and his gestures as well, and they became cruder and more primitive as the days went on and his early fear of her and the social position which she represented dropped from him. But she considered each step as a rising above stupid social subservience and she thrilled to his crudity especially when he broke into a long string of profane oaths in telling her about something which annoyed him. Day by day he became less the perfect servant and more the man, the real, lustful he-man of her desire. In the face of that satisfaction how little the sly comments of people mattered.

And now, even as she was sure Jane would not interfere with her, so also it was impossible for Thor Bronson to do so, since he had returned to Palm Beach only to set out immediately for Havana, taking Olive Smith with him. There was no one now to interfere with her doing exactly as she pleased. Her mother's indifference was a thing to be counted upon and as a test of it she told her that she was going to drive up with Timothy in the car when they were planning their trip north late in March. She did it deliberately when Jane was in the room on one of those rare occasions when the three of them were alone together.

"Mother, I think the ride up will do me good and I am
1 no hurry to get back to New York, anyway. I haven't
thing in the world to hurry back for."

Mrs. Bronson stifled a delicate yawn. "Well, I suppose
is a bit unconventional for you to drive back with just a
hauffeur, but I dare say Timothy is a good boy and will
ake care of you in any emergency. Don't you think so,
ane?"

Miss Talbot laughed her strange raucous outburst with
hich Aurelia Bronson was so familiar that she ignored
s probable significance at that moment. "Why do you ask
ie anything like that, Aurelia? I should think Cynthia
as the best judge of what she wanted to do herself."

"That's exactly what I say. Just the other day Mrs.
mithson was trying to tell me some silly idea about why
id I let Cynthia drive around all the time and why was
he never home. I said, 'My dear Mrs. Smithson, I'm sure
ynthia is very well able to take care of herself.' And that
as all there was to that. I might have gone further had
cared to do so and said that Cynthia seems to be very
apidly growing into a complete woman of the world and
f she makes any mistakes in judgment she knows how to
ectify the matter perfectly."

Cynthia laughed cynically. "Thanks ever so much,
10ther, I didn't know you were quite so clever in defend-
ng me against stupid gossips like Mrs. Smithson. I dare
ay if I were flat-chested, bow-legged and had buck teeth
ike her daughter, I'd be a very model of circumspect pro-
riety. But inasmuch as I am only as God made me I
uppose I can't help matters. As to my mistakes, as you call
hem, which do you mean, Dale, or Dick, or both?"

Her mother waved a magnificently manicured hand.
'My dear Cynthia, I would certainly not be so vulgar as to
efer specifically to anything you may or may not have

done, in front of a woman like Mrs. Smithson. Her father actually made his money in a brewery."

Jane Talbot snorted. "And I suppose that accounts for Mrs. Smithson being so full of gas most of the time." Mrs. Bronson looked up a little in bewilderment.

"Is that supposed to be funny, Jane?"

"Dear, dear, no. Nothing that has any relationship to beer is considered to be funny these days."

A moment later the girl ran out of the room and back to the garage to tell Timothy she had been successful in her arrangements. He was wearing dungaree pants and an undershirt and was busily engaged in washing the car which they always used. He grinned at her when she told him everything was all right.

"Okay, kid, what it takes to fix things up you sure got it." He winked at her. "Say, how do you manage to get this car so dirty every night? Boy, you must have a lousy chauffeur who doesn't know how to take care of it at all. It looks like Hell."

She went closer to him and brushed her cheek tenderly against his brown bare arm, looking at him with glowing eyes. "Yes, he's what you call him, 'a lousy chauffeur,' but I think he's the best lover in the world, so I'm afraid I won't need any one else, at least for the present."

He lowered his voice a little. "Hey, don't talk like that out here. Morgan's liable to be back any minute now, and he's gettin' too damn nosy as it is. This morning he wanted to know where I drove you every day, and I told him to go to Hell and try to find out."

She made a laughing face at him and leaned against the car. "You just go around spoiling for a fight, don't you?"

"No, it ain't that, but that Morgan's too God-damn fresh. I'm gonna smash his puss for him yet."

Cynthia laughed gayly. This was the mood in which the

nan pleased her most, when he was an unadulterated man
f the people, ready to settle all discussions and arguments
vith his fists. "Well, I hope you let me know when the
ight comes off because I'd like to see just how good a
attler you are. You know you talk a great deal about it,"
he added mockingly.

Tim fairly bristled at her words and she had somehow
ludicrous impression of a dog scenting a rousing fight.
'Yeah, so you think I shoot my mouth off too much, don't
rou?" His eyes were blazing.

She thrilled to the sheer physical virility of his sudden
inger, and taking a step forward, caught his slightly
lushed face caressingly between both her hands. "What
ι man you are, Tim. I've never known any one in the least
ike you. As for shooting your mouth off too much, as you
:all it, I think mouths were just made for kissing, and
hat's all. Now give me a real kiss to show me you're not
ingry because I tried to tease you."

He bent over and kissed her swiftly then stood away
igain, his hands still clutching the sponge and chamois.
She pouted her lips at him.

"Is that what you call a real kiss?"

"Sure. Didn't I tell you Morgan was gonna be back any
ninute now? You gotta be a little careful, ain't you?"

"Careful?" She laughed loudly. "I just feel I want to
shout from the housetops and never be careful about any-
:hing else in the world. Don't you feel that way?"

"Shhhh! There comes Morgan now. What'll he think?"

"Morgan think?" The girl was frankly incredulous.
'Don't flatter Morgan. He hasn't had a thought since the
World War, and even then he thought he was fighting to
make the world safe for Democracy." She turned swiftly
toward the door as a short, heavy-set chauffeur entered.
"Hello, Morgan. Are you going to be busy this morning?"

The man was of the type whose deference is extreme, at least in public, no matter what he might say about his employers when he was sure of not being overheard. "No, Miss, I won't be very busy. Is there anything I can do for you?"

"Yes, you can take me shopping over in West Palm Beach right away. Will that be too much trouble?" She smiled at him in her most captivating manner.

The man squared his beefy shoulders and said rather eagerly, "No trouble at all, Miss. My car's in the driveway now all ready to go."

"Thank you so much, Morgan, you're a great help. Here I expected Timothy to be all ready to go and you see he hasn't even washed the car yet." She winked lovingly at Tim in a way which the other man could not see and then tripped demurely out of the garage. Her chauffeur stood for a moment looking after her with wide open eyes. Timothy O'Flaherty was of that large class of people who are utterly dumfounded by any show of cleverness and diplomacy. He had never seen Morgan quite so humble and oily before. Maybe he wouldn't have to fight with him now after all, seeing he was starting to drive North in two days. He rather regretted the lack of opportunity, but he did manage to realize that this was no time for him to embroil himself in garage squabbles.

So there was no display of fisticuffs before Cynthia's departure for New York two days later. She sat demurely in the back of the car with the luggage piled alongside of Timothy on the front seat, and she smiled as she thought how short a time such a formal arrangement was going to last. They would drive up to New York slowly, taking four or five days, and she would be able to sit beside him with her arm about his neck during all the long hours of travel, even as she would lie beside him at night, defying all the stupidities of the social code which would try so valiantly to keep them apart merely because her mother paid Tim a salary. She knew that he had another suit with him, a regular civilian's suit which bore no marks of his service or occupation, which he would put on as soon as they were out of town. Then there would be nothing to proclaim to the world that they were not other than she would pretend to be, a young bride and groom driving back to New York after an ardent honeymoon. Her mother and Jane, with the prince in tow, were leaving the same night by train and of course would be there days ahead.

For a moment she sat and wondered as to just how much the prince knew of what she was doing. She had not seen very much of him lately because of the long drives which had occupied so much of her time, and because he had been away for two or three weeks on a yachting cruise. But whenever they were together he was as deferential and ceremonious as ever, in no wise changed from the man whom she had always respected and admired since her childhood.

Meanwhile what of Timothy sitting rigidly in the chauffeur's seat, driving the big high-powered car with his customary care and precision? Now that he was actually on the road to New York he couldn't help thinking a little more than he had of late about his wife and two children. He suddenly realized how much he wanted to see them all again, how anxious he was to sit in his big Morris chair with one of his boys on each knee and feel their chubby fingers on his cheeks. He was anxious to see Nora, to have her retail the neighborhood gossip in her loud, happy voice while he sat eating some of her good Irish cooking, dressed only in his pants and undershirt with his shoes kicked off under the table. Working as a chauffeur he didn't get so much chance to get tired of his family circle

as some men did. Only last night he had made up sufficiently with Morgan so they had each shown the other
snapshots of their family groups.

As the car ran swiftly over the smooth roads his mind
was increasingly absorbed with thoughts of Nora and the
kids so that he was almost startled when he felt Cynthia's
hand caressingly on the back of his neck and heard her
voice in his ear. He slowed down mechanically at the side
of the road.

"Well, Tim, old boy, here we are on the 'love tour' to
New York. You'd better drive up the first little side road
you come to and that'll give you a chance to put on the
other suit and move the luggage into the back of the car."
She brushed her cheek lovingly against the back of his
sleek head. "Oh, it has seemed such a long time waiting
until we could really be together like this. Five, six, maybe
seven days, to just laugh at the world and live completely
in our love for each other. Tell me how glad you are. I
want to hear you say it."

He still sat with his hands on the wheel staring straight
ahead of him and the feeling of her arms about his neck
from the back of the car was like a touch from another
world. He finally managed to say the one word, "What?"

"What?" Cynthia thought she could not believe her ears.
She had been looking forward to this first stop as soon as
they were out of town so that he could crush her again
with his crude, mauling embraces that were so much like
the hug of a bear. She had been waiting for his passionate
wet kisses on her mouth, and eyes, and throat, and the
strange little way he had of groaning faintly when he
kissed her breasts and his face was almost buried in the
softness of her body. She found herself trembling a little
as she began to talk quickly.

"How terrible you are! Here I've been telling you of my

love and yearning for you, and all the while you've been staring ahead of you without listening to a word I was saying. For weeks now I've been looking forward, almost hopelessly, to a time like this when for a few days we could be alone together with just our love surrounding us, away from the conventions and mockeries of the whole world. I've been yearning to sit beside you all day with my arm about your neck, and to lie with you all night absorbed in your alternate passion and drowsy tenderness." She paused for a moment wistfully. "Now you don't even hear what I'm saying to you. I don't think you even understand what I'm telling you. You should be thinking of me and nothing else but me at a time like this; instead, you act as if your mind was a thousand miles away. What are you thinking about?"

"I'm thinking about Nora and the two kids," he said simply.

She stared at him in amazement. "Thinking about your wife and family! Oh, Tim, what a fool you are. What do they matter now that I'm with you? What does anything in the world matter, now?"

He shook his head doggedly. "They'll always matter. They're my wife and kids, and I can't forget about 'em, especially when I'm going home to them. Just think, I ain't seen the youngsters for four months, pretty near, an' every time I come back and see them again they seem to be so much bigger and huskier than they were when I went away. Gee, I bet you'll like my kids, too."

For a moment Cynthia sat back in the car dully trying to comprehend the mad things this man was saying to her. Then she climbed out and stood on the road, still without speaking. It was a quiet road lined on each side with scrub palmetto, one of those rather lonely roads which are so usual in Florida once one has turned off the main highway.

There seemed to be something brooding and sinister in the deathlike stillness which hung over the flat uninteresting land, and the heat of the early afternoon seemed to settle down crushingly, breathlessly. With a tremendous effort she swung round and laid her hand on the door of the car.

"Are you going to change your clothes, Tim?" Her voice was very quiet and the words fell from her tight lips in dull, measured cadence.

"Sure." She smiled a little because it was his usual word, but it was not spoken in his usual almost truculent way. She watched him climb out of the car and pull out a small suitcase which he opened on the running board. He took out a light gray suit and stood holding it in his hands as if doubtful just what to do or just how to effect the necessary change. She watched him with a mocking twist to her lip, but in her heart there was a new heaviness which no mockery could lighten.

"Are you waiting for me to walk up the road or look the other way while you change?"

He looked at her a moment steadily, then dropped the clothes in a little heap and caught her in his arms almost savagely. "What do you want to torture me for? Can I help it if I think about the kids when I start out for home? They're my family, ain't they? What am I gonna do about it?"

She wound her arms about his neck and clung to him. He squeezed her tighter and pressed his lips crushingly, brutally, upon her upturned mouth. For a full minute they clung to each other in the full abandonment of emotion and then quite suddenly stood back looking hungrily into each other's eyes.

"What am I gonna do?" He repeated the question haltingly, helplessly now like a man in a daze.

She flung back her head and her glorious laughter rip-

pled out in a stream of silver tone. "Do?" The word
fairly gurgled into laughter as she pronounced it. "Why
you're going to change your clothes, of course, and you'd
better hurry or we'll never make St. Augustine by dark,
or even Daytona for that matter." She caught the lapels of
his uniform jacket and ripped it open. "Throw it away,"
she laughed. "Throw away the cap, the puttees, the
breeches, all of the stupid uniform, and let me see if you
can forget you ever wore them."

CHAPTER TWENTY-FOUR

TIMOTHY sat in his big easy chair reading a newspaper. He was wearing an old pair of khaki trousers and an undershirt but had discarded his outside shirt in the interest of what he considered complete home comfort. His bare feet were stretched out before him quite innocent of shoes or socks, and an old pipe was clenched in his teeth. Timothy was back home again, back in the bosom of his family and very glad indeed he was there. The reading of the paper was really only a desultory method of distracting his mind from thinking too much about how glad he was to be home. Everything here was peace, and contentment, and quiet. It was the sort of life he really wanted to lead, the leisure to which he looked forward every day after the day's work was done. A little while before he had had what he considered a real man's meal, a big bowl of Irish stew with all kinds of vegetables in it, and afterward two big pieces of home-made apple pie covered with whipped cream, and two big cups of coffee, not the silly little things that they served you in hotels and restaurants. Nora and the two boys had joked about the size of the cup as they put it on the table and he had caught all three of them together and kissed them rather indiscriminately in his happiness at once more indulging in such foolish laughter. To be teased about his big cup of coffee and about how much pie he could eat meant being really home.

He dropped his paper on the floor, and leaning his head back against the cushion, closed his eyes in meditation. How different this was from the five days spent on the

trip north with Cynthia. He had only been home for three
days now, yet already that trip was assuming the propor-
tions of a nightmare. There was no use trying to deny
that he had lived on a plane of ecstatic passion, but now
that he had a chance to think it over quietly he realized he
had not been happy. Happiness was something quite other
than that mad delirium of sex, at least for him. Last night
he had awakened long before dawn and lain wide-eyed in
bed for an hour. In the darkness of the room he had
imagined he saw Cynthia with her wild, passionate eyes
and voluptuous body, holding her arms out to him, enticing
him out of himself. The agony had continued for so long
he had felt it would never end and if he dared to close his
eyes he could feel her arms about his neck, her delicate
hands running lightly over his body, her lips warm and
moist leading him on to madness. And all the while his
wife had lain calmly beside him, her regular breathing
indicating the quiet placidity of her slumbers. Finally he
had not been able to stand it any more and he had seized
Nora in his arms holding her close to him. It was in no
sense a lover's embrace but the desperate clutch of fear
with which a child clings to its mother when awakened by
some midnight terror.

Nora had only rolled over sleepily, muttering, "Now,
Tim, behave yourself." No more than that and yet the
crude simplicity of the phrase bore the mark of security
of accustomed things. A few minutes later he had fallen
into a deep, troubled sleep. That was all, and yet it was
enough. It mustn't happen again to-night. He couldn't bear
the thought of it.

At this point in his meditations there was a loud ring of
the door bell which was so startling in its suddenness that
he jumped to his feet. He wondered who it could be and
was sorry that Nora had taken the two children with her

to the movies even though she had done so at his expressed request. He had wanted a chance to think things over quietly, though of course he had not been able to tell Nora that, and had merely said that there was a good picture, one which he would like to see himself if he were not so tired after a long day's work. After the years of their marriage he knew there were certain things he could not tell Nora without a great deal of explanation. She would never have comprehended the idea that he wanted to sit home quietly and think, but to her it was quite sensible that he should want to stay home, read his paper, and smoke his pipe. Sometimes he regretted her simplicity of mind, but to-night he was grateful for it.

While he stood and tried to collect his thoughts the door bell rang louder and more persistently than before. With a muttered exclamation he walked across the room and into the little hall. Just as the bell started to ring again for the third time he pulled open the door and then stood back in open-mouthed astonishment. Of all the people in the world he least expected to see Cynthia in the flesh at that moment.

"Well, Tim, why are you gaping at me so? You'd think I was a ghost. Aren't you even going to ask me to come in?"

He stood aside without a word and she passed through the little hall into the living room. Mechanically he closed the door into the outer hall and followed her. For a moment the two stood looking at each other and he flushed a little as he realized she was slowly scrutinizing every detail of his costume, his bare feet—his stained khaki trousers and sleeveless undershirt. He still held his old blackened pipe clutched in one hand.

"You certainly look very comfortable here, Tim." Cynthia's tone was most matter of fact but he gave no answering smile. He shuffled a little on his naked feet.

"Nora took the kids to the movies. She ain't home."

"So much the better," the girl exclaimed, "then I won't have to go through any grotesque mockery of social politeness." With her characteristic gesture she snatched off her hat and flung it on the table. "Aren't you going to ask me to sit down?"

"No, I don't want you to stay. Nora may be home any minute, or maybe one of the neighbors'll drop in."

Cynthia looked around the room carefully and then sat down in the big chair the man had vacated. "Thanks so much for your cordiality, Tim. And now that I am comfortably seated may I know just why you don't want me to stay because your Nora may come home or some neighbor may come visiting? Are you classifying me as a skunk, or what? You sound exactly like mother when she rides her social high horse the hardest. I hadn't realized that Mrs. Nora O'Flaherty was so very exclusive."

Timothy knocked out his pipe in a bowl which was always kept on the table for that purpose and then faced his guest stolidly. "It ain't because of Nora at all, but because you shouldn't be here. It ain't right you should come to see your chauffeur, especially when I'm dressed like this and my wife ain't home."

Cynthia waved her hand flippantly. "Dear me, dear me, what a stickler for etiquette you have become. You haven't perchance forgotten that night in the hotel at Richmond? What a mad boy you really are when you forget your job, and your dignity, and your Nora, and all the rest of it. Do you remember how we bathed in that funny big old-fashioned bathtub together and anointed each other with bottles of Coca-Cola? How perfectly stupid it was and how glorious at the same time because you were just a big boy able to play whole-heartedly and see life as the merry gamble it really is."

"I'm sorry I acted like that. I wish you'd forget about it."

She laughed loudly. "How funny you are to ask me to forget one of my most precious memories. I'd rather forget almost anything in the world. That's why I had to come here to-night, because I couldn't get you out of my mind, because I had to see what your home life was really like and how you and Nora got along together."

"Leave Nora out of it," he growled truculently.

"I don't see how we can leave Nora out of it, especially since you are the one who insists on bringing her into it. Even when we were in bed you used to insist on turning on the lights and showing me pictures of your 'two kids,' as you called them. I feel I know your family so well that I'd recognize them sitting in the bleachers of a World Series baseball game. I should think you'd be anxious to have me meet Nora so we could be friends."

"Well, I'm not. I don't want you to meet nobody. It wouldn't do no good for you to come here and mix up in my life."

"Why Timothy, I can't quite make up my mind whether you're being philosophic or just deliberately rude. But you see I'm so crazy about you I'm ready to forgive you everything." She arose languorously from her chair and crossed to him, walking on the tips of her toes. Her hands were on his shoulders an instant later and she was looking deeply into his eyes. "When will Nora be home?"

He stood with his head slightly lowered and his hands limply at his sides. "I don't know exactly, a coupla hours, I guess."

"Then you have time to show me how much you love me, to show me you haven't forgotten our glorious trip together. Oh Tim, don't you realize it's three whole long days since I felt your hands and arms crushing me and your lips pressed on my heart?" She laughed shortly. "Three days, but it seems like three years, three eternities. You see I simply couldn't keep away from you. I have to have you now that I've learned what you're really like."

For a moment the man continued to stand stolidly without speaking, though Cynthia could feel the nervous movement of the muscles of his arms and knew he was holding himself rigid as if in actual physical resistance. Finally he shook his head slowly from side to side, muttering, "No! No! This craziness has got to stop. I'm home now and I can't be a damn' fool any more."

With a soft, caressing movement she drew her body against his and wrapped her arms closely about his bare neck. There were tiny beads of perspiration on his forehead and suddenly he raised his hand to brush them away and smooth his sleek black hair.

"Tim!" There was an ecstasy of passion in the short word as she pronounced it, her body clinging to his, her lips yearning toward him. Then suddenly his arms shot about her and a moment later he had bent her body back in his powerful grasp and was showering her upturned face with wild kisses.

She laughed in reckless abandon as she clung to him, her heart thrilling to the triumph over his domestic feelings which she had so much feared. But even as she did so the doorbell rang violently, peal after peal in rapid succession, and there was a brisk rattling of the knob. He loosened his grasp and sprang back with startled eyes.

"What is it?" Cynthia whispered.

"I don't know." The man was visibly shaking.

"Is it Nora?"

"No. She has a key." He spoke very softly and his voice trembled a little.

The rattling and ringing began anew, now with increased violence, and after a normal space there was a heavy pounding on the door. The girl shook herself as if waking from a bad dream and then turned resolutely. "Tim, you've got to go to the door and see who it is. What are you afraid of ?"

With halting steps the man crossed the room and the little entrance hall while Cynthia leaned heavily against the table in the center of the room. She watched him with fascinated eyes as he pulled himself together and then suddenly flung the door wide open. An exclamation burst from her lips as she saw who the impatient visitor was.

Mrs. Bronson fairly bounced into the room and almost flung herself physically at her daughter, her eyes blazing in unaccustomed wrath. The girl sprang back a step from the astonishing apparition, exclaiming, "Mother, what's the matter ?"

"Where's Mrs. O'Flaherty?"

Receiving no answer from the girl who continued to stare at her in bewilderment she turned around to face Timothy who had shuffled after her into the room. "Where's your wife?"

"Gone to the movies." The man's voice was barely audible and the meaning of his words was almost lost in the woman's angry snort which followed immediately.

"I thought so. And while she was gone you have so far forgotten yourself as to take advantage of my unfortunate daughter's sex-madness. You, my chauffeur, have actually seduced my daughter because she is unable to control her impulses."

Before the man could speak Cynthia sprang forward

with a cry. "Mother, you're crazy! How dare you talk like that?"

"I dare talk any way I please now that I understand exactly what my position is. I was quite willing to blind myself to your affairs with Dale Eustis, and then with Dick Sperry, and even with Prince Ladislov. But when it comes to your becoming the mistress of my chauffeur it's time to put a stop to everything. I've been suspicious of you ever since you came home from that automobile trip. I've had your whole trip investigated by detectives and at last I know exactly how mad you are." She stretched out one hand in a feeble gesture which failed to express anything more than a rather pathetic futility. "Cynthia, oh Cynthia, how could you do such a horrible thing? How could you go night after night to hotels with such a man, your chauffeur, a mere paid servant?"

The girl faced her squarely. "I love Tim, and that's all there is to it, so you'd better make up your mind to it. There's nothing you can do to prevent me from having the man I love, or any number of men if I want them. I'm a normal, healthy, full-blooded woman, praise God, and I intend to live and practice the fullness of my normalcy. All my childhood, all my early days were crushed by your neglect, your lack of understanding, your abnormality. Now I'm going to live as I see fit and with no interference from you or any one else. You feel you're very clever because you followed me here to-night, but now that you are here what are you going to do to stop matters?"

Mrs. Bronson looked sadly at her enraged child. "I've expected very little from you during all the years of your life but I had supposed that by the mere matter of birth you had acquired a certain semblance of decency, a certain sense of proportion. I've asked nothing more than that of you heretofore, and I shall ask nothing more in the future, but so much I do insist on. I will not have you carrying on an affair under my very nose with my chauffeur. As to what I can do to stop it, that's very simple. To begin with I'll wait until Mrs. O'Flaherty comes home and have a talk with her."

For the first time the man started forward and cried in an agonized voice, "Oh, you couldn't do that, you really couldn't do that."

Mrs. Bronson faced him haughtily. "And pray why not? I usually do exactly what I feel to be necessary. If I can't appeal to my daughter's sense of honesty and decency I must appeal to your wife to exercise some sort of command over you." She paused a minute and then went on in a lower but still more biting manner. "How dared you take advantage of my easy-going ways to seduce my child? You poor miserable fool, what did you hope to profit by that? Has your brain been turned by stupid newspapers to some mad belief that I would give you money to bring you to your senses?"

The man stood with bowed head as he muttered his new appeal. "Please, Mrs. Bronson, please don't tell Nora. She wouldn't understand at all."

"Tim!" The young girl's voice rang out like the snap of a whip but he had no eyes for her now, his whole attention being centered on Mrs. Bronson who stood icily facing him.

"To begin with I certainly shall stay to see your wife, and of course you are discharged. And I'll give you no reference."

"No! No!" the man cried. "You've gotta give me a reference. I can't get a job without a reference—not these days. I gotta wife and two kids to support." Somehow his bare feet made his appeal ludicrous.

"You should have thought of that before you started

amusing yourself with Cynthia or letting her amuse herself with you, which is most likely what happened."

With an angry cry the girl pushed between her mother
and the chauffeur and caught him by the arm-hole of his
undershirt. Her face was blazing with anger. "Tim, are
you going to stand there like a fool and let her talk to you
like that? You always told me what a fighter you were and
now is your chance to prove it. Tell her to get to Hell out
of here before you kick her out, and I mean *kick her out*
in the exact sense of the word." She paused gasping for
breath and then continued a little more quietly: "Tim,
listen to me, listen to what I'm telling you. Just throw her
out, physically, if necessary, out into the street. Then we
can go away and be happy together forever. Then I'll
know you're a real man, the kind of a man I need, the kind
my heart cries out for. Don't you realize she's standing
here insulting you because you happen to be her chauffeur?
Because she happens to pay you a salary she feels entitled
to drag your very manhood through the mud. Don't you
realize that she and all her kind are like that? What does
her job, or her references, or anything else she has, matter
if you have me? Let her stay here to tell Nora what she
pleases, especially to tell her that you and I have gone
away together to find real happiness."

For a moment the man stood watching her with dull eyes
and then brushed her aside abruptly, callously. In her
astonishment her grasp on his undershirt relaxed. She
couldn't believe it possible that with a single movement of
his arm he was thrusting her and her love aside as a thing
of no consequence. She stood astounded as he began to
plead with her mother. It seemed incredible, but his hands
were trembling.

"Don't listen to her at all, Mrs. Bronson. Please listen
to me. I'm so sorry anything happened to make you feel

bad. I know I done wrong, but I couldn't help myself, believe me I couldn't. I'll do anything in the world for you if only you won't discharge me and won't tell Nora. I've got my two little kiddies to feed and I wouldn't be able to keep them alive if I lost the job now. There wouldn't be any place for me to go, nothing to do but beg on the streets. And I love Nora, too. We've been so happy together up to now and if she finds out what I been doin' it'll break her heart. Please, please don't tell her. I'm askin' for her sake. I'll do anything to make it up to you."

Mrs. Bronson's face lit up with triumph but before she could speak Cynthia stepped forward and caught Tim by the arm, pulling him around roughly to face her. "You poor miserable worm! Why did I ever think I could care for a man like you? Take your pants off and throw them away because you're a disgrace to them. Oh God, how utterly sick I am of miserable creatures like you, with no force of will, no force of character, nothing to carry them through life but a kind of cringing fear of death which makes them afraid to live completely. You live in a filthy little flat here and you plead for it as if it were the palace of an emperor. You plead to keep your job, only a rotten servant's job at that, just so you can have a stupid woman to cook for you and a place to sit around in your bare feet and smoke a stinking pipe. That's all life means to you, that and nothing more than that. And I, poor fool, thought you were the kind of a man with whom one might climb the very stars to find happiness. Go ahead, crawl on your knees to mother, lick her feet for her. She'll like it, and you'll probably revel in it. She was clever enough to see you for what you really are, a servant with the soul of a servant, good for nothing but to be a servant."

With a choking sob she flung herself out of the room and out of the apartment. Mrs. Bronson watched her go with heightened color and took a deep breath once the door had slammed loudly. But the chauffeur had no eyes for the retreating figure. His gaze was centered on the woman who gave him his weekly checks, who paid for the little home for which he was fighting. He clasped his shaking hands tightly together and spoke piteously, "Please say you won't discharge me, you won't tell Nora."

Mrs. Bronson looked him slowly over from head to foot and her lip curled in a sarcastic smile. "You *are* a poor fool, aren't you? Now that Cynthia's through with you do you suppose I care a bit about you, or Nora, or anything connected with you? If you want to come to work as usual, come ahead. What do I care one way or the other? I need some one to drive a car and now that Cynthia is safe it might just as well be you as any one else."

She started for the door which he ran to open for her obsequiously. There was a choke in his voice as he cried, "God bless you for being so kind." But the woman only laughed lightly as she passed out of the door. To her his feelings of gratitude or hate, likes or dislikes were equally unimportant. She had accomplished what she set out to do and nothing else mattered. She would drive around to Jane's at once and let her know everything had been straightened out. It was rather annoying to think that Jane hadn't told her about this affair or given her any warning concerning it. Perhaps that was why it was so good now to be on the way to see Jane, to tell her she had discovered it herself and within a few hours put a stop to it once and for all. She laughed short. How stupid all men looked in their bare feet.

CHAPTER TWENTY-FIVE

CYNTHIA and May-May sat side by side at one of the little wicker tables of the Veranda Café. Other people sat near them laughing and joking and a large crowd swirled about here and there through the great social rooms and along the scrubbed decks, for a late April sailing of a ship like the *Majestic* is always a gala occasion. Several acquaintances of Cynthia had greeted her gaily and rushed over to shake hands, but she had been indifferent in her reception of them, and having assured them that she was not sailing they had sensed she wished to talk to this quiet gray-haired woman and so had run away in search of more livening company and the probability of a cheering drink. Now the girl sat in a corner to be sheltered as far as possible from such casual contacts. She did indeed want to talk seriously to May-May before the ship sailed and the first whistle had already blown.

"I feel rather sad about your going away like this, May-May. I know I haven't been very kind or attentive to you for several months now because I've been so distracted by my own affairs, blown about here and there like a dried autumn leaf. That's over now and I know I'll miss you. Above all I think you were one of the few real anchors I had to tie me down, to keep me from losing my head entirely. Even if I saw little or nothing of you I could always feel that you were there ready to help me if I called on you. I mean it, mixed metaphors and all."

May-May's face flushed with pleasure. "That's awfully nice of you, Cynthia, and I can't tell you how much I appreciate it. I feel as if I had completely failed to do any good in the way I intended when I came here, and it only makes it worse to be showered with gifts by you and your mother. Here I am going back on the *Majestic* with a private bath and all kinds of luxuries which I'm not used to, to say nothing of the check your mother gave me which was so large that I was almost frightened when I looked at it. Far from just being able to live the rest of my life quietly I should be able to live in absolute luxury now, if I should be so foolish as to want to."

The girl put her hand earnestly over Miss Downer's lying near her on the small table. "May-May, never feel for a second that you have failed in your mission here because you've succeeded gloriously." She paused a moment, then went on more slowly. "I sometimes wonder if you haven't succeeded almost too well; if in order to save me from Charybdis you haven't succeeded in handing me over to Scylla." She looked up at her former governess with a faint smile. "You've been very loyal to mother and all that, but I do know she sent for you and why she sent for you. The full realization of that has only come in the last few days, since I've been able to view mother in a different light than ever before. Do you know anything about my playing the fool with Timothy?"

Miss Downer flushed painfully. "Yes," she said in a small voice.

Cynthia laughed lightly. "I thought so. When that happened a couple of weeks ago I thought I'd never be able to even look at mother again as long as I lived, but even a few quiet hours alone showed me what a fool I was. Mother rose to the occasion superbly and because I had never believed it possible I behaved like a little beast. There's no other word with which to express it. I was running around in circles like a sex-crazed dog. Do you remember how wildly I talked to you that night after our walk through the park? Well, I've been living just the way I talked then, and now suddenly the whole thing seems so very stupid, so completely worthless."

May-May patted her hand gently. "My dear little girl, I always knew everything would come out all right."

Cynthia looked at her quizzically. "How I envy you your optimism, May-May, and your sense of duty which I used to find laughable. I used to think Duty was such a stern god to kneel to, but Pleasure is still sterner because he is only a chimera, never to be firmly grasped by his suppliants. Oh, but I'm so terribly lonely now that I have nothing to turn to."

"Then why not come to England with me?"

For a moment Cynthia sat up with a happy startled look and then slouched down on her chair again. "No, May-May, that would never do." She shook her head sadly. "If I'm to find happiness I've got to find it here because I'm a stubborn little fool at heart and I insist on believing it is here and I shall find it. If I lose that hope I think I'd be willing to jump over the side of the boat right now and be lost. It wouldn't matter, then. In England I'd only make you miserable without helping myself at all."

For a moment there was a strained silence which seemed to hang like a cloud over the two women, then Miss Downer leaned forward and almost whispered, "What about Dale Eustis? Where is he?"

The girl laughed bitterly. "It's rather funny you should bring that up. Don't you realize Dale Eustis is the man who started me on my downward path, if you want to call it that?"

Miss Downer shook her head slowly from side to side. "No, Cynthia, you're absolutely wrong. I don't know about these other men who have come into your life. You must remember that down in Palm Beach even though I was living in the same house with you I wasn't part of your life as I was in New York, but I was near enough to see certain things even there, to see that these men didn't matter. Dale Eustis did matter. You really loved him. I think you love him now."

The girl took so long in speaking that Miss Downer began to fear she was not going to say anything more on the subject, but like a wise woman she kept very quiet, waiting, hoping for a reply to her statement which was almost a leading question. At length Cynthia raised her eyes from the deck and looked at her squarely.

"I don't know, May-May, I really don't know. I used to think I hated Dale Eustis more than any man on earth. Now I know I don't hate him at all. That's rather funny, isn't it? But there's no use in my trying to be a logical person, for I'm not, and in my heart I dare say I'm rather glad I'm not. Since I've come down to earth and decided to be sensible these last few weeks I can't help thinking about Dale."

But she got no farther in the analysis of her thought. The final blast of the whistle trembled through the air and she realized she must run or she would be taken out to sea. She held out her hand warmly.

"May-May, you've been a darling to come all the way over here to help me out. I'll never forget it."

Miss Downer walked swiftly with her to the head of the gang-way. "Try to come to see me in England, as soon as you can."

"Oh, I will, I will," the girl cried. "If I ever find my happiness I'll have to rush over to tell you all about it," and she ran gayly down the long covered gang-way.

A few minutes later she stood on the end of the pier, a part of the large throng waving handkerchiefs and shouting good-by. May-May was gone, and she felt she had lost the one person to whom she could always turn. For a moment she feared the tears were going to well up in her eyes but with an effort she controlled her emotions, shouting, "Good-by, May-May, good-by." She still stood waving her handkerchief as the tugs straightened out the giant liner in mid-stream and it moved slowly down the river, flags flying and music playing triumphantly. May-May was gone.

She walked slowly the long length of the pier and found her car waiting outside. As she lay back on the cushions being driven uptown she thought for a moment of Timothy. This new chauffeur of hers was just a man who drove an engine and she wondered how she could ever have conceived of Timothy as anything else. In a way this new man did not look like him and at the same time there was something about him which was strangely familiar The clothes, the gestures, the mannerisms, the speech were identical, outward manifestations of the genus chauffeur to which they both so patently belonged. This one was short and blond and of German descent. Timothy was tall and dark and of Irish descent. There was no other difference.

Her mother had not discharged her erstwhile lover as she had rather suspected she wouldn't. Instead she had given him a handsome present to pay expenses and gotten him a job driving for a woman in Chicago. That was almost a thousand miles away and according to Mrs. Bronson far enough to mitigate any danger of a recurrence of her daughter's foolishness. Those were almost the exact words that she had used in telling Jane about it and of course Jane had retailed them to her with great gusto. The girl sighed. "Poor mother, she doesn't quite realize that if I were alone with Timothy on a desert island he would have no more attraction for me than a cocoanut tree. Indeed, far less, because cocoanut trees are not only beautiful but useful as well."

When she arrived home she found Greenleaf, the old family butler, waiting for her in the hall. She looked up at him in surprise. "Greenleaf, I'm sure you have something to tell me, it's just written all over you."

The man bowed calmly but there was a little light in his tired eyes which indicated her perspicacity was not lost on him. "Yes, miss, I have several messages. While you were at the steamer your mother suddenly decided to go to Philadelphia. She left a message for you to have a good time while she was gone."

The girl grinned. "Very like mother, I'm sure, Greenleaf, and I'm equally sure that isn't the important message. What next?"

"Prince Ladislov telephoned to ask if you would have dinner with him. He said something about having 'captured a Soviet poet' whom he thought you might like to meet."

"Thank you, Greenleaf. That was very well done. And now I think that you have prepared the way beautifully for a real dramatic statement. Please don't keep me in suspense any more. Just what has happened?"

"Mrs. Eustis is waiting for you in the small drawing room."

"Mrs. Eustis!" The girl repeated the name incredulously. "Do you mean Dale's mother?"

"Yes, Miss Cynthia. Mrs. Clorinda Eustis of Tuxedo." The girl stood silent for a moment, her eyes dark with concentrated thought. Then suddenly she twitched off her hat and flung it away from her as if it suddenly had become too tight and was hurting her head. "Has she been waiting long?"

"Almost an hour, Miss Cynthia."

"Thank you." She repeated the words almost mechanically as if her mind were far away and then suddenly crossed the hall and entered the small drawing room with her head held very high. She walked straight up to the seated figure dressed richly in black, holding out her hand in welcome. "How do you do, Mrs. Eustis. I'm so sorry to have kept you waiting. I just got back this minute and heard you were here."

The old lady looked steadily at her for a moment and then said slowly, "You're looking very lovely, Cynthia."

The girl sat down in a near-by chair with a little laugh. "I'm feeling very well, thank you, Mrs. Eustis. How have you been,—and Dale?"

The old woman settled herself more comfortably and her aged fingers fussed a little with her dress as if she were finding it difficult to frame in words exactly what she wished to say. Finally she said, "I've been very well, thank you. But Dale has not been."

Cynthia gasped a little involuntarily and her hands clasped nervously in her lap. She tried to control them from trembling because she knew her guest was watching her closely, but she feared her efforts were not altogether successful. Finally she managed to say, "Has he been sick?"

"Sick?" The old lady repeated the word in a strange tone. "I don't know whether you would call it sick or not. From the doctor's point of view he is very well. Maybe if I called it 'sick at heart' that would be the best description. I've just come from seeing him to-day. He's living in a cabin up in the Adirondacks, all alone. He won't take a friend with him or let me send a servant. I went up there yesterday myself hoping to distract him just a little because he's been up there alone three months now, and I'm beginning to be afraid. I stayed there last night and then to-day he made me come away early this morning." She paused a moment for breath, then continued with a little sob in her voice.

"Cynthia, I never knew my son could look like he looks now. His hair hasn't been cut since he left Tuxedo. He has a stubble of beard. I'm sure he hasn't shaved in a week. He was wearing old sloppy corduroy clothes and worse still I'm sure he wasn't even clean. He had that strange dirty look a man has sometimes when he lives all alone without any woman's care and influence. I kept looking at him and saying over and over to myself, 'This is Dale, this is my boy.' You see I was trying to convince myself I wasn't talking to a tramp, to some one who had forgotten the meaning of all the decencies of life." She tried to wipe the tears out of her eyes furtively but the girl was watching too closely to miss even her slightest movement. After a moment the woman continued.

"It wasn't anything he said that made me worry half so much as what he didn't say. He said he was quite contented, perfectly satisfied to go on there living alone. But he wouldn't let me try to reason with him at all. Somehow when we sat there, one on each side of the big log fire, I had an idea that he was trying not to hate me, and not succeeding very well. I felt that he kept reminding himself every minute that I was his mother, that I had cared for him, that I had given him birth, all these things to keep from wanting to drive me out of his life forever. I sat there trembling, afraid to say the wrong thing, something which might drive him to active anger against me, and at the same time still more afraid of the long, dreary silences when his weary eyes were fastened on me as if trying to remember just who I was and why I was there at all. Cynthia, he's not even eating enough to keep alive.

I know that now. He's up there alone in the woods—dying."

The girl sat tensely through the long tirade, her eyes fixed intently on the old woman's face, her body leaning forward nervously. Her throat felt so tight she feared for a moment she wouldn't be able to frame her thoughts in words, but finally she managed to say faintly, "Didn't he go back to college?"

Mrs. Eustis shook her head. "No. He managed to keep up his spirits through the Christmas week, but after that was over he went completely to pieces. I was such a miserable fool and stood there with him day by day, unable to see what was happening, unable to see how he was torturing himself. My stupid vanity blinded me so I actually thought he was happy because he was laughing and dancing and going through the gestures in all the sports. He won the speed skating contest and I, like the silly old woman I am, thought that meant he was happy. Now I know it only meant that he was flying away from the terror in his heart, trying to escape from himself. Toward the middle of January even I couldn't blind myself any more to the truth and then before I had time to think he went away. For a week or two I didn't know where he had gone, and then a letter came, telling me he was at the cabin in the Adirondacks, but forbidding me to come to see him. All winter he has been forbidding me in the same way, until yesterday I couldn't stand it any more and I went up there to see for myself just what had happened to my boy." She shook her head dolefully. "He isn't my boy any more. He's an unshaven, unkempt, rather brutal stranger who makes me afraid, and early this morning he made me leave him. I had nowhere to go, no one to turn to, so I came here."

"What's the matter with Dale?" The words fell haltingly from Cynthia's lips.

The old woman leaned forward eagerly. "Don't you know? Doesn't your heart tell you? He loves you. He is dying because he feels he has failed you and driven you away from him. He feels that without you life isn't worth living, not anywhere, not even alone up there in the mountains. Look into your heart and ask yourself if you don't love him, too; if your life hasn't been as broken as his since you drifted apart."

The girl jumped to her feet and stood with clenched hands in the middle of the room. "How can you say he loves me? How can you dare to ask me if I still love him under the circumstances? That night he chose your love in preference to mine, he chose to be your son rather than my lover. What right has he to complain of that choice now? If he has suffered I've suffered, too, in a different way. He's only beginning to learn what it means to really love some one who is indifferent to him. What does he want now? Or what do you want? Why have you come here at all? If he has messed up his life, what can you expect me to do now?" Her voice broke in a sob.

The old woman rose unsteadily to her feet with the aid of her ivory cane. It seemed a matter of minutes rather than seconds before she finally was standing steadily, but Cynthia still stood with clenched hands and taut body, making no movement toward her. Mrs. Eustis stretched out an appealing hand and the girl could not help noticing how it trembled.

"Cynthia, I have come to the end of my pride. There is no strength left now to try to deny what you and he and I should have known all along. He loves you, loves you with all the strength of his ardent nature; loves you the more desperately because he does not know as I do how much you really love him. I know that now because I, too, have suffered, because for these months I have been a miserable old woman, repenting for my folly day by day and hour by hour. I drove you apart. Yes, I'm willing to acknowledge that now. I waited night after night to catch you in some such unexplainable predicament as I did that last night, that awful Christmas Eve. I was like a spider in a web, waiting my time to drive you away from my son because I wanted him all for myself, because I was afraid he would love you so much he would completely forget me. The morning after you left I told him he had to choose between us. I was so proud of my trickery and because he was not man enough to thrust me aside. He gave way and allowed me to prevent him from going after you. That's why he never came to explain, on his knees, if necessary, how much he loved you, how much his fault was the fault of my training, my upbringing."

There was a moment's heavy silence and then the old woman continued more calmly. "Cynthia, I'm pleading with you for forgiveness. I am an old, proud woman and I have never before asked any one for forgiveness, never even thought of such a thing. I've come to you now because three lonely months have taught me I love Dale unselfishly as well as selfishly, and I want him to be happy even if his happiness means my never seeing him again. I'm willing you should hate me and never speak to me as long as you live, if you will only go to him now. He needs you so much, and I think you need him, too, if you'll only look into your heart. I'm pleading with you for his happiness, his very life, perhaps, and for your happiness, too. If you want me to do so I'll go away somewhere and never bother either of you again. I mean that exactly."

Slowly the girl's tenseness relaxed while the woman was speaking and finally at the end she stood limply, her body sagging. Her eyes hung on the old woman's suffering countenance, drinking in the passionate appeal that rolled from her lips. When she had finished, the silence of the room rolled heavily between them, but finally her lips moved.

"Where is he?"

The woman took a step forward in her eagerness. "My car is outside, and the chauffeur knows just where to go. Will you really go to him, now, immediately?"

"Yes! Yes!" and the girl flung herself sobbing into a chair. Mrs. Eustis crossed to her and patted her shoulder gently, but her lips were unable to speak any words. She knew that the girl's sobbing meant that she did love her son, that she was going to him, that everything was going to be all right, now. This time she had really succeeded.

CHAPTER TWENTY-SIX

THE rain had fallen all day in a kind of steady, sickening drizzle and Cynthia was glad it was night now, and she could light the lamps and shut the heavy curtains to exclude the dreariness of it all. The last vestiges of the snow had melted and the world outside was a sad rainsodden place which it was good to try to forget. Spring was in the air, but it was the late soggy spring of the mountains which held for the moment little promise of the cheer to come once the rain ceased.

She closed the door and began lighting the lamps in the cabin. She expected Dale's return any moment now and the day had been so dreary she looked forward to it. The smallness of the cabin with its three rooms, a living room, bedroom, and a tiny room for cooking, had begun to crush her spirit and render her anxious for anything to happen which would break the monotony. She wondered if Dale would be as dour and disagreeable as he had been since her arrival a week before. She shrugged her shoulders sadly. He probably would be, but in a week she had already come to accept that almost as a matter of course. In a week her whole view of life had changed.

She smiled a little sadly as she remembered how eagerly she had rushed up here after her astonishing conversation with Mrs. Eustis which had driven away so many of her doubts and fears. She had rushed up here thinking to be welcomed with open arms by a man whose love for her was driving him to desperation. His mother had said just that, not once but several times, his mother who supposedly knew him better than any other person on earth. How different her reception had been from that of her imaginings. She felt she could never forget even the minutest detail of it. It had been after dark when the car managed to drag its weight up the final slope and with a glad cry she had plunged in at the door. A single glance had sufficed to show that his mother had not exaggerated his condition. He looked far more like a tramp who had wandered in there seeking shelter from the storm than like the handsome, immaculate man she remembered. She had stood in the doorway for a minute watching him while he sat half huddled over a dreary fire, just looking at her without a word of greeting or welcome. Finally she had held out her arms to him, crying, "Dale, I've come to be with you."

She was sure she would never forget his reply. He had said coldly, "You needn't bother. I don't want you here at all. I don't want anybody here. Go back immediately the way you came."

And that had been all. She wondered now what she would have done at that time had she known what the last week had taught her. It was impossible to say, impossible to figure out. She only knew that then she had laughed at his surliness and merely returned to the car in order to send the chauffeur away with it, telling him to return to Tuxedo at his convenience; telling him to call Mrs. Eustis at the first town with an available telephone and assure her that everything was all right. The man had saluted and gone and she had walked slowly back into the cabin and closed the door firmly after her.

It was easier now to remember what had happened rather than what she had expected to happen, but she was sure she had expected his attitude to have changed at least a little during the time she had spent dismissing and in-

structing the chauffeur. How foolish she had been. He
had not so much as moved from his place by the fire, nor
did he rise to welcome her. He had merely said, "Well,
what do you want?" And she had said, "I've just sent
away the chauffeur and I'm going to stay with you."

That had been all. Since then he had only spoken to
her when necessary and for hours they had sat one on each
side of the fire, looking drearily into the heart of the blaze.
His mother had described him looking at her with eyes in
which he strove to control his hate, but she could not complain of that. He had not looked at her at all. Except when
absolutely obligatory there had been no conversation whatsoever, no outbursts of rage, no recriminations. When she
tried to talk to him at all he answered sometimes in mono-
syllables, mere Indian grunts, and sometimes not at all. In
her desperation she had tried to make herself mean something to him, tried to force his appreciation. She had
cooked and cleaned up the cabin, filled the lamps, even
scrubbed the floors so that he might see exactly what she
meant when she said she had come to be with him. She
had never done an hour or a minute's work until now. He
surely understood that, and must appreciate what it meant
to her that she should cook meals for him and keep the
cabin clean and orderly. But he never so much as grunted
a thank you, though he ate the food she set before him
and slept on the couch in the living room, which she prepared. His only gesture of decency had been giving up
his bed to her, but even that had been done in a kind of
scornful, insulting way which had hurt her far more than
if he had flung a blanket on the bare floor before the fire
and bade her sleep there like an Indian servant or a dog.

She walked slowly to the window and stood looking out
into the drizzle a moment before dropping the curtain and
returning to her seat before the fire. Nervously she threw

two or three logs into the blaze to make it flame higher, to throw the lurid gleams of firelight farther into the corners of the room. This light seemed more alive, more companionable than that of the lamps which she had lit so carefully. It might mean a little more to him when he entered soaking wet from the dreary walk of many miles to and from the nearest village for supplies. The added fuel would make the room warmer and it was too warm already because there was a touch of spring in the air in spite of the dreariness and the drizzle outside, but the added warmth and the glow of light might touch his heart a little and in a strange way teach him something of what she meant by her persistency in staying there.

Suddenly, without warning, she buried her face in her hands and began to sob quietly. Where could she find the strength to keep up this cruel, unequal battle with a man whom she loved so much and who seemed resolved to ignore her completely, to treat her as if she were a piece of furniture which one walked around, not from any sense of kindness or feeling, but merely lest one bruise oneself by contact? Yet now that he was treating her so, she realized at last what he meant to her, that in his body and mind was the answer to all the love she had to give to everything which cried out in her own heart. With the sobs choking her she could understand at last how little Sperry and Timothy had meant, how little Dale himself had meant before. Through the long months she had cherished the memory of what she called her "glorious night" at the little road-house in Connecticut. What a poor thing that seemed to her now that she had come to a realization of this new emotion which transcended all passion because it was the outgrowth of passion, the very distillation of her heart's desire. Now she wanted him not for his magnificent body, powerful arms, crisp yellow hair, flashing blue eyes, all of those things which had seemed to mean so much for her before; now she wanted him for something which was far more than all these because it was the essence of all these, because it was the very soul of the man himself. Now she wanted him to lie in her arms, not so her flesh might tingle to the touch of his hands or join itself with his, but so that something which was herself might mingle with that equally indescribable something which was himself, might mingle and form that incredible union which was both of them, which was Love.

The door was suddenly flung open violently and he strode heavily into the room. She sprang to her feet and stood facing him, her back to the fire, her heart racing wildly with some instinct to which she could give no name because she had never known it before. For a moment they stood facing each other, she with her head held high, the leaping flames silhouetting the elegant lines of her figure and casting dancing shadows on the low walls, he with his head down and eyes lowered.

"Well, are you still here?" he growled.

"Yes, Dale. I told you I had come to stay."

"Suppose I don't want you? I've told you that all this week. I'm sick and tired of saying it over and over again. I went away to-day to give you a chance to be alone all day, to give you a chance to think things over and realize I don't want you here. Now, will you go?"

"No, Dale, I will not go." She said the words very slowly and quietly, but there was a strange conviction about them which was almost surprising to her own ears. It seemed almost as if some one else were speaking, some very determined young woman who was something like her and yet entirely different.

"What'll I have to do to convince you I don't want you here? I'm not a fool and I'm not going to let you drive *me* away. That's one thing you may rest assured about. This is my home, the only home I have, and I intend to share it with no one. I insist upon your going in the morning."

She shook her head slowly. "It won't do, Dale, because I'm not going. At least not when things are as they are now. I've come here to save you from yourself and I won't go away until I've succeeded."

He leaped forward with startling suddenness and caught her roughly by the arm. "Be careful how far you tempt me. What's to prevent me from throwing you out of the house now, out in the rain? I don't think you'd ever find your way to the nearest village; it's miles and miles away. I guess you know that. You'd probably die out there on the mountainside, die of exposure because there's no one to take you in. Not even the offer of all your money or your body could get you a night's shelter out there on the mountain. You wouldn't even interest a living creature out there except the wolves, and they've probably gone further north at this time of the year. There's nothing, no law or any other power, to prevent me from doing what I please up here. You taught me to laugh at all conventions and decency, and now I've learned your lesson only too well. You've come to share this den with a beast. Now the beast is tired of looking at you and is going to throw you out. What can you do to stop it?"

"Nothing. I wouldn't want to do anything. If you want to throw me out, go ahead. I'm here because I love you and if you don't care to have me it doesn't matter very much where else I am. I've been waiting a week to tell you that, and now I'm glad I've been able to do it. You may be excited and not know exactly what you're saying, but I'm perfectly calm and I'm weighing every word very carefully."

With a sudden convulsive movement he shook her rapidly and then flung her away from him. "Love! That's the sort of thing you would say, the sort of thing I expected you to say the very minute you got here. You've probably had a succession of lovers and tired of them. Now you come back to me. You heard I was up here all alone, that I've seen no one for months, and you probably figured I'd be glad to see you, waiting like so much gunpowder to be set off by the blaze of your eyes. Well, it hasn't worked, has it?"

"Dale, why will you persist in refusing to understand? I did come up here because I heard you were alone and unhappy, but it was only with feelings of love and tenderness in my heart. I was a fool before, but I've suffered, too, these last few months, and I've learned a great deal about what life really means, and about myself. I've learned how mad I was in my discovery of sex. I've learned you can't bow down and worship the body without paying for that worship in suffering. I thought that we two, who had been so unhappy apart from each other, might learn real happiness together."

She finished with outstretched hands of pleading, but even as the last words left her lips she knew she had failed.

He caught both her hands in a vise-like grip so strong that she barely managed to keep from screaming aloud with the pain of it. His eyes were blazing now, and there was a wild look about him which flooded her heart with terror. He began to talk slowly and brutally between his clenched teeth. "I've learned a lot of things, too, since I've been up here alone. I've learned the only one thing women are good for, especially women like you. When I was home and happy I had faith in women and what they signify in life. You broke down that faith and destroyed my happiness. You insisted on giving yourself to me because like so many women you had learned no control over yourself, no law in life except the law of getting whatever pleased your fancy at the moment. Well, two can play at that game. Just for the moment you please me in a way. I happen to like the idea of having you around here washing dishes and cooking and scrubbing floors. It's the only damn thing you're good for anyhow. That, and one other thing. Do you know what that is?"

Receiving no answer, he dropped her hands suddenly and caught her by the throat, shaking her back and forth in unsuppressed fury. "So you don't know any more what I'm talking about," he cried hoarsely. "You used to know well enough what men wanted from women like you, especially men who have lived in the woods alone for months without seeing any kind of a woman. Now you don't know, and yet you were the one that taught me what it means to drop all decent considerations in life and just revel in being an animal. Now do you still want to stay up here with me?"

Her eyes were almost popping from her head from the pressure of his cruel hands about her throat, and for an instant after he released her she couldn't form words to speak. He stood back a little with hate and mad desire mingled in his glaring eyes, his hands hanging at his side, his knees a little bent like an animal about to spring. Chokingly she managed finally to gasp an answer.

"Yes, I have come here to stay. I told you—I love you."

For a moment he hesitated, then leaped forward with a wild animal cry. With both hands he caught her dress at the neck and ripped it down the front. She stood rigidly with closed eyes while he continued tearing every shred of clothing from her body, flinging the ragged pieces on the floor madly. In a moment she stood naked in the fitful light from the fire, her beautifully formed body casting grotesque shadows on the walls and ceiling of the room. Her head was thrown back, her eyes closed, her heart stricken with terror, but by a mighty effort she managed to keep from trembling. She could feel his hot breath on her throat and breast, his powerful hands, roughened by a winter in the woods, running roughly, brutally, over her delicate flesh.

Suddenly his hands were gone and she opened her eyes. He was standing a few paces away, looking at her intently with strange, unfathomable eyes. She felt his gaze running over her steadily, minutely, but she neither spoke nor moved. Finally he took a hesitant step forward and spoke, this time in a low voice which barely reached her. "What now? Do you still want to stay?"

"Yes."

"Do you still think you love me,—now?"

"I know I love you—now."

For a moment he stood bent forward looking at her, looking into her eyes as if he could not believe what he had heard, as if he doubted his senses. Then with a sharp, agonized cry he swung around and dashed out of the room, out into the drizzling wet night. She stood astounded by his swift, unaccountable action, then ran, all naked as she was, to the open door, crying, "Dale, Dale, come back!"

For at least five minutes she stood there peering out into the soaking darkness, calling his name as loudly as she could, but there was no answer, not even an echo to mock her. The sound of her voice was swallowed up by the sodden trees, and standing there in the doorway she shivered, afraid of the ominous dreariness. Slowly she turned back into the room and crouched trembling before the fire, needing its warmth and companionship. When the chill had passed she gathered up the rags of her clothing and flung them into the blaze. There was a sudden smudge of smoke and then the flames leaped up brighter than before, richer for the unaccustomed fuel. It was symbolic to her, symbolic of the smudgy passion which was gone and the clear flame of her love now that she understood what things really meant. She passed into the bedroom and returned immediately with a blanket which she wrapped around her. She sat down on a low stool before the fire to wait, her mind almost numb. Vaguely she wondered why she felt no resentment against this man, but there was no answer to that either in her mind or in her heart. She only knew she wanted him to come back. She threw another log into the flames.

CHAPTER TWENTY-SEVEN

SOMETIMES after a night of rain the new day dawns with an almost undreamed of loveliness, the whole world refreshed and invigorated in consequence of the storm. Especially in spring this is true, in the mountains where the trees hold the last lingering drops to glitter in the first rays of the sun.

But a room from which the beauty of the new day is excluded seems to hold a dour memory of what was, unrecognizing that yesterday is part of the endless past. So it seemed to Dale as he slowly pushed the door open and looked into the living room of his cabin. The once sparkling fire was now a gloomy heap of gray ashes and the heavy curtains so carefully drawn to exclude last night's dark drizzle now shut out the glory of the sunshine. The lamps had gone out, too, having used up their quota of life-giving oil, and were now dead. One of them was still smoking a little, sending out a pale, sickening fume that poisoned the air.

Then he saw Cynthia sitting on a little stool before the fire, her head bowed over her knees. She was wrapped in a blanket, a blanket his mother had brought back from Mexico for him after her trip there several years before. He wondered why that should all be so clear to him now, why his mind should grope trying to find some meaning in the fact that Cynthia was sitting wrapped in a blanket which his mother had brought from a far country to give to him.

"Cynthia," he whispered softly.

The crouching figure never stirred and he knew, she was asleep. An indescribable wave of emotion swept over him as he stood for a moment looking down upon her huddled figure. The whole pathetic scene was so clear without a word of explanation. She had wrapped her naked, abused body in this blanket and come to sit before the fire to wait for him. He was sure of that, surer than he had ever been of anything in his life before. How many hours she must have sat on that little stool waiting before Nature stepped in and soothed her exhaustion with this trance-like sleep. Only a person incredibly tired could possibly sleep in such a position, so crouched and bent over.

His hand reached forward nervously to touch the soft brown head bent trustingly toward what had been fire and warmth, and was now only gray ashes. A delicate tendril of hair wrapped itself about his fingers ere his hand could actually touch her and he drew back from the faint touch as if he had been stung. After what had been last night he had no right to touch a single hair of her head even in his present mood of contrition and suffering. He had no right to assume that she would even wish him to touch her ever again, to imagine that she could do other than shrink from the impact of his callous hands that had shamed her. He held them out to look at them, the two offending hands, crude servants of his passions and blundering willfulness. It seemed impossible now that last night he could have sunk them cruelly into her soft flesh. With a faint shudder he dropped them to his side again and walked swiftly to the windows.

He drew the heavy curtains aside and opened the windows. The sun flooded in warmly and the balmy spring air seemed to dissolve and destroy the atmosphere of the night before which still clung to the room. The faint wisp of smoke from the burnt-out lamp was thrust aside and even the dead ashes on the hearth were stirred. For a moment there was no sound, then suddenly the girl started up from her crouching position with a faint cry.

"Dale!" She breathed his name in a tone of wonderment and he turned around slowly to face her.

"I've come back again, Cynthia. I couldn't stay away. All night long I wandered out there through the woods. It was dark and cold and endlessly dreary, but I couldn't come back because out there in the darkness I realized what I had done to you, what a disgusting beast I had been. Two or three times I came close to the cabin and once I even listened at the door and touched the latch with my hand; but I hadn't the strength to open the door and there was no sound, nothing to tell me either to come in or to go away. The curtains were drawn so tight that not a glimpse of light reached outside. I tried to look in at the windows, but I could only see into the kitchen and I only dared to look in there because I knew you couldn't possibly be there. Then I wandered away again. I never knew that a night could be so long, that hours could pass so slowly. Just before dawn the rain stopped, and then the sun came up like the light of new hope in a world that had grown old, and weary, and hopeless. The air grew suddenly warm, and mild, and gentle. For the first time in my life I knew what the poets used to mean by the word 'Spring,' and I came back here, and came in this time because the sun had given me courage."

She stood looking at him with glowing eyes of infinite compassion. When he finished speaking in his quiet, weary voice a very faint smile touched her lips and she moved slowly toward him, one hand stretched out before her, the other holding the blanket loosely about her body. Then her hand touched his coat sleeve lightly and she exclaimed, "You're wet, soaking wet. You'll be sick."

He laughed shortly. "I'm not afraid of that. I almost hope I am. I wish my body could shake and suffer to match my feelings."

She shook her head slowly and said, "Dale, now that you've come back you mustn't talk like that. You must take off your clothes at once and get into bed. I'll fix a hot drink for you."

He drew back a step. "No! I can't do that. I'm going to go away."

She looked at him tenderly. "You poor boy. You're still fighting against reason and understanding, aren't you? Surely you can't hate me enough to wish to make yourself sick just to annoy me."

"I don't hate you," he cried. "I hate nothing in the world but myself, because nothing in the world is so hateful as myself."

"And nothing in the world so lovable." She almost whispered the words, then walked up to him resolutely. "Dale, I'm telling you you must take off your clothes and get into bed or you'll be sick. That's a very simple thing to understand, and there are no two ways about it."

"But—" he began.

"There are no buts in this, Dale; no possible objection you could have to behaving sensibly." She caught his coat deftly by the collar and drew it slowly from his shoulders. He was quite limp in her grasp and in a moment the garments lay in a sodden mass on the floor. They both stood silently watching it for a little space before she raised her eyes to his. "Now, Dale, will you please do as I tell you?"

He walked slowly, hesitantly across the room, dragging his feet as if the high leather boots were weights holding them down, and passed into the bedroom, closing the door softly behind him. The girl picked up the coat and hung it carefully over the back of a chair. It was so wet it hung there limply and she watched it with fascinated eyes until a faint sound from the next room recalled her to herself. She passed into the kitchen and lighted the oil stove to boil water for the hot beverage. She didn't know exactly what you gave a person to drive cold out of his body, but she felt sure very hot tea or coffee would help some, and she knew there was plenty of whisky to add to it. In the kitchen she found the little dress she had been using while washing dishes or cleaning, and dropping the blanket she slipped into it quickly. Then with a calm smile on her lips she walked to the bedroom door and knocked softly.

No answer came, so she pressed the latch and entered. The curtains at the window were still drawn and the room in semi-darkness. Coming from the bright, sun-flooded living room it seemed doubly dark in there and she waited an instant to accustom her eyes to it. Dale had removed all his clothing and left it in a pile on the floor. She crossed to the bed and saw he was lying there on his back with the bedclothes pulled tightly up to his chin. His eyes were wide open and he was staring at the ceiling. She sat down on the edge of the bed, resting her hand lightly on his body.

"What now?" he asked dully.

She laughed lightly and the sound rang in the dusty room. Her laughter was astonishing even to her own ears because she had almost forgotten she could laugh happily and easily like that. "Why Dale, everything is perfectly simple now. You're just going to lie here all day in bed to make sure you didn't catch cold. You need the sleep, you know. You see, you were wandering around all night while I was home here sleeping."

He turned his head slowly to look at her and she saw there were tears in his eyes as he murmured, "Poor Cyn-

thia, sitting all night long in front of the fire. Why didn't
you go to bed?"

"I was waiting for you to come home," she said simply.

"Home?" He repeated the word dubiously.

"Yes, Dale, this is our home. That is, until we go to
Tuxedo for the wedding."

"Wedding?" He raised himself up on one elbow to
look at her.

"Exactly. As soon as we're both rested we must go
back to your mother, now that we understand each other,
and start in all over again to realize our happiness."

"But, Cynthia, surely you wouldn't marry me now, now
that you know what a beast I am. Remember how I
treated you last night."

"What children men are, every one of them. You don't
understand us and still less do you understand yourselves.
Whatever doubts I might have had of your love, your
brutality last night drove them away. When you forgot
your politeness and every last vestige of civilized conduct,
when I became for a moment merely a female at hand
to satisfy your lust, a creature whose clothes you could
tear off to expose a body you could use, then for a moment
things hung in the balance. When you dashed out into the
rainy night I knew I could never doubt you again, no
matter how long we live, no matter what may happen.
You tried to brutalize your love. You tried to frighten
me with a false brutality, but I was not frightened, not
in my heart. Now I won't even let you try to say anything
to explain your conduct, because my heart understands so
much better without the silly words which so often clog
and distort the meanings of what we say.

She twisted her body around and lay on the covers
beside him, putting her arms gently about his neck, twin-
ing her fingers in his crisp, yellow hair which was so long

and unkempt now. Slowly, tenderly she pressed her warm lips against his and the touch of his unshaven chin and cheeks thrilled her. The end of the search for love had led back to the beginning, the circle had been completed and once more she knew this was her man, that and only that. Everything else, all foolishness and pride and spent passion, had been only a valley of suffering through which she had to pass to find the meaning of things.

He drew his arms from beneath the covers and pressed her body closer to his, her lips more firmly upon his own. With a deep sigh she lay beside him, both their heads, yellow and brown, resting on the single pillow.

"Dale," she whispered, "tell me you love me."

He turned his head a little so that his eyes could smile into hers, so that his lips might reach for hers and almost touch them. "Cynthia, darling, don't you know I've always loved you?"

THE END

www.ingramcontent.com/pod-product-compliance
Lightning Source LLC
Chambersburg PA
CBHW030939260626
47169CB00002B/539